SHOW ME THE PLACE

SHOW ME THE PLACE

Book 3 of the Storyteller Trilogy

---

pHil Rittenhouse

Written Books

For information, contact inquire@writtenbooks.com

All statements of fact, opinion, or analysis expressed are those of the author and do not reflect the official positions or views of the Central Intelligence Agency (CIA) or any other U.S. Government agency. Nothing in the contents should be construed as asserting or implying U.S. Government authentication of information or CIA endorsement of the author's views. This material has been reviewed by the CIA to prevent the disclosure of classified information.

*

Book Cover design by the Author

First edition 2026

ISBN: 978-1-970322-06-4

*

Written Books

www.writtenbooks.com

For Lois Chang.
None of this would have come to be had you not shown such faith in the boorish, infantile scribblings of a snot-nosed teenage punk so long ago. I think I'm older now than you were then. How is it that you were so wise, and I'm still just me? Thank you, Mrs. Chang.
You are missed.

PREFACE

ROUND THREE. ONCE more into the fray.

Of the Storyteller trilogy, this was both the book that I most looked forward to writing and the one I most feared to pen. Type. You know what I mean; don't be so picky.

The question of Ashe's origin inevitably comes up, some would say on the first page of book one. I've danced around it for hundreds of pages and have made the hard decision to simply depict it and leave interpretation to the reader. That was one of the hardest lessons to learn as an undergrad pursuing a degree in art a few of my own lifetimes ago. When you have an idea, and a strongly felt conviction, it can be a difficult thing to leave things open to the whimsy of the observer.

But... Here is Ashe, exposed by his own words. Make of him what you will.

After this, the real fun begins.

This page intentionally left blank.

Prologue: Scorched Earth

1998

THE CHIHUAHUAN DESERT stretched out before her, shimmering in the heat of late afternoon that sought to roast her alive in the black uniform. The shadows of the mountains cut jagged shapes across the valley floor, and a hot wind stirred the dry, scorched earth beneath her feet. The air smelled of dust and smoke, as well as countless other, more noxious, fumes: remnants of the inferno below.

Supervisory Special Agent Dani Linder stood atop a low rise, her boots planted on the baked ground. A hot, dry wind tugged at her tactical field gear, rattling the wires of her comms against the FBI patch clipped to her plate carrier. Her dark aviator sunglasses reflected the scene below: a wreckage of ash, twisted metal, and blackened craters, where death had swept through the valley like a storm.

Her gaze followed the contours of the valley. To the north, the Sandia Mountains stood like solemn sentinels; to the east, the lower but equally rugged Manzano Mountains caught the fading light. South and west, a series of jagged lava escarpments loomed, their shadows sharp against the sand. The geography funneled everything into a single point. It was a place of endings, desolate and indifferent: certainly the last place dozens of cartel chemists, guards, and dealers strewn across the valley floor would ever have seen.

She exhaled slowly, letting her eyes settle on the charred remains of the meth lab. Like so many others cropping up across the state, it had been a production hub, using ephedrine reduction methods. Dangerous, volatile work that often ended in accidents. But this scene was larger than most, and it told a different story.

She scanned the burned-out vehicles scattered across the valley, her mind piecing together the attack like a puzzle. The patterns were clear. Machine-gun fire had torn through the trucks. The vehicle nearest her had taken a direct hit from an RPG.

Dani took a step down the hill, her boots crunching on the dry earth. She moved carefully, weaving through scattered debris, scanning the wreckage with a practiced eye. Near the edge of the site, she stopped beside the burned-out pickup truck, its frame twisted and riddled with .50-caliber holes. Not the kind of firepower you'd expect in a cartel skirmish. Dani crouched, brushing dirt away from a jagged fragment embedded in the ground, turning it over in her hand. She brushed dry earth from the numbers on the hunk of metal with gloved fingers.

Military tactics. Military weapons. This was not cartel work.

Dani stood slowly, her mind ticking through possibilities. Whoever had hit this place hadn't been interested in a messy shootout or a chaotic firefight. This had been brutal and precise, taking out the vehicles and guards en masse before they had a chance to mount an effective defense.

A familiar pattern. This wasn't the first time she'd seen a scene like this in recent months. It was part of a growing trend that had left the DEA scrambling, forced to admit they were far out of their depth.

The FBI had agreed to assist by sending a CIRG—Critical Incident Response Group—team to assist. CIRG was a fairly new endeavor of the FBI, less than five years old, formed in response to the fiascos in Ruby Ridge and Waco. The purpose of the group was to provide tactical and investigative resources and expertise for critical incidents where an immediate response from law enforcement authorities was required. The DEA had so far been unable to mount that immediate response, and so CIRG was called in. And of late, Dani with it.

Dani had been in CIRG for four of its five years and wasn't here just because she could breach doors or rappel down buildings. Pushing fifty, her days of those activities were probably approaching an end. No, she'd been recruited because she could shoot better than anyone else in the Bureau, plain and simple. Her precision was unmatched, whether she was scoping in at 800 yards or putting down a close-range threat with her sidearm. That in itself might even have been enough to land her a spot in the elite group. But that wasn't the only reason. Dani had been a trauma surgeon before she joined the Bureau. And she was cool-headed. She knew how to keep people alive under fire, make decisions in the chaos of combat as well as any others in the group who'd served multiple tours in the military.

The others had all come to respect her. Some more slowly than others, but that was not surprising. She'd proven herself to them, and to herself, too many times for doubts to play into the picture any longer. If the Bureau needed a sniper, a surgeon, or someone who could cut through a mess of internal politics or operational chaos, they came to her. Every time.

She wondered if this time might finally prove the exception. This was a disaster.

According to the briefing her team had received that morning from the DEA agent in charge, the meth lab had been a major site for the Juárez Cartel, producing methamphetamine for distribution across the Southwest.

The Juárez Cartel was struggling to rebuild after the death of their leader, Amado Carrillo Fuentes, the year before. Their rivals? The Félix brothers' Tijuana Cartel and the upstart Sinaloa Cartel, led by Joaquín Guzmán, known as "El Chapo" were circling like vultures. The power vacuum had triggered a wave of violence and retaliation, each cartel trying to outdo the other in a brutal contest for dominance.

But this attack didn't fit the usual patterns. It wasn't part of the turf war. Someone else was in the mix: a fourth party.

Her hand tightened around the RPG fragment. Her team had already been briefed on the rumors. Military-style tactics, high-grade explosives, ruthless efficiency. A new player had arrived, and they'd been quick to make a name for themselves.

And the name of their leader was known.

Wyatt Ming.

Dani's lips pressed into a thin line. Her eyes swept across the wreckage once more, cold and calculating. If Ming was here, she suspected things would get worse long before they got better.

She dropped the RPG fragment into a pocket and turned back toward the waiting vehicles at the base of the hill. The wind carried a new gust of ash and smoke, stinging her eyes and biting at her exposed skin.

Ming had been off-grid for years. She'd let herself believe he was gone for good. But this was his signature, clear as day. He was back.

And Dani wasn't about to let him slip away again.

THE JOINT OPERATIONS center hummed with restrained tension, voices low and clipped, movements edged with fatigue. The converted conference room at DEA headquarters was crowded, the air heavy with the smell of stale coffee and stress. Agents from two sides of the country gathered around the long conference table. The eyes of the hosting agency betrayed their exhaustion, physical and mental. Their postures slumped with the weight of too many battles lost.

The conference room had been converted into a makeshift command center. The west wall was lined with several large maps of the Southwest, each one dotted with colored pins marking cartel-related incidents. A projector flickered at the front of the room, cycling through slides filled with grainy surveillance photos, intercepted communications, and outdated intel.

Dani leaned against the wall at the back of the room, arms crossed, observing silently. Her CIRG team sat scattered among the DEA agents. She caught the occasional sidelong glance from the DEA officers: a mix of skepticism and resentment.

They didn't like needing help, but they'd accepted it. Some hosting agents in these situations called them the cavalry, others called them something less polite.

She couldn't blame them. The DEA had been fighting this war for years, and it was only getting worse. Many of them didn't want outsiders coming in, especially not a team like hers. CIRG agents had a reputation for being parachuted into chaotic situations, stirring things up, and then leaving others to clean up the mess - even though the exact opposite was true.

But she and her colleagues weren't here to make friends. They were here to clean up the mess.

Dani could feel the tension crackling in the air, sharp as static. Every agent in the room knew the stakes, but no one said it out loud.

They were losing.

She glanced at the wall maps, the red, blue and green pins spreading across the landscape like infected wounds, each one indicating a differing degree of violence and ruin. The drug war was still raging, but few outside rooms like this seemed to care anymore.

The news cycles had moved on to scandals and other distractions. The press was consumed with the latest developments in President Clinton's messy personal life, replaying the same headlines over and over. Every talking head wanted to dissect the details, speculate on impeachment, infidelity, and appearances.

And the politicians? They were probably too busy covering their tracks, worried that if anyone looked too hard at the president, skeletons might tumble out of their own closets just in time for November's midterm elections. No one cared to spotlight a war America was quietly losing on its own soil.

Her lips narrowed to a bloodless line. At least the FBI director, with his reputation as a tough-on-crime prosecutor, hadn't forgotten what mattered. He had been only too happy to loan her CIRG team to the DEA, knowing they could make an impact where it was most needed. For now, that was here: New Mexico, at the crumbling edges of cartel territory, where things were spinning out of control faster than anyone wanted to admit.

A DEA supervisor stood at the front of the room, flipping through briefing slides with the precision of a man who'd spent way too much time performing similar presentations.

"Let me paint the picture," he began, his tone dry but edged with frustration. He gestured at the map littered with recent incidents, each one clustered around cartel strongholds and key distribution hubs.

"Juárez, Tijuana, Sinaloa—those, we understand. We know how they operate, how they fight, how they think." He clicked to the next slide, a grainy surveillance photo of the meth lab Dani had just visited. Its wreckage was stark against the desert landscape.

"This? This is something else. No clear pattern, no defined strategy. Just overwhelming force and chaos. Whoever hit that site wasn't interested in posturing or sending a message. They came to annihilate."

He let the weight of his words settle before flipping to the next slide: a surveillance image—a fuzzy one—of Wyatt Ming, stepping out of a black SUV.

"Rumors are that this is the man behind it." The briefer tapped the screen. "Wyatt Ming. The tactics match, although the scale is greater than it ever was in the Midwest. Thought is that he's seeking to take advantage of the power vacuum and dominate traffic here in the Southwest."

A murmur rippled through the room, voices exchanging whispers. Dani could feel the unease shifting into something colder. Ming's reputation preceded him. The man had been a ghost for half a decade. He'd consolidated power in the lower Midwest and then faded from view, his influence known and ever-present, but the man himself fell out of the public eye. He'd unified the drug landscape across half the country, but his influence had been anything but stabilizing.

Dani's jaw tightened. Her eyes fixed on the useless image of Ming on the screen. She'd never seen him in person, missing him that day in a Chicago dockside firefight. All she had to go on was her memory of a much older photo from Ashe's collection, and the resemblance was there. But his appearance was inconsequential; his methods were distinctive.

The briefing wrapped with the scrape of chairs on tile. Dani slipped away from the group, weaving through clusters of agents until she reached a borrowed desk at the edge of the room.

Her ThinkPad greeted her, a boxy black brick that she resented a little less when away from D.C. Authenticating past the Windows NT prompt, she connected to the network and ran several queries. She pulled the RPG fragment from her jacket pocket, running her thumb over its jagged edge. The serial number was faint but visible, stamped into the metal near the base.

The number was cut off, but she was willing to take the chance that it was missing only a single digit. She knew it was a long shot, but it was something to focus on: a thread she could follow, however thin.

❧ • ❧

DANI WORKED FOR almost an hour, cross-referencing databases from the FBI, military procurement records, and DEA asset logs. The search took time: dead ends, corrupted files, outdated links. But eventually, she found a purchase requisition bearing a serial number that was a solid match, along with several others. The line item read: M136 AT4, Single-Use Anti-Tank Weapon.

She grabbed her phone and punched in a number, waiting as it rang. On the third ring, a tired voice answered.

"Los Angeles National Guard Armory," the voice said. "This is Sergeant Hale."

"Supervisory Special Agent Dani Linder, FBI," she said, keeping her tone calm but direct. "I need to check the status of an item in your inventory. M136 AT4, serial number Delta-Romeo-13592."

There was a brief pause, followed by the sound of keys clattering on a keyboard.

"One moment, ma'am," Hale said. His voice returned a few seconds later, cautious but steady. "Okay, that item's listed as still in inventory. No recent activity. Checked and logged in place during the last physical audit two months ago."

Dani frowned. "You're sure?"

"Yes, ma'am. It's right there in the system," Hale replied.

Dani glanced down at the fragment in her hand again, the faint serial number staring back at her like a challenge. She didn't need to check twice. This wasn't just any stray fragment, it was part of the AT4 Hale claimed was sitting in the armory, safely accounted for.

"Thanks," she said and ended the call before Hale could ask questions of his own.

She sat back, her eyes locked on the fragment. There were only two explanations: Either someone had doctored the records, or someone had walked that AT4 right out of the armory and replaced it with a ghost entry in the system. Neither option was good.

She grabbed her phone again and dialed Assistant Special Agent in Charge Bill Rourke, who was stationed at the FBI's field office in El Paso. Rourke was Dani's commander for this operation.

"Rourke," Dani's temporary boss answered, his voice clipped and businesslike.

"Bill, it's Dani," she said. "I just tracked the RPG fragment from the site. It's an AT4, current military issue. Supposedly still in inventory at the Los Angeles National Guard Armory, but it's not. Same serial number. No mistake."

There was a pause. "You're sure about that?"

I just said I was, didn't I?

"Positive. Ming's moving military-grade weapons into the field, and it looks like somebody's covering his tracks at the source. If this is happening at the armory, it's bigger than we thought."

"You're right," Rourke said, his tone growing less skeptical. "Probably not a coincidence. I want you there in person. I'll arrange the clearance. Go to L.A. and find out how big this is."

"On it," Dani said.

The line went dead, and Dani set the phone down. She slipped the fragment into her jacket pocket and closed her laptop, scanning the operations center one last time. The noise washed over her: agents on phones, printers humming, chairs scraping against the floor. But Dani had already left that space behind in her head.

L.A. had answers. She just had to find the right questions to ask.

☙ • ❧

THE LOS ANGELES National Guard Armory looked like any other nondescript government building: a squat, rectangular structure with tan walls, razor wire lining the top of the perimeter fence, and fading signs. A couple dozen Humvees sat parked in front, their camouflage paint blending with the dusty lot.

Dani stepped out of her SUV and grabbed her CIRG badge. The sun hung high, baking the pavement beneath her boots as she scanned the lot. Wilkerson and Dyer, the two of her team members she'd brought on this trip, were following up on leads elsewhere. She'd wanted to handle this first visit alone, to avoid raising too many alarms.

The main entrance loomed ahead, its steel doors partially open. Dani strode toward it, ignoring the bored glance from the guard stationed nearby.

She was halfway down the corridor when she saw him.

Ashe.

He stood near a bulletin board cluttered with training schedules and equipment memos, his back to her. He wore an olive-green uniform, the fabric worn but perfectly tailored to his broad frame.

For a split second, Dani froze, her breath catching in her throat. Ten years. Ten years since she'd shot him on the docks in Chicago. Ten years since she'd watched him fall, thinking she'd killed him. Thinking that was the last she'd ever see of him.

And here he was. Alive.

"Ashe?" she said, approaching, her voice just above a whisper.

He turned slowly, his eyes locking onto hers with a gaze that felt like a gut punch. His face was harder than she remembered, sharper, the kind of face that had seen too many things and survived all of them.

"Doctor Linder." His voice was rough, edged with something colder than she'd expected.

She took a step closer. "You're alive."

"Yeah. It's a problem I have."

Dani opened her mouth to say more. To explain, to apologize for Chicago, for everything that had come after, but Ashe's eyes narrowed. The words died in her throat.

"What are you doing here," he demanded.

"What are you doing here?" she asked, shifting into investigator mode. It was safer ground. "You're not military. It's a crime to impersonate a serviceman."

Ashe smirked, the same smirk that had annoyed her a decade ago. "Who's impersonating?" He spread his arms. "I'm not on any active duty roster, sure. But I've served in more uniforms and earned the right to wear 'em than you'll ever be able to count. What's one more?"

His words hung in the air like a challenge. Dani felt her pulse tick up. He was evading, deflecting, and she knew exactly why.

"You're after Ming." It wasn't a question.

Ashe's expression barely flickered. He made no reply.

"You're still chasing him. Just like back then. That's why you're here."

Ashe crossed his arms, standing on spread feet. "Maybe I am. What's it to you? You've got your methods; I've got mine." His tone turned sharp. "But don't get in my way, Dani."

Her temper flared. "Don't get in my way?! You think this is still some personal vendetta? This isn't just about you and Ming anymore. People are dying. More will follow if it's not handled the right way."

Ashe's eyes burned with an intensity that made her heart skip. "Handling it the right way means killing the scum. I'm not here to play by your rules, Dani. I'm here to end this. Period."

Dani stepped closer, her voice dropping to a hard whisper. "You still think you can do it all by yourself, don't you? Like you did in Chicago. Well, as big as your head is, this situation is bigger. I've watched what Ming has done to every city he's touched: people he's slaughtered, lives he's destroyed. You think I haven't carried that with me every day?"

Ashe's jaw tightened, but he said nothing.

"And you?" Dani pressed. "Gone for a decade. No contact, no explanation. Just gone. You don't get to show up now and act like you've got the moral high ground."

Ashe glared at her, the air between them crackling with tension. "You shot me, in case you forgot."

Her breath caught. "I didn't think I had a choice. You were in the—"

"You had a choice," Ashe cut her off. His voice dropped to something low and dangerous. "And now, so do I. Stay out of my way, Dani. Ming is mine. Thirty years. He's mine. I'll finish it without you."

Dani stood her ground, refusing to blink. "And what if you screw this up?"

Ashe turned, already walking away. "Then that's my problem, not yours."

"You're wrong. If you get in my way, it becomes my problem."

Ashe paused at the end of the corridor, casting her one last glance. "Then I guess we'll see who wins that argument, won't we?"

Without another word, Ashe pushed through the exit, leaving Dani standing in the empty corridor, her heart racing and her mind spinning.

He hadn't given her a chance to explain, to apologize, or to settle anything from the past. And now, Ming was still out there, and so was Ashe, running headfirst into whatever chaos came next.

❧ • ❧

DANI MOVED QUICKLY, her boots striking the pavement with loud reports. The tension in her chest hadn't eased since Ashe had disappeared into that corridor, leaving her with a mix of frustration, confusion, and far too many unanswered questions. That had all faded, at least for the moment, when a call had come in from Sergeant Hale that they had her suspect in the east warehouse.

She rounded a corner and sprinted toward the far end of the compound, her breath coming steady and controlled despite the adrenaline spiking in her veins.

The east warehouse loomed ahead, its corrugated steel doors partially closed. A cluster of soldiers from the base had already taken position around it. Dani could see a second group of men moving to the back corner of the building.

She skidded to a stop beside Hale. "Is he in there?"

Hale nodded. "He's inside. Moved fast when your alert came through. Looks like he was trying to destroy records. We've got him boxed in."

The doors burst open, and Hale's team poured into the warehouse, footsteps echoing in the cavernous space. Fluorescent lights flickered overhead, casting shadows across rows of crates and supply racks.

Dani's eyes swept the area, her instincts razor-sharp. Near the back of the warehouse, she spotted a man crouched beside an open file cabinet, rifling through papers with frantic energy.

"Freeze!" she barked, her weapon trained on him.

The man spun around, eyes wide with panic, his hands flying into the air. "Don't shoot! Don't shoot!"

"Step away from the files. Now," Dani ordered, her voice cold and steady.

The man hesitated for a fraction of a second too long. Two soldiers rushed forward, forcing him to the ground and zip-tying his wrists. Dani holstered her weapon and crouched beside him, her eyes narrowing.

"Who are you working with?" she demanded, knowing the answer.

The man shook his head, his breath coming in short gasps. "I don't know what you're talking about."

Dani looked at Hale, who simply shrugged. The young sergeant was not entirely sure of the jurisdiction here, but since Dani knew what she was looking for, he decided to let her take the lead.

"Really?" Dani said to the man on the ground, her tone dropping into a lower register. "Because from where I'm standing, it looks like you were about to torch those records. Covering your tracks, maybe? Or Ming's?"

The man's eyes flicked up at her, fear flashing across his face. "I—I don't know anything about any Ming."

Dani leaned closer, her voice dropping further to a hard whisper. "Lying to me is the worst decision you'll make today. You think Ming's scary? You have no idea what I'm capable of if you push me. Now talk."

The man swallowed hard. "Okay, okay! Ming... he gets some stuff from me on occasion. Moves it out. I don't know where he takes it. I don't know any details. Says he's got some kind of transport that can't be traced."

Dani's eyes narrowed. "What kind of transport?"

"I don't know!" The man shook his head, desperate. "I swear! I just get him stuff. He doesn't tell me anything."

Dani pushed back to her feet, her mind racing. She turned toward the rows of supply crates and racks lining the warehouse.

"We need to search everything," she said to Hale. "I need to know what's missing."

Hale's team moved quickly for two hours, tearing through the storage area with military precision. What they found confirmed Dani's worst suspicions.

Hale called out from the far end of the warehouse, holding up a clipboard. "We've got a problem."

Dani joined him, her eyes scanning the list. Missing inventory jumped out at her in bold red text: thirty-seven assault rifles, eleven anti-tank weapons (AT4s and other variants) various plate carriers, night-vision goggles, and tactical gear. PETN 20 g/m detonation cord. Dani's mind flashed back to Ashe's tale of Ming's "compliance belts." A thousand feet of it, on two spools. And...

And almost two hundred kilograms of Composition C4.

Dani stared at the list, her mind piecing it together. This wasn't just a simple theft, this was a fully-equipped strike force's worth of supplies.

Dani muttered something unladylike, rubbing her temple. Hale nodded.

Walked back to the crooked supply officer. "You! The transport he's planning? What's the timeline?"

The man shook his head. "I don't know. Soon, I think. He doesn't tell me anything. Just said no one would ever find the stuff once it's on the move."

Dani stared down at the man for a long moment, then turned to Hale. "He's yours."

THE CONFERENCE ROOM at the Los Angeles FBI field office was a sterile, windowless space, the kind of room that could have been in any government building across the country: grey walls, a scuffed table, flickering fluorescents, and an ancient coffee machine humming softly in the corner.

Dani sat at the far end of the table, her laptop open in front of her, maps and notes spread out across the polished surface. Her eyes flicked between tabs on her screen: intel reports, missing munitions logs, personnel lists. But her focus kept slipping back to the same thought: *Ashe was alive.*

She leaned back in her chair, rubbing her temples, trying to push the memory of his face from her mind. It wasn't working.

The call came at exactly 10:00 a.m. *Had she been sitting here for three hours?* The mid-morning sun streamed through the large windows, casting warm light across the polished floor, but Dani had barely noticed its march across the floor. Her mind had been in overdrive for days.

So had the phone she'd commandeered as her personal line.

That phone buzzed now. She glanced at the number: ASAC Rourke.

Dani lifted the handset, fearing what was coming.

"Linder," she said, keeping her voice low.

"Morning, Dani." That wasn't a good sign. Rourke's voice came through, calm but clipped. The kind of tone he used when delivering bad news. "Listen, I just got off a call with the AD. Effective immediately, you and your team are standing down on the Ming investigation."

Dani straightened in her seat. "What are you talking about? Standing down? Bill, Ming's building something, and those stolen munitions—"

"Not your problem anymore," Rourke cut her off. "At least not directly. You're being pulled off drug-related operations and reassigned to cover a critical transport operation."

Dani closed her laptop, suddenly very aware of how many people were around her. She lowered her voice further. "A what?"

"Yeah, I knew you weren't going to like it," Rourke said, exhaling sharply. "You and your team are being tasked with traffic control and overwatch support for a classified transport operation. Nuclear waste."

Dani froze. *This job just keeps getting better and better.* "Nuclear waste?"

"Yeah. SONGS to Yucca Mountain. They're running a transport this Sunday. The route passes around the east side of L.A., and with those stolen munitions still unaccounted for, everybody's freaking out. They want CIRG covering two key points along the route."

Dani sat back, processing. SONGS, the San Onofre Nuclear Generating Station, was one of the biggest nuclear facilities in the country. Moving waste from there to Yucca Mountain was a logistical nightmare, planned down to the second. Postponing it wasn't an option.

For the most part, Dani understood the politics of the situation. The stolen AT4s, PETN det cord, and C4 were suddenly in sharp focus. The kind of munitions Ming had access to were insanely dangerous on a good day. On a day with a transport like that laid in, the risk alone was a political nightmare.

Nonetheless, Dani rubbed her temple, her frustration simmering beneath the surface. Roadblock duty. It wasn't why she'd joined CIRG. CIRG didn't sit on the sidelines and hope things didn't go wrong. CIRG stopped bad things before they started.

"Why us?" she asked, keeping her voice calm. She knew the answer.

"The brass wants eyes and boots on the ground," Rourke said. "Your presence in the area was too appealing to pass up. Your team's roadblocks will cover two critical access points. One at the eastern checkpoint, one at the southern junction. Your backup team leader is already en route. You'll meet him there and prep the operation together. The rest of your team's already on the way as well."

"And then what?" Dani asked, her tone sharper than she should use with a superior. "After we play traffic cop for the weekend, do we just forget about Ming?"

"If the transport goes smoothly, you'll be back on him first thing Monday," Rourke said. He hadn't missed her tone. "Until then, this is priority one. Get it done."

Dani exhaled through her nose, a sharp, controlled breath. "Understood."

"Linder," Rourke snapped. "Stakes are high on this one, and optics couldn't be worse. Make sure it's done right."

"Got it," she said quietly.

The call ended, but Dani stayed seated, staring at her phone. Her thoughts drifted back to the armory, to Ashe's face, his voice, the tension that had hung between them balanced on a razor's edge.

Ashe was alive. After all these years. After everything.

And the first thing he'd done was push her away, just like he always had. He hadn't asked questions, hadn't given her a chance to explain, and now he was out there somewhere in Los Angeles, chasing the same ghosts they'd both been running after for years.

Her jaw tightened. She didn't have time for distractions, not with a nuclear waste transport to secure and her team expecting her to lead. But the distraction was there, nagging at her like an old wound that refused to heal.

Dani closed her laptop and slipped it into her bag, standing slowly. If this was the job, she'd do it right. Still… Roadblock duty? It was beneath her team's skill set, a babysitting job that no one would ever thank them for.

Politics. It always came down to politics.

Her phone rang again and she answered. It was Mitchell. He and the rest of her team were leaving Albuquerque now. She acknowledged and placed the handset on its cradle.

Her tactical mind was already switching gears, thinking through the logistics of roadblocks and access control. But in the back of her mind, Ashe lingered. He was out there now, somewhere in Los Angeles, chasing Ming the only way he ever had: reckless, stubborn, and alone.

She wasn't sure what scared her more: running into him again, or not running into him at all.

•

THE STREETS WERE empty, wrapped in shadows and silence. The air felt heavy, tinged with the faint scent of burned trash and something metallic that clung to the back of Dani's throat. Streetlights flickered intermittently, casting pools of pale light on cracked pavement and sagging rooftops.

The safehouse stood at the end of the block: a two-story husk of a house, its once-white paint peeling in long strips, the windows boarded up with mismatched sheets of plywood. Layers of graffiti fought for dominance across the walls, an intricate mix of tags and warnings, the signatures of gangs that repeatedly traded control over this part of the city.

It looked like a place people came to disappear.

Dani stood just outside the chain-link fence, her eyes sweeping the property. Clarke and Ororo flanked her, their movements silent, practiced. The glow from the streetlight flashed briefly on the white FBI letters on Ororo's plate carrier patch and his whiter teeth, but otherwise, Dani and her men blended into the shadows.

"You sure about this, boss?" Clarke asked, his voice a low whisper.

Dani nodded. "Wilkerson's been tracking leads on Ming and the munitions all week. Safe houses make sense. This place fits: quiet, easy to overlook. We check it out, confirm it's clean, and head back."

Ororo's smile widened further. "And if it's not clean?"

"Then we've done our job," Dani said, her tone neutral. "We're not breaking orders. The shipment's not until

Sunday. We've got time to clean up a loose end or two. Besides, this is just recon."

"Until it's not," said Clarke.

Ever the optimist, Dani thought.

The gate creaked as Dani pushed it open, and the three agents slipped inside, weapons drawn, every movement deliberate and controlled. Weeds had overtaken the yard, strangling the chain-link fence and winding around the base of the house. A rusty swing set leaned to one side, its chains tapping gently in the night breeze.

Clarke took point, his pistol held steady, eyes sharp as they approached the door.

"Locked," he said quietly, glancing back at Dani.

Dani counted down in silence, using exaggerated hand signals. Three… two…

Clarke kicked the door in, and they swept into the house.

The interior was worse than the outside: walls stripped down to scraps of drywall, the floor littered with broken furniture, beer bottles, and cigarette butts. The stench of mold and rot hung in the air.

Dani's team moved room by room, clearing each one with quick, methodical precision. The house was empty, its silence thick and oppressive.

"Clear," Clarke said, lowering his weapon. Ororo checked the last corner and gave a nod.

Dani frowned. Her gut told her there was something they'd missed. She was about to call it when a sharp noise broke the stillness: a muffled thump from the back of the house, barely audible but enough to snap her attention to the hallway.

"Clarke, Ororo, flank the door. I've got the exit," Dani said, already moving toward the far end of the hall.

Clarke and Ororo moved into position, weapons up. The door loomed ahead, chipped and sagging on its hinges.

"Go," Dani said softly.

Clarke kicked the door open into a room they had already cleared. Dani looked through the doorway and her vision seemed to blur for a second: a sudden flurry of movement, the dull sound of impacts, the crack of bone against drywall.

And silence.

"Clarke? Ororo?"

No response.

Dani rushed forward, turning the corner into the room just in time to see Ashe standing over the two unconscious agents, his face shadowed but unmistakable. He held a Glock G23 identical to Dani's in his right hand: Clarke's gun, with the extended 22-round clip. Ororo, for some reason, had always liked the older, bigger S&W 1076 he'd received when joining the Bureau a decade earlier. Since he somehow consistently qualified with the inferior weapon, she let him keep it.

She saw it now over in the far corner, where Ashe had kicked it after incapacitating the big black man.

"You've got to be kidding me," Dani said, raising her weapon. "Drop it."

Ashe's eyes locked on hers, sharp and unrelenting. "What's the matter, Dani? Going to shoot me again?"

Her finger tightened on the trigger. "Don't tempt me."

For a moment, neither of them moved. The room was charged with tension, the weight of a decade's worth of anger and regret pressing down on both of them.

Ashe slowly lowered the gun, tossing it onto the ground with a metallic clatter. "You haven't changed much, have you? All that talk about going back to doctorin'."

"Don't do this," Dani said, her voice calm but hard-edged. "You're in over your head. We're on the same side, Ashe. We want the same thing."

"No, we don't," Ashe said, stepping closer, his voice rising. "You want to catch Ming. You want to arrest him, make him answer for his crimes, and wrap it all up in a neat little package." His eyes burned with something raw, something deeply personal. "You want to get yourself another promotion. I want him gone. For good. I want to bury my hands in his guts up to the elbows as I rip out his insides and stuff them full of his own drugs. I want to paint the walls in his blood. You think prison can stop someone like Ming? You don't know him like I do."

"He'll pay for what he's done," Dani said, holding her ground. "But we do this the right way. No more bodies, Ashe. No more collateral damage."

Ashe laughed bitterly. "The right way? Since when has the right way ever worked with these guys? All it does is give them time to regroup, rebuild, and kill more people. I'm done playing by your rules, Dani. I was done a long time ago. And Ming was done with those rules long before that. The only way to stop Ming is to stop him permanently."

"That's not justice," Dani shot back. "That's revenge."

"Yep," Ashe growled. "And it's the only thing that's going to work."

They stood there for a long moment, locked in a silent battle of wills. Finally, Ashe shook his head, his expression hardening.

"Stay out of my way, Dani. Last time I'm sayin' it nice. I'm going to finish this. One way or another."

Before she could respond, Ashe turned and walked toward the exit, his footsteps echoing down the hall. Dani's heart pounded as she watched him disappear into the shadows, anger and frustration swirling in her chest.

Her grip tightened on her weapon.

"This isn't over," Dani whispered to no one.

THE RAIN HAD started as a drizzle just after dawn, soaking through their clothes and making everything miserable. Now, hours later, it was a steady downpour, pounding on the roof of the SUVs and turning the dirt road into a slick mess of mud and puddles. The flat terrain on one side of the road served as a makeshift landing zone for the helicopter on loan from the Surveillance and Aviation Section, its blades idling, ready to lift off at a moment's notice. The other side dropped off into a shallow embankment, rainwater coursing down the slope in silvery streams.

Dani stood in front of the roadblock, her hood pulled low over her face, blinking through the rain. It was just past eight in the morning, and the convoy wasn't expected for another hour. But Dani's nerves were already on edge, and the steady hammer of rain wasn't helping. She envied the helicopter's pilot. He might be dying of boredom, but he was dry.

She and her sub-team—Ororo, Stevens, and Murray—had been in place since an hour before dawn, their vehicles parked at angles to block the narrow desert road. The second half of her team was positioned seven miles away, led by Graves, the new B-team leader, and assisted by Clarke.

Dani had questioned the wisdom of splitting Clarke and Ororo, but they were pros, and both had been smart enough to keep their mouths shut about the Friday night safehouse disaster.

She'd barely slept since then, of course. Every moment replayed itself in her head: the confrontation with Ashe, the arguments, the sound of big Ororo hitting the floor. And now, the knowledge that Ashe was out there, somewhere, as unpredictable and dangerous as ever.

"Incoming!" Murray suddenly called out, raising his hand toward the road.

The rumble of approaching diesels snapped Dani back into focus. Two sand-colored HMMWVs appeared at the top of the hill, rolling toward the roadblock with slow, deliberate precision.

"Eyes up," Dani said, her tone sharp. The team moved into position, weapons ready but lowered.

The lead vehicle stopped just short of the SUVs positioned across the road.

Dani stepped forward, waving Murray to approach the driver's side of the lead vehicle. A man in camouflage fatigues leaned out the window, rain dripping off the brim of his cap. He held up a laminated ID card.

"Leapfrog escort for the SONGS transport to Yucca," the man said flatly.

Dani exchanged a glance with Murray, who keyed his radio. "Stand by," he said, calling it in. "ASAC Rourke, confirm we've got two HMMWVs. Say they're escort vehicles for the transport."

The answer came back quickly, but Murray still appeared indecisive. "Yes, sir," he said. "Driver's badged... No, I don't know."

Murray leaned out to look past the lead vehicle at the second. Its driver flashed another set of credentials. "Yes, sir. All of them."

The call terminated, and Murray stepped back. "They're clear. Let them through."

Murray gave the lead driver a quick nod, waving them on. "You're good."

The first HMMWV rumbled past, water spraying in low plumes around its wheels. Dani squinted at the trailing vehicle, her instincts prickling. There was something about the older man in the passenger seat: something off. His face flashed through her mind like a half-forgotten memory, but she couldn't place it. Maybe someone she'd seen at the Armory.

The HMMWVs disappeared down the road, leaving only a cloud of mist and the sound of rain hammering on the SUVs. Dani's eyes lingered on the empty stretch of wet asphalt, doubt gnawing at her.

The sound of a roaring engine snapped Dani back to the present. A sedan tore up the road toward the roadblock, engine and tires straining as it careened around a curve.

"Crap," Dani muttered, raising her weapon. By the time that every other gun in the place snapped to the car, hers had already fired a single shot.

The sedan slipped sideways and skidded to a stop just shy of the roadblock, its driver-side front tire blown to ribbons. Dani lowered her weapon, recognizing the driver immediately.

Ashe. Of course.

He threw open the door and he stepped out, seemingly before the car had even come to a stop. *He doesn't even have the common sense to raise his stupid hands,* thought Dani.

When he spoke, his voice was anything but calm.

"You've got to let me through!" he yelled, his eyes blazing. "Now!"

"Stand down, sir!" Murray shouted, assault rifle trained on him. "Get on the ground!"

"Ashe!" Dani barked, stepping forward. "What are you doing?"

"You have no idea what's happening right now, do you?" Ashe snapped back. He jabbed a finger toward the direction the HMMWVs had gone. "Those two Hummers? That's Ming. He's already past your roadblock. Let me through now, or you'll lose him for good."

Dani opened her mouth to respond, but Ashe didn't give her the chance. He took a step toward Murray, his voice rising. "I don't have time for this, kid. Move!"

Murray, in his late thirties and easily a head taller than Ashe, braced himself, ready and willing for things to turn ugly. Dani saw it coming a second before it did.

"I got this," she said, stepping between them and pushing Murray back with a sharp glance. "Stand down. He's... an old informant of mine."

Murray shot her a look but complied and lowered his weapon.

Ashe turned back to Dani, his eyes still blazing. "You've been playing catch-up this whole time, Dani. Did you think that guy you found at the armory was the only source Ming had on the inside?"

He stomped back toward the immobilized sedan. "I've got another one for you."

The trunk popped open, and Ashe dragged out a middle-aged man in bloody fatigues. The man's hands were zip-tied. His face was pale, sweat dripping down his forehead and mixing into the rain.

"He's logistics and planning from the armory," Ashe said. "He knew all about the nuclear transport. Ming's been planning this for months. While you've been chasing weapons, he's been prepping stolen vehicles to blend into the convoy. That's how he's getting out of L.A.: posing as part of the escort."

Dani's stomach dropped. Stolen vehicles. It seemed so obvious now, and yet she'd overlooked the possibility, too distracted by Ashe, too focused on the missing weapons to consider the broader picture.

"You missed it," Ashe said, his voice biting. "Rookie mistake."

Dani's fists clenched at her sides, anger rising, but she couldn't deny it. He was right.

Ashe could see it instantly on her face.

"Because you were too busy worrying about doing things the 'right way,'" Ashe said, his tone dripping with sarcasm. "Typical."

Dani shoved her anger down and keyed her radio. "Rourke, this is Linder. The two HMMWVs that you just had us let through the eastern roadblock? Yeah, they're carrying the stolen munitions. Ming is using them to blend in with the convoy. Requesting immediate pursuit."

"Stand by," said Rourke.

There was a pause, followed by her superior's voice, sharp and angry. "Stand down, Linder. You're not authorized to engage."

"What? Roarke, he's past the roadblock! We need to stop him now!"

"I said stand down," Rourke snapped, his tone rising. "You've already made enough of a mess out there. We'll handle that later. Hold your position."

Dani's fingers tightened on the radio's switch. "You don't understand—"

"No, you don't understand!" Rourke barked. His voice was wavering now, on the verge of losing control. All of his prospects for a bigger, better office were drying up hundreds of miles from him in a pouring rainstorm. He wanted his pound of flesh. "You've been freelancing for days, Linder. You think I don't know about your little side quest? Do not make me repeat myself. Hold your position and await further instructions while we figure out what to do. And we'll be having a conversation about you letting him through the roadblock later."

He was going to pin this on her. She had no doubt of that.

The rain suddenly intensified, pouring down in heavy sheets. Turning, Dani caught the brief shift in Ashe's body language, the way his shoulders tensed, his eyes flicking around.

"Ashe, don't—"

He moved fast. Too fast.

He grabbed the captive by the collar and belt, hurling him at Murray and Stevens. The three men went down in a heap of writhing arms and legs, sliding around on the muddy ground.

Ororo stepped in to intercept, but Ashe lowered his shoulder and barreled into him, using his lower center of gravity to knock the larger man off balance. Ororo hit the ground hard, the rain splashing around him.

Dani raised her weapon but hesitated, the chaos in front of her making a clean shot impossible.

"Ashe, stop!" she shouted.

He didn't. He dove into one of the SUVs, slamming the door shut. The engine roared to life.

"Ashe!" Dani screamed, but it was too late.

The SUV shot forward, ramming into the second vehicle. The force sent the second SUV rolling down the embankment, coming to rest on its side in the muddy runoff at the bottom.

Ashe's vehicle straightened and peeled out, tires spinning, kicking up mud and water as it tore down the road. Within seconds, it disappeared into the rain.

Ashe was gone. Again.

❧ • ❧

RAIN POURED DOWN in heavy sheets as Dani sprinted toward the waiting helicopter, her boots slipping on the mud-slick pavement. The Surveillance and Aviation Section helicopter sat with its rotors already spinning, the downwash kicking up water and loose debris. The pilot leaned out, his face grim beneath his helmet.

"We're moving!" Dani yelled over the roar. "Get me in the air now!"

The pilot nodded, his voice barely audible. "Strap in!"

The Bell 412 helicopter lifted off with a shudder, rising above the flooded terrain and banking hard toward the road. Dani strapped into the tactical seat, her radio crackling to life as she adjusted her headset. The rain lashed against the canopy, the wipers struggling to keep up as they climbed higher.

"Local law enforcement is in a stolen FBI SUV," she called into the mic. "We're in pursuit."

"Local law enforcement?" Rourke's voice was strained.

"Undercover." Dani told herself she wasn't so much lying as she was polishing the truth. "Guy was embedded with Ming and holds a Godzilla-sized grudge against the guy."

Her voice was calm, steady. More so than she felt.

Below, the desert was a patchwork of waterlogged roads, muddy embankments, and low-lying streams overflowing with rainwater. The chopper pilot was able to track Ashe's SUV's headlights flickering through the storm, a faint glow in the gray expanse.

"Command, we have visual on the target," the pilot confirmed.

"Maintain pursuit," Rourke's voice snapped over the channel. "Dani, you're tasked with stopping that vehicle. I can't have some local cop taking his vendetta up to a truckload of nuclear waste. The B helicopter will continue after the HMMWVs. They're ahead of you and in a better position to intercept Ming."

Dani bit back a curse. Every instinct told her this was the wrong call. Ashe was reckless, but he wasn't the priority. Not when Ming was out there, hauling enough munitions to level a city block.

Knowing what had to be coming, Dani adjusted the heavy .50-caliber Barrett M82 that had been fitted out as the helicopter's complement. Sighting through the massive rifle's scope, she swiveled it on its mount to track Ashe's vehicle. The helicopter banked slightly, allowing her to line up the shot.

Dani instructed the pilot to drop as low as possible. Switching radio channels, Dani tried to appeal to whatever reason Ashe still had.

"Ashe!" She called out, over the internal channel that would transmit her message directly to the radio in the black SUV below her. "You need to break off, now. You have no idea what you're headed into."

"I'm the one who told you, remember? I think I got it." Reaching a straight patch of road, he sped up.

"No! Ashe! You are not going to be allowed to reach Ming! Please, just pull it over."

There was no immediate reply and the SUV slowed slightly, weaving side-to-side for several yards. For a brief moment, Dani thought she might have gotten through to him.

Then, Ashe's arm appeared, flinging the radio he had torn from the dash out of the vehicle. It hit the pavement and shattered to a thousand pieces.

What happened next was the subject of much investigation, the ending of several careers and a long congressional inquiry.

Normally, this situation would have been manageable. The helicopters were in sync, the ground teams coordinated. But a pair of matching communication failures sent everything spiraling toward disaster.

The first failure had occurred on the ground some time earlier and had nothing to do with Dani's team. The driver of the nuclear transport truck, carrying spent nuclear fuel rods encased in heavy casks, had unknowingly lost radio contact with his controller more than twenty minutes earlier. His vehicle continued its preset route, oblivious to the chaos approaching from behind him.

The second failure was either a slip of the hand or a panicked oversight. It was never determined which, but no member of the Congressional inquiry board had any doubt that it came at the worst possible moment.

"Take the shot," Rourke barked into his mic, his voice cracking under the pressure. He intended to transmit only to Dani's helicopter, ordering her to disable Ashe's vehicle while others farther up the food chain struggled with how to handle the bigger problem of the two HMMWVs. But in the chaos, he accidentally broadcast the command to both helicopters simultaneously.

Dani heard the command and nodded, allowing her training to take over. "Taking the shot. Targeting the engine block."

Dani breathed out slowly.

"Target acquired," Dani said, her voice calm. "Firing."

The high-velocity round left the barrel with a crack like thunder, punching through the engine block of Ashe's SUV and shredding the left front tire.

The vehicle skidded violently, tires losing traction on the rain-slick road. It spun once, twice, before tumbling end-over-end into the shallow ravine, landing like a dead tortoise in a torrent of water and mud.

Dani's breath caught in her throat as she watched the SUV come to a halt, mostly submerged in the rushing water of a flash flood.

"Ashe," Dani muttered to herself, leaning into the rain, her pulse racing.

Eight miles ahead, the second helicopter crew also heard Rourke's order. Special Agent Wilkerson, already tracking one of the HMMWVs, locked onto it with an identical Barrett rifle just as it rushed past the nuclear transport truck in its attempt to escape according to Ming's meticulous plan.

"Taking the shot," Wilkerson confirmed, unaware the order hadn't been meant for him.

He squeezed the trigger.

The round punched through the rear of the HMMWV, striking a spool of PETN det cord stowed as part of the stolen munitions cache. An explosion ripped away from the bullet along the coiled cord at a rate of approximately 6,400 meters per second, essentially flashing the entire 500-foot spool into a single burst of energy over fifty times faster than human neurons can transmit thought.

As fast as the detonation cord was able to transfer energy in a linear direction, its blast was able to travel outward even faster, reaching the ninety kilograms of Composition C4 before the vehicle containing both explosives could travel a hair's breadth farther down the wet road.

Once the resultant chemical reaction began, the C-4 decomposed to release a variety of gases—most notably, nitrogen and carbon oxides—and energy. The gases expanded at over 26,000 feet per second, applying cataclysmic force to everything in the surrounding area in an expanding sphere. At that expansion rate, there was no vehicle on the planet and few outside its atmosphere that could hope to outrun the blast wave.

To any observer, the explosion would have been instantaneous: one second, the HMMWV was passing on the left, and the next, it was replaced by a blinding flash of orange and white light.

From this point, the explosion had two distinct phases. The initial expansion inflicted most of the damage, enough to reduce a large house to small fragments at a distance of twenty meters. This first explosion was a concentrated fireball, sending shrapnel and white-hot debris in all directions. The C4 destroyed everything within a 30-yard radius in an instant. A secondary, less-destructive inward energy wave followed next, but the damage had already been done.

The shockwave ripped outward, slamming through the nuclear transport truck just as the HMMWV passing it was converted to shrapnel and energy. The heavy casks inside shifted violently, several of them rupturing instantaneously. Spent nuclear fuel rods—long, cylindrical assemblies of enriched uranium encased in zirconium cladding—were flung into the air like giant javelins or shattered into jagged shards.

The explosion's directionality sent them hurtling across a wide arc of desert, embedding in the soft earth at random intervals. The rods hissed and cracked in the rain, their protective cladding compromised, releasing a faint but deadly blue glow of ionizing radiation.

The rain carried the radioactive particles, washing them into nearby ravines and dry riverbeds. The water, once a harmless runoff, became a conduit for death, spreading radiation downstream into previously unaffected areas.

The flash of light from the explosion was immediately seen by Dani, but not before the helicopter's pilot had already reacted. Banking sharply, he threw the Bell 412 hurtling toward the deck and in the opposite direction of the explosion as fast as its whupping rotors could carry them.

Dani knew that Wilkerson, her counterpart in the lead helicopter, was already gone. The truck moving the spent nuclear fuel was gone. At long last, Ming was gone.

And so was Ashe.

PRESENT DAY

THE RAIN PATTERED softly against the windows of Dani's office, blurring the view of the Virginia hills. Gray clouds hung low, pressing against the horizon. It was the kind of rain that soaked deep into your bones, lingering long after the storm had passed.

Dani Linder, Assistant Director of the FBI's Counterterrorism Division, sat behind her desk, her eyes skimming a classified report spread out across the polished surface.

The Los Angeles Exclusion Zone. No one had ever settled on a single name: The Zone, the Fallout Zone, the Dead Strip. But for Dani, it was always just the aftermath of that day in 1998.

She picked up the top page of the report, her thumb brushing absently against the edge. Recent drone activity over the containment zone. Nothing overtly dangerous, but enough to raise red flags. Increased chatter among extremist groups, some with a known interest in radiological material for dirty bomb construction.

They'd never be able to piece anything together to amount to any real risk, but it was still the responsibility of her office to ensure no one tried. Over ninety percent of the spilled waste material had been recovered and allowed to finish its interrupted trip to Yucca Mountain. The remainder was so integrated into the desert that her office would keep the Zone closed to human habitation or passage for the next million years or so.

The margins of the report were filled with handwritten notes from analysts, each one circled in red.

Potential risk.

Surveillance recommended.

Further investigation required.

Dani set the report down with a sigh, leaning back in her chair. Decades later, the Los Angeles Exclusion Zone was still a problem. Still her problem.

Her office had long since become the unofficial nerve center for everything related to containment, monitoring, and security in the exclusion zone. It fell at least partially under the purview of her counter-terror operations branch, not because it was radioactive, but because it was an irresistible target.

Terror groups had been circling the zone for years, looking for ways to breach its perimeter, to harvest materials they could turn into weapons. So far, the safeguards had held. But Dani knew the only real safeguard was that the remaining material was in no state to be useful to anyone for anything. That, and it was so integrated with the very earth that just going to look would either kill you or make you wish it had.

Somehow, that didn't deter everyone, so she had a job to do.

She reached for the next report, flipping it open with a practiced motion. The words blurred slightly as her thoughts drifted. Rain always brought her back to that day.

The memory was clear despite the years: a desert road soaked with rain, the sound of shouting over the radio, the roar of an explosion that shook the earth and scattered spent nuclear fuel rods across the southern California desert.

She could still smell the ozone in the air, feel the heat of the blast on her face, see Ashe's SUV tumbling into the ravine in a torrent of mud and water.

Dani stood and moved toward the window, folding her arms as she stared out at the rain-wet complex below.

Ashe. She hadn't spoken his name aloud in years, but it was always there, lingering in the back of her mind. A ghost that refused to rest.

She'd convinced herself that he was dead. The wreckage of the SUV had been found days later, submerged and crushed. No sign of him. Nothing to prove he was gone for good, but nothing to suggest otherwise.

He was gone. He had to be. And still, she refused to let him go.

She'd spent years thinking about that day, about everything that had gone wrong. Her decisions. The chaos. The moment she'd pulled the trigger on that sniper rifle.

She'd killed him. Twice. Chicago, 1988. There, on that road, in the rain, a decade later.

The guilt had softened over the years, worn down by time like a jagged stone turned smooth in the current, but it had never disappeared. It never would.

Her computer chimed softly on the desk. Dani crossed the room and clicked the mouse, glancing at the notification. An email from her deputy: a routine personnel update, new assignments for high-priority cases. And a few not-so-high-priority ones.

She opened it absently, her eyes skimming the list of names. That one was strange. Special Agent Lamentation—seriously? What was this guy's mother thinking?—Standish. Temporarily re-assigned to the Los Angeles field office.

Dani's pulse ticked up, a slow thrum in her chest. The attached file referenced a cold case she wished had stayed buried.

"Standish," she muttered, rolling the name on her tongue like a bad taste.

Chapter 1 : ASHES OF TIME

THE SUN LOOKED down on the man without mercy.

It pressed down with the weight of ages, a molten eye in a colorless sky, burning away softness, moisture, all pretense. The air shimmered over the cracked earth; ghosts wandered through the hollow husks of forgotten canyons. There was no sound here but the dry rasp of wind and the slow, patient scrape of metal against sand.

The man worked alone.

He crouched low, a vague, armored silhouette against the bleached horizon, chipping away at the compacted earth with a hand pick. His work was slow, meticulous, methodical. It had to be, considering the object of his search. Strike and stroke combined to break through years of sediment, of history, of catastrophe covered over by the desert winds and long-ago rain. A small, military-issue shovel lay discarded nearby, its green edge dulled by its struggle against the sunbaked ground.

His suit, thick and lead-lined, white as a funeral shroud, bulged at the joints as he moved. It was a cumbersome thing, built for survival, not comfort. The boots were reinforced, heavy enough to slow him down but necessary to keep him alive long enough to complete his quest. The gloves, thick with layers of polymer and lead weave, made his grip clumsy, but he had long since learned to compensate.

Across the man's chest, a dosimeter blinked lazily, its needle fluctuating as it measured the ambient radiation still trapped in the land. This, he disregarded. Even if it reached a dangerous level, he would continue to work. All that mattered to him was the prize. And even that was simply a means to an end.

Beneath the suit's tinted faceplate, his breath came slow and controlled, though beads of sweat gathered along his forehead, trailing down the bridge of his nose. The world inside the helmet was an oven, the filtered air stale and recycled, every breath warmed by his exertion. His lips curled in discomfort, but he did not stop. He had come too far to stop.

His pick struck something.

Not rock. Something else.

He scraped gently with the pick and paused. Tilting his head slightly, he listened to the change in tone, the way the sound carried differently through the dense material beneath the surface. He switched to his hands, digging now, carefully brushing away the layers of history with slow, deliberate strokes.

And then, at last, there it was.

A sliver of dull silver-green, long and slender, was exposed as he brushed away decades of dust and sediment. Its smooth, weathered surface was jagged at one end.

The last breath he took before reaching for it was slow, reverent.

And then, in the silence of the wasteland, his gloved hands reached for the prize.

THE HANDS REACHED into the earth, brushing away the last layer of soil.

They moved with the delicate precision of a surgeon, fingers working carefully to avoid damage to the object buried beneath the weight of so many years. The morning mist curled in slow ribbons across the grassy hilltop, whispering through the folds of the excavation site as the soil released its treasure.

The pale prize emerged. Smooth, cool, impossibly intact.

The archaeologist paused, holding his breath, before gently lifting the object free.

The bust, a woman's face, rose from the grave of time. The morning light, soft through the haze, caught the fine curvature of her cheekbones, the subtle parting of her lips, the smooth, confident arc of her jawline. Reddish ochre pigment still clung to the carved strands of her unruly hair, frozen mid-motion, spilling in thick, curling waves that had once been fiery in color. Despite the years, the artistry had survived; each strand of hair testified of the delicacy of the sculptor's hand.

The archaeologist exhaled, rising to his feet, cradling the bust in his hands as though it were a newborn child. Dirt still clung in the crevices of the stone, but the woman's likeness remained pristine, defiant of time.

He stepped carefully over the churned earth and the yellow cords segmenting it into a grid. He moved toward the table beneath a canvas awning where a padded sling had been prepared. He lowered the bust into its protective cradle, then reached for a clean brush to dust away more remnants of the clinging soil.

The Gloucestershire landscape stretched beyond the excavation site, rolling green hills bathed in patchy morning fog, the distant outlines of hedgerows and stone fences barely visible through the shifting white veil. The cool air carried the scent of damp earth and nearby farms, mingling with the faint musk of overturned soil.

Wheeling the artifact past the main tent, the archaeologist pushed on down the path to the main house and the barn the farmer had allowed to be used as a more secure storehouse for the history being exhumed. Within the barn, the man approached two other busts, similarly set in protective slings on a long, well-lit worktable. He carefully added today's addition to the pair. The three statues, reunited after nearly two millennia, now sat side by side: silent echoes of a family lost to time.

A young woman stepped up beside him, pushing back the hood of her jacket as she peered at the newly recovered bust.

"Two days well spent," she mused, inspecting the delicate features. "And I guess we've confirmed your suspicions." She motioned to the other two busts.

The first, a man's likeness, was strong, resolute, chiseled in both form and expression. His broad forehead and angular cheekbones were marked with the fine artistry of its Roman sculptor, capturing not only strength but something deeper: endurance, perhaps, or the weight of too many years. The eyes, though empty now, had been carved with remarkable depth, their gaze intense and unwavering, set beneath slightly furrowed brows. His nose, slightly aquiline, bore a small irregularity, as though shaped by an old break. The mouth, firm and unsmiling, was set with determination of a man who'd seen war but found peace.

His hair was rendered in cropped curls, the Roman style of a soldier, but worn longer than regulation. Traces of dark pigment remained in the carved strands, faded but still clinging to the stone.

The Latin inscription beneath the bust, though partially worn, remained legible, as did the words on the two other busts.

"This one..." the assistant ran a finger along the new bust's inscription, eyes alight with excitement. "Aurelia.

It's exactly what we thought. Feminine version of the paternal nomen gentilicium, Aurelius. She's his daughter."

The archaeologist nodded. "His wife and daughter. A rare familial grouping." He glanced at the third bust, the female counterpart to the man. Her features were equally preserved, her expression softer but no less resolute.

He let out a slow breath, stepping back to take in the trio. "A husband, a wife... and now their daughter." His eyes lingered on the newest bust, her features so hauntingly familiar, her expression so close to the father's—but younger, unmarked by the same burden of experience.

The assistant grinned, shaking her head. "This is big, Ari. Really big."

The archaeologist nodded absently, still staring at the three of them.

Somehow, after nearly two thousand years, this family had found their way back together. He had an article to write.

❧ • ❧

THE AFTERNOON SKY hung low and heavy over the Gloucestershire dig site, its slate-gray weight pressing down on the rolling green landscape. The scent of manure from pastures beyond the excavation perimeter lingered heavy in the air. The autumn chill had settled in, curling mist around the hedgerows and stone fences, whispering through the ruins of a house that had stood proudly in another age.

Inside the barn, now repurposed as the excavation's main cataloging site, dim yellow light cast long shadows over wooden tables cluttered with fragments of history: ceramic shards, rusted tools, and stacks of brittle parchment covered in careful notations.

Aristophanes McGinnon was a man in his mid-fifties, lean and sharp-eyed, with a weathered, perpetual squint. Ari to all who knew him, he deliberately used the more pretentious name his mother had given him to great effect in every article he sent to various and sundry journals of archaeology. He stood across from his visitor. His hands, stained with the perpetual grime of the field outside, were tucked into the pockets of his canvas jacket as he regarded the dark figure before him.

The visitor had given no name.

He had arrived unannounced, his presence an intrusion into the quiet rhythm of the excavation. Dressed in an impeccably dark suit, severe and unyielding, he had the air of a man accustomed to authority, but something about him suggested something colder. His skin was pale, his features sharp and watchful beneath the brim of his hat. He had the air of a man who hunted things in the dark.

Ari McGinnon shifted uncomfortably beneath the weight of the visitor's stare, clearing his throat. "We've been working on this Roman-era house for a few years now," he began. His voice was calm, but something in him disliked the way the other man listened: so intently, so completely. "Started when a farmer out here turned up the first bust of the woman of the house in his field. Thought he'd plowed up a pile of old stones. Turns out, he'd driven his tractor straight over a piece of local history."

The dark man said nothing. Instead, he reached into his coat and withdrew a thin envelope. With precise, deliberate movement, he pulled free a pair of photographs and placed them on the table.

The archaeologist leaned in, frowning. The photos were of paintings, two of them, side by side. In the first, a woman in Roman dress, her hair a dark storm of wild curls, her features fierce but striking, bent lovingly over a cradle holding a red-haired child. In the second, the woman was younger, softer, but undeniably the same person.

"These are... remarkable," the archaeologist murmured, his fingers tracing the edges of the prints. "Where did you say these were painted?"

The dark man spoke at last, his voice smooth as a blade sliding from a sheath.

"I did not."

The archaeologist glanced up, puzzled, but the visitor offered nothing further.

Instead, Ari turned back to the photos, eyes narrowing. He flicked a glance over his shoulder at the row of artifacts cataloged along the back wall of the barn. Three marble busts sat in individual fabric slings, carefully placed under soft light. His gaze moved between the painted faces in the photographs and the middle of the three carved visages in stone.

His eyes widened slightly.

"This is uncanny," he admitted, stepping away from the table. His boots scuffed against the packed earth floor as he led the visitor toward the busts. "The resemblance is..." He shook his head. "It's right near perfect."

The visitor followed without a sound.

McGinnon stopped before the busts, gesturing. "We recovered these over the course of three seasons. The first was the woman, the one the farmer found. Then, the male bust, her husband, we presume. The third, just a few months ago. Their daughter."

The visitor's gaze lingered on the daughter's bust briefly and all but ignored the mother's.

His attention fixed instead on the male bust, his gaze boring into it like a man searching for the shape of a nightmare in the dark.

It was old, yet astonishingly well preserved, a fact that had become even more clear after the busts had been carefully cleaned by Susan, McGinnon's capable assistant. The face of a Roman man, likely upper middle class, his features carved with masterful precision. Early to mid-forties, broad forehead, angular cheekbones, a strong, resolute jawline.

A scar ran along his right cheek: a small, almost incidental detail, but one that made a style of art that could often be sterile into a very personal record of a specific person. The eyes, though worn with time, had been sculpted with depth, a piercing, unwavering gaze frozen in stone. His hair, once painted dark, was cropped in loose curls, longer than a soldier's but still disciplined.

Beneath the bust, carved into the worn marble base, was an inscription. The visitor whispered the name under his breath.

"Appius Aurelius Cinis."

A moment passed.

Then, softly, he repeated the cognomen, the third part of the tria nomina. It would have been the name used by those closest to the man. "Cinis."

Ari McGinnon folded his arms, nodding. "Yes. I know it sounds odd coming from an archaeologist, but I've never bothered much with Latin. My intern, bright girl, did the translation. 'Cinis' can mean 'grave,' 'ruin,' or even 'spent love,' if you want to be poetic. She liked that last one best, so that's what we put in the journal article. Gave it a flair, she said."

The visitor did not look at him.

His gloved fingers traced the name along the marble base, his jaw tightening as if the words had weight, as if they had meaning beyond time itself.

Finally, the visitor spoke, his voice even colder than before.

"Your assistant is wrong."

Ari blinked. "What?"

The visitor straightened, refusing to lift his gaze from the stone face before him.

"Cinis," he said, his voice a quiet verdict. "It translates to 'Ash.'"

The wind shifted outside, rattling the barn's tin walls, sending a shiver through the archaeologist.

Ari McGinnon could not shake the peculiar feeling that the visitor wasn't simply looking at the bust. At the long-dead Roman's face.

He was remembering it.

Chapter 2 : HISTORY ON THE ROCKS

AMBER BARELY HAD time to grab her menu before a waitress in a button-bedecked polka-dot uniform swaggered up to their booth with an attitude that was possibly lethal at close range. She planted a hand on her hip, popped her gum like a gunshot, and gave them a once-over that somehow managed to insult them without using a word. She rolled her eyes in Ashe's direction like she'd already decided he wasn't worth her time.

"You two look positively thrilled to be here. Let's ruin that. What do you want? Make it quick, I have people to ignore."

Amber grinned immediately; she automatically loved this place. Ashe, meanwhile, looked like he wasn't pleased at being back in Chicago, let alone at having walked through the neon-lit door of the restaurant. He set down his menu with the same energy as a man surrendering to fate.

"Route 66 Burger, no onion. Chili cheese fries. A Reuben. Side of onion rings. And a pitcher of water."

"Don't trust her to order for herself, huh?" mouthed the waitress, gesturing at the third, unopened menu on the table next to Ashe. Amber had informed the hostess another member of their party would be arriving soon.

Ashe looked up at her name tag, then to her face. The waitress' name tag read, "Velveeta," and Amber was disappointed when he declined to engage.

"That's for me. Dunno what she wants," he muttered.

Velveeta blinked, then barked a laugh. "Oh, okay, Hoss. Taking one to go for feeding your army, or is it just a 'live fast, die bloated' kind of day?"

Amber tried not to laugh. "Oh, he's serious. He eats like this all the time."

"Sure. That's normal," the waitress said flatly, scribbling notes like she was documenting a crime scene. "You want me to get you a trough, or are we still pretending this is human behavior?"

"Just bring the food. And the water. In a pitcher," Ashe growled at the woman.

"Oh, right. In a pitcher, like that's the weird part." She turned to Amber. "What about you, Red? Ordering for a normal person or joining the food hoarder here?"

"I'd like a BLT, but no tomato, please."

The waitress stopped writing. Blinked. Amber wondered if she'd swallowed her gum. The woman looked up from her notepad. "I'm sorry, a what?"

"A BLT, but I don't want tomato," Amber repeated.

Velveeta slowly dragged a hand down her face.

"So… a BL."

Amber shook her head. Curls flopped about in merry assent. "I still like calling it a BLT."

"Why? You literally removed the T. The T is gone. Do you just like extra syllables? You want me to call his water 'dihydrogen monoxide' for funsies?"

"No," Amber said matter-of-factly. "I just don't like tomatoes."

Velveeta scoffed. "Who doesn't like tomatoes?"

Amber sat up straighter, fully prepared for battle. "They're poisonous."

The waitress froze. Her pen hovered like it had thrown itself at the notepad and missed. "I'm sorry, what?"

Amber nodded solemnly. "Tomatoes kill people. It's a documented, historical fact."

Ashe sighed. Loudly. "It wasn't the tomatoes," he muttered. "It was pewter plates."

Velveeta turned to Ashe, smacking loudly on her gum. "Oh, great. Here we go," she said. "Please, professor. Give carrot-top here a history lesson."

Ashe rubbed his temples, grumbling as if he already regretted speaking up. "We've been over this. Sixteen, seventeen-hundreds. Wealthy Europeans used pewter plates. Pewter contained lead. When they ate acidic foods, like tomatoes, the acid would leach the lead out of the plates. People were poisoned. They blamed the tomatoes, not the plates."

Amber crossed her arms. "That's all propaganda. That's what Big Tomato wants you to think."

The waitress stared at her. Then at Ashe. Then back at Amber.

"For cryin' out loud," said Velveeta. "I can't believe I have to say this, but... Tomatoes. Are. Safe. They are not murder berries."

Amber shook her head. "You can eat whatever you want, but I'm not taking the risk."

The waitress turned to Ashe, looking for backup.

Ashe simply exhaled and tried to hand his menu to the woman. "Don't look at me. I stopped arguing about this three weeks ago."

The waitress threw her hands in the air. "Oh, fantastic! So this is a thing with you two? A doomsday prepper and a tomato truther?! What a fun house that must be." She scribbled something down. "Fine. Enjoy your BL-not-T. I'm gonna go try to process whatever just happened."

"Wait," Amber said. "I'd like a coffee."

The waitress whipped around. "Oh, you're not done ruining my night?"

Amber held up a finger. "Not just any coffee. Dark roast. French press, if you have it. No cheap diner sludge, no burnt espresso, and don't you dare bring me anything instant. I want something rich, smooth, full-bodied—"

Velveeta cut her off with a pained groan. "Oh boy, we got a coffee snob. Lady, this is a place that puts paper hats on people and publicly shames them. You think we have a French press back there?"

Amber shrugged. "Hey, it's worth the ask."

"No, it really isn't." The waitress scribbled in her pad and read off what she'd written. "Coffee, pretentious, extra delusion. Okay." Satisfied with her work, she pointed again at the bench next to Ashe. "What are we doing about this invisible third person?"

Amber and Ashe exchanged glances. Ashe took the lead.

"She'll be here soon. No idea what she wants," he said.

The waitress sighed like this news completed the ruination of her day. "Oh, awesome. I love mysteries. Nothing better than hovering at a table while someone asks me, 'Uh, I don't know, what do *you* like?' like we're about to get engaged." She tapped her pen against her notepad. "Tell you what, I'll be back when your missing friend gets here, and I fully expect her to be just as much of a pain as you two. Don't let me down."

She turned and started to walk away—then paused, giving Amber a sidelong glance.

"Wait a second. You look familiar."

Amber smirked. "Yeah? I've spent some time working as a waitress myself. Ever been to L.A.?"

Velveeta's eyes narrowed slightly. "Wait. That's not it." She snapped her fingers. "I've seen you on TV. Cable news."

Amber nodded, enjoying this too much to feel awkward about the circumstances that made her face recognizable to the waitress. "A couple times. I'm writing a book. Got some attention after… well, after some things happened."

The waitress snorted. "Yeah, 'some things.' I remember now! That whole corporate meltdown thing, right? The billionaire. 'Some things.' Wow. Hope you write better than you understate."

Amber waved her hand. "Oh, it's not about that. I'm writing a novel."

The waitress crossed her arms and deadpanned, "Oh good. Another up-and-coming victim of the five-minutes-of-fame-to-novel pipeline. I bet it'll be 'raw' and 'brutally honest.'"

Amber nodded seriously. "And 'unflinching.'"

The waitress groaned. "Saints preserve us. I hope you fail just so I don't have to look at your face on a bookshelf." She shook her head. "Great, I've got an ex-waitress cable news reject writer and a doomsday prepper with a drinking problem at table seven. It's gonna be a long night."

Velveeta slapped her notepad shut. "Alright, I'm gonna go put this order in and contemplate every poor life choice that led me to this moment. Try not to die of boredom before I get back."

She spun on her heel and disappeared toward the kitchen.

Amber turned to Ashe, barely containing her glee. "I love this place."

Ashe picked up a sugar packet and crushed it between his fingers.

"I hate it."

* • *

THE UNMISTAKABLE SOUND of heels clicking on tile preceded the new arrival at their table. Amber glanced up from her just-delivered tomato-free sandwich just in time to see the tall, poised woman in a leather jacket and tailored slacks step past the hostess station unassaulted. Dani Linder moved with the effortless authority of someone who had spent a lifetime commanding rooms, and even in a place as chaotic as this, heads turned as she walked past.

Amber had met her once before, briefly, but the woman's presence left an impression. Dani had a certain magnetism, the kind that made her seem both approachable and impossible to rattle at the same time.

"Ashe, darling." Dani's voice was warm, but her sharp blue eyes flicked to him with something that seemed like half challenge.

Ashe, for his part, barely looked up from the basket of onion rings he was plowing through. "Mrs. Linder."

Amber almost choked on her coffee at his casual, deadpan response.

Dani turned to her next, offering a charming, easy smile that brought a dance to the crow's feet at the corner of each eye. "Amber, right? We met under less-than-ideal circumstances, but it's good to see you again. I'm glad you're joining us." She smoothly unfastened and doffed the thin scarf wrapped loosely around her shoulder-length waves of silvered hair.

Amber returned the smile, immediately liking the older woman. "Yeah. You were kind of busy with that creepy Standish guy that night. I won't hold it against you."

Dani slid into the booth beside Ashe, graceful even as she casually nudged his leg out of her way. "Good. No more of that nonsense now, thank goodness. I'm finally retired. No more jumping in to fix messes."

Amber perked up. "Retired? No way! How's it feel?"

Dani sighed dramatically, reaching for her menu. "Like I've been released from captivity. No reports, no late-night briefings, no more chasing ghosts." This last, she directed at the man sitting next to her. "Just... peace."

Ashe made a noncommittal noise that could have been either agreement or skepticism.

Amber raised an eyebrow at him. "You're not congratulating her?"

He grunted. "She'll be back at work inside of six months."

"And what's that supposed to mean, young man?" quipped Dani with mock outrage.

"Some jobs, it's just who you are. You can't escape, you can't get away. You can't retire. It's just part of you."

Dani rolled her eyes. "Don't listen to him. He's just bitter that I get to sleep through the night now."

"I know, right?!" exclaimed Amber. "What is it with this guy and not sleeping?"

"Actually, I have a theory—"

"We are not talking about me," declared Ashe with finality.

Dani winked at Amber. "Well, then, I guess I'm sure I just wouldn't know," was Dani's coy reply.

Ashe's eyes narrowed.

Amber watched their exchange, fascinated. The way they talked: it was familiar, effortless, edged with a dry fondness. Not quite romantic, but... not the opposite, either.

She was about to probe further when their waitress, Velveeta, sidled up, snapping her gum loudly to announce her return.

"Oh, fantastic. Another one. Can't say they didn't warn me." She eyed Dani up and down. "I don't know who you are, lady, but I assume you're just as annoying as these two."

Dani blinked, then laughed. "That seems like a safe bet."

Velveeta crossed her arms. "Alright, what's it gonna be?"

Dani glanced at the battlefield of plates that held Ashe's excessive order, then at Amber's oddly specific coffee. She shook her head. "Just a club sandwich and black coffee, thanks."

Velveeta narrowed her eyes. "Oh wow. No tweaks? No hand-picked coffee beans? An actual normal order? This is a historic moment." She scribbled something down, then noticed Ashe's empty pitcher. "What's with your weird water thing, by the way? You allergic to taste?"

Ashe didn't even blink. "I like water," he mumbled around a mouthful of food.

Velveeta scoffed. "Yeah? You know we have actual drinks, right? Things with flavor? I'm just saying, any time you wanna grow up and branch out a bit... It's a choice; I'm just saying."

Dani grinned, nudging Ashe's arm. "Did he at least tip you well?"

Velveeta snorted. "He's still eating. Jury's out. But judging by how much food he ordered, I'm sure he'll be leaving enough for a table of six, or I'm tracking him down."

"Yeah, good luck with that," Dani said with a smile.

Velveeta threw Ashe a mock salute and disappeared back toward the kitchen.

Amber, grinning, turned to Dani. "So, did you know Ashe was such a bottomless pit before tonight?" she asked gesturing broadly at the crowded table.

Dani sipped her coffee, completely unfazed. "You should have seen him in '88. Twice as reckless, just as hungry."

Amber perked up. "Ooh, history. Do tell."

Ashe refused to look up. "Actually, don't."

Dani only smirked, jabbing Ashe with an elbow. "Oh, come on, you're fascinating." She turned back to Amber. "Did you know he used to be clean-shaven?"

Amber gasped. "No. You're lying."

Dani grinned wickedly and ran a playful hand through Ashe's hair, ruffling his already unruly locks.

"I much prefer this version, though. Scruff suits him."

Amber covered her mouth to hide her laughter, but Ashe scowled, smoothing his hair back down immediately.

"Stop that."

Dani sighed dramatically. "Fine, ruin our fun."

Amber leaned forward. "So you two...?"

Dani didn't miss the implication. She gave a pleasantly neutral smile. "Ashe and I have a lot of history. I respect him a great deal."

Amber wasn't buying it. "That's a very diplomatic answer."

"That's a very intentional answer," Dani grinned.

Amber glanced at Ashe, who hadn't looked up from his food. His silence spoke volumes.

Before Amber could press the issue, Dani reached into her bag and pulled out a folded magazine.

"Speaking of history," Dani said, placing it on the table. "I saw this when I visited my dad for his birthday. He just turned ninety-nine."

Amber whistled. "That's incredible. Ninety-nine. I don't think I ever met anyone that old."

Ashe glared at her.

Dani nodded. "Sharp as ever, too. While I was there, I flipped through last month's copy of the Journal of Field Archaeology." She tapped the open page. "And, well..."

Amber leaned over to look at the magazine article and froze.

The photograph beneath the abstract showed an ancient Roman bust. The subject was a man in his forties with strong features, sharp cheekbones, and a timeless, intense gaze.

Amber's eyes widened.

"Holy—"

It was Ashe.

Or rather, it was a two-thousand-year-old marble sculpture of Ashe.

Dani sat back, observing the expressions of both Ashe and Amber.

"So… turn the page," she suggested, too casually.

Amber did so and was greeted this time by a pair of busts, two women. Regarding the younger of the two was not unlike looking in a mirror, except Amber's skin had never been that perfect.

Amber just gawked at the photo. "Okay. I have questions."

"Me, too," said Dani. "Who's up for a little side trip to England on our way to Paris?"

Ashe finally looked up.

He sighed.

And took another bite of his onion rings.

Chapter 3 : BURIED

AMBER STOOD AT the base of the dry-rotted wooden steps, staring up at the long-abandoned row house. Even in the dim glow of early evening, it was obvious the place had been left behind by time. The brick was faded, the mortar lines dark with years of Chicago soot and neglect. The third unit from the left sagged deeply at the edges, its once-proud Victorian details worn smooth by decades of wind and weather. Only the second unit showed any sign of human habitation, but even that was of the long-gone variety. The curtains behind the upstairs windows hung limp, untouched by recent life inside.

The place looked haunted, in a way. But not by ghosts, she didn't think. By something too stubborn to die, but too tired to hold on.

The breeze kicked up, swirling a few crispy brown leaves past Amber's sneakers. The thick cloud cover above shifted uneasily, hinting at approaching rain, and the street lamps flickered on and off in the twilight, casting pale pools of light onto the cracked pavement.

Amber wasn't the only one looking at the house.

Amber could feel the eyes on them: residents taking notice of three strangers standing outside a place that had been empty for decades. A few kids on battered bikes slowed as they rode past, their heads turning. An older woman across the street, wrapped in a shawl, paused in her doorway, her eyes narrowing slightly before she shuffled quickly inside.

But none of them watched with interest as pointedly as the man in the shadowed entryway of the brownstone across the street.

Middle-aged, black, maybe late fifties or early sixties. He leaned just inside his doorway, arms folded, not hiding his interest at all. He wasn't just curious. He recognized them.

Or rather, he recognized Ashe.

Amber wasn't sure if that should trouble her or not.

She turned her attention back to the house. The stairs creaked as Ashe climbed them, his worn boots heavy on the wood treads.

That's when she noticed the flowers.

A window box, perched just beneath the dusty, streaked front window, sat full of white lilies. They stood in delicate contrast against the worn, peeling paint of the railing, their stems strong despite the season. Someone had been tending them.

Amber frowned. The lilies reminded her of another place, of a cluster of white flowers growing against the skeletal mouth of a cliffside cave.

The sight of them here felt impossibly out of place.

She opened her mouth to ask, but Ashe reached the door and turned the key in the lock.

"So," she said instead, flipping open her notebook. "You've had this place since the eighties? You just... left it sitting here all that time?"

Ashe didn't answer, working the key as if the lock had fused from disuse.

Dani, still lingering at the base of the stairs, flashed a knowing grin. She started up to join them. "Oh, he's left behind dozens of places over the years. This one's just in slightly better shape than most."

Amber snapped at the bait immediately. "Oh? How many 'places' are we talking?"

Dani looked thoughtful. "Let's see, two apartments in D.C., a cabin in Virginia, that weird place in Arizona..."

Ashe shot her a sharp look. Dani just smirked.

Amber her eyes wide, looked at Ashe. "Wait... for real?"

Dani shrugged dramatically. "Who can say? Maybe all the evidence is buried in the deepest depths of the FBI's archives... Or maybe I'm making it up just to watch him squirm."

Amber grinned, scribbling furiously. "Noted: check for secret bunkers."

Ashe sighed and rubbed his temple.

Amber flipped a page. "Okay, so when you two met, he had, what, a cabin? A bunker? A lair?"

Dani grinned wider. "Oh no. When I first met him, he was a bum. Then next, shaved bald and face-down on an operating table."

Amber froze mid-scribble.

"Wait, what?"

Dani nodded, looking pleased with herself. "Yeah. Strapped down, half-dead, looking like someone had tried to blow him in half. Which they had. Very different from the man you see before you today."

Amber's eyes flicked to Ashe, who, to no surprise, was not elaborating.

"Maybe not so different," Amber offered after a brief moment.

Dani's laugh tinkled like a silver bell. "No, not so different after all, I suppose."

Ashe finally got the door open and nudged it open just enough to let the musty scent of abandoned space and old books spill into the evening air.

Amber turned back to Dani. "I have so many questions."

Dani grinned. "I bet you do."

Ashe sighed, stepping into the darkness of the house.

"Come on. Let's get inside," he muttered. "Before I regret letting you two talk."

Amber flashed a delighted grin and hopped slightly, bouncing her curly mop of hair before following them inside.

Best. Novel. Ever.

THE STAIRS GROANED under their weight as Ashe led them up the half-flight to the main level.

Amber followed just behind him, Dani at her side, as they entered what had once been a parlor or living room. A dim gold glow from the streetlights outside barely pierced the dust-covered windows, leaving the space murky and gray. The house had the heavy quiet of abandonment, but something about it felt... not quite forgotten.

Without a word, Ashe strode to the far corner of the room, ran his hand along the wall, and slid back a small wooden panel.

Amber caught the faintest glimpse of wires, switches: some kind of control panel. There was a soft click before he sealed the panel again as if nothing had happened.

"What was that?" Amber asked, flipping open her notebook.

"Nothing," Ashe muttered. "Stop it with the notes."

Dani tilted her head, grinning. "Oh, sure. Just a random, unnecessary hidden switch in the wall. Totally normal. I never saw that one before..." She let the unspoken question hang in the air.

Ashe ignored it. He continued onward, leading them through the rooms.

The living room gave way to a dining area, its oak table covered by a cloth cover and that by a thick layer of dust. Chairs sat haphazardly pushed back like people had once stood up from dinner and never returned. Beyond that, the kitchen, its counter lined with old coffee tins and sealed storage containers that looked like they hadn't been opened in years.

At the far end of the kitchen, they reached the main stairway. It was narrow and steep, an old Chicago-style stairwell that dropped downward into darkness and thrust upward to the upper floors.

Without hesitation, Ashe turned to move downward.

Amber followed, Dani right beside her, as they wound their way into the basement. The air grew heavier, cooler; the scent of aged wood and old dust was even thicker in the space below.

As soon as they reached the concrete floor, Amber's brows furrowed. Something felt off.

She glanced around the rows of boxes, the dusty old oil drums stacked neatly against the walls. There should have been something else. Something was missing.

"I don't know why," she said slowly, "but this place feels weird."

Dani nodded. "It does."

Amber turned to her. "What is it?"

Dani tilted her head, scanning the space. Then her eyes narrowed.

"No cobwebs."

Amber's jaw dropped slightly. That was it.

It was dusty, sure. It smelled old. But the expected layers of neglect: the creeping webs, the dangling dust strands? They weren't there.

Ashe, now halfway across the basement, didn't even pause as he muttered, "I was here a couple months ago. Packing some things."

Amber scribbled a note. "Packing things... for what?"

"Sent some items to Paris. For a traveling exhibit from the Hermitage."

Amber's hand froze mid-word. She blinked. "Wait. The Hermitage? In Russia?"

That caused Ashe to stop in his tracks. He turned to face her, a questioning look plastered across his face.

Amber looked at him. "Yeah, I don't know how I knew that. Fry must've mentioned it or something."

Dani shrugged. "Maybe you just read about it somewhere."

Ashe made a sharp noise that resembled a laugh.

"Okay, mister wise guy. Just keep going on your journey to the bottom of your junk," Amber snapped at the old man. She was about to launch into more questions when Ashe came to a sudden stop in front of an old brick wall.

He pressed his hand against one section, then pushed inward.

Amber squealed in delight as the hidden doorway swung open.

"No way," she breathed, furiously scribbling. "You have a hidden door?!"

"No."

Amber grinned. "Oh, man, this is so much better than I imagined."

Ashe rolled his eyes and stepped inside, leading them down a narrow passageway carved from the shared basement walls of the row houses. Dim bulbs were strung overhead on a wire. Most of these had long since burned out, but those remaining buzzed faintly and cast jittery shadows across the stone floor and walls as they progressed.

Amber glanced at Dani, who appeared to be remembering another time. It was clear that the older woman had made this journey before.

"So," Amber prompted, flipping pages in her notebook. "Are you going to explain what this is?"

Ashe exhaled. "Built these passages in the 1930s, during Prohibition. Speakeasy setup. Friend of mine ran one out of here."

Amber's eyes widened. "You built this?!"

Ashe ignored her awe and kept walking.

"I bought the buildings after the war. Taxes and costs are covered through automatic drafts: investments, pensions, whatever."

Amber furiously scribbled. "Wait. So you own all four row houses?"

Ashe nodded.

Dani's eyes sparkled in the flickering light. "I guess that explains a lot."

Amber scanned the narrow corridor as they passed a bricked-up door. "So… you just lived in one and let the rest rot?"

"Rot? They didn't rot," Ashe muttered. "They're functional."

Amber arched a brow. "They look condemned."

Dani looked at Amber. "I think that was the point."

Amber blanched. "Wait, are you saying he did that on purpose?"

Dani looked at Ashe with what could only be described as respect. "Amber, you don't survive that long without some contingency plans."

Ashe said nothing.

But when he reached another reinforced door, he paused, resting his hand on the steel.

Amber held her breath. A long moment passed.

"What's in there?" she whispered to Dani.

Ashe gripped the handle, twisted the lock, and swung open the vault-like door.

Amber's pulse quickened.

Dani smiled, "Let's find out."

And they stepped inside.

❧ • ❧

AMBER STEPPED THROUGH the threshold, barely breathing as her eyes adjusted to the dim space beyond.

She had expected... well, she wasn't sure what she had expected. A hidden bunker full of weapons? Some paranoid prepper's fortress? Been there, done that. Maybe even something clinical and organized, like a museum storage facility.

What she found instead seemed like a tomb.

The space felt eerily preserved, like a room sealed away from time itself. Dust hung in the air, disturbed only by their entrance. Crates, stacks of boxes, old trunks lined the walls, some bearing labels, others left untouched as if their contents hadn't been disturbed in years.

Several shelves and cubbies with mounting brackets were stripped bare, save for a few scattered remnants of military equipment.

Art stood against the far wall, covered in heavy cloths, the outlines of paintings barely visible. Amber didn't have time to linger on that thought, because everywhere she turned, history stared back at her.

Bronze statuettes. Ancient texts, their bindings fragile with age. A row of sealed wooden cases, each labeled in precise, blocky handwriting. Things that should have been in a museum but were only now headed there, after untold years in Ashe's possession.

Dani let out a low whistle, crossing the space with familiar ease. She ran a finger along one of the crates, frowning when she came away clean.

"Nice packing job. Meticulous as always," she murmured. "You've been a busy boy."

Ashe's voice came from somewhere behind her. "Yeah, a couple months ago. Moved a lot of things out."

Amber turned toward him, her pen already flying across the pages of her notebook. "Like what?"

"Tools, remember?" Ashe said tersely. "Donated some art. Some artifacts."

Amber's memory flashed back to Ashe's storage unit in Texas. Presumably, that was the new home for Ashe's supplies. At least the more "functional" ones.

Amber's eyes landed on something curious.

On a metal workbench, among scattered tools and a few loose artifacts, sat a metal rod, blackened by time. It was notable for a leaf-shaped blade attached to its metal shaft. The other end bore an empty bracket, as if it had once been affixed to something larger.

She reached for it out of curiosity.

"What's this?"

She had just barely run her fingers down the metal when Ashe was beside her.

In a blink, his hand closed around the metal shaft. Not hard, but firm. His grip carried an edge of warning.

Amber froze.

For the first time since stepping inside, she noticed how tense Ashe looked. His jaw tight, shoulders rigid, eyes sharper than before.

Something was wrong.

"That's nothing," Ashe said, voice low, clipped. He tossed it with a deliberate motion into an open box.

Then, he shut the lid. And just like that, the subject was closed.

Amber blinked, thrown off by the reaction. Dani noticed it too, her eyes narrowing slightly.

Then, a sound. Faint. Mechanical.

Amber didn't notice it at first, but Dani snapped to attention immediately.

Beep.

Amber frowned. "What was—"

Beep. Faster this time.

Ashe went still.

Then, without hesitation, he grabbed both of them by the arms and yanked them toward the side wall, not the way they'd come.

"Move," he ordered.

Dani didn't question it. She grabbed Amber's other arm, dragging her along as Ashe pressed his hand against a section of the brick wall.

Beep. Beep. Beep.

Amber's heart lurched. "Wait, wait! What's happening?"

"Someone's been here since I was."

Dani swore under her breath. "Someone broke in?"

"More than just broke in," Ashe growled, shoving them through the new passageway. This one was nearly pitch black, lit only by the faint light spilling through the door they had just rushed through.

BeepBeepBeepBeep.

The sound receded, but the pitch changed, growing more rapid, urgent.

Amber barely had time to stumble forward before Ashe slammed a metal lever downward.

The wall behind them slammed shut. Amber was mystified as the group found itself in a broad alleyway behind the block of buildings. Ashe shoved Dani ahead of him and dragged Amber unceremoniously along, stumbling and scrabbling for balance in his haste.

The world exploded and the darkness of the night vanished along with it.

Amber didn't register the impact so much as she felt the air disappear. The ground rumbled violently, the very bones of the row house shaking as a wave of pressure ripped through the structure behind them.

She barely heard Dani shout before a secondary blast followed.

Dust. Heat. Darkness.

Silence.

Amber coughed, lungs burning as the last of the dust settled. Somewhere behind her, rubble shifted.

She felt Dani's hand on her shoulder as the older woman struggled to her feet.

"Ashe?" Dani called out, her voice rough and urgent.

"I'm here," Ashe muttered, voice tight with something unreadable.

Amber coughed again, her throat raw. "Did the entire block just collapse?"

Ashe didn't answer immediately. But when he did, his voice was flat and cold.

"Yeah."

Amber swallowed hard, trying to calm her breathing.

"Was that... was that your plan?" she asked weakly.

"Not mine."

Ashe finally turned toward them, brushing dust from his clothing.

Amber just stared at him.

This hadn't been just an old bunker; this place had meant something to Ashe.

And someone had been here.

And now, whoever they were, they had just wiped the place off the map.

Chapter 4 : FOUND AND LOST

THE ENGLISH COUNTRYSIDE unfolded beneath her, a patchwork of rolling green fields, winding rivers, and hedgerows that looked too precise to be natural, but too ancient to have been made by any kind of machinery. From this high up, the landscape looked like a quilt stitched together from every shade of green imaginable: deep emerald farmlands, soft sage meadows, and the dark, dense green of forests that had probably been home to Robin Hood and his Merry Men.

The roads snaked between the fields in narrow, meandering ribbons, some so thin Amber guessed they had been carved by centuries of foot traffic rather than designed for modern cars. Small villages dotted the landscape, clusters of buildings with steeply pitched rooftops, their pale stone and brickwork glowing softly in the golden haze of the setting sun. Church spires stood tall among them, silent sentinels watching over lands that had weathered the wars and struggles of countless generations.

Amber pressed her forehead against the airplane window, watching as they drifted past centuries of history, moving deeper into England. They had passed over Ireland a while back; she had barely noticed, too caught up in the rhythm of her thoughts. But now, as the reality of landing in London set in, she felt an unexpected mix of excitement and uncertainty. And even though she had been thrilled when Ashe and Dani asked her to come along, she still wasn't entirely sure where she fit into it all.

This wasn't a vacation. She wasn't entirely sure what it was, but it wasn't that. The trip was supposed to have started in Paris, but it hadn't, of course. Dani's discovery of that article about the statues and the events in Chicago had led Dani and Ashe to make that detour to Gloucester after all. At first, Amber had surmised the reason to have been curiosity—she was bursting with it, after all—but Ashe had made some comment about wanting to be as unpredictable with their travel plans as they could. Something he called "operational security."

Ashe was funny that way.

He was also a convincing actor when he had to be, as Amber had discovered. Amber had found herself ducking questions from Chicago PD while Ashe calmly and convincingly lied through his teeth about a "gas leak" that had somehow demolished an entire row of houses. She still wasn't sure how he had pulled that off, but he'd almost convinced her.

Amber sighed, rubbing a smudge of oil from the glass with her sleeve. She wasn't even sure whose idea this trip had been in the first place. Dani had framed it as Ashe wanting to move on, to step away from his past, to distance himself from his former life as an isolated vigilante. That didn't sound entirely like Ashe to her, but she went with it.

Whatever the reason, Amber wasn't complaining. Far from it.

She'd been thrilled when they had asked her along. Completely, ridiculously thrilled. She had leapt at the chance to travel, even if she had no idea who was paying for it. That was the real reason she was sitting back here, in coach, while Ashe and Dani were up front in first class, drinking expensive champagne—well, champagne and top-shelf bottled water—and enjoying their hero's journey.

Amber had spun it well, she thought, claiming she wanted to "experience everyman travel" for the sake of realism in her writing. But the truth? She hadn't wanted to be a burden, to cost more than she needed to. She had no idea what the financial arrangement was between those two, but she wasn't about to start racking up debts she couldn't pay back. Besides, eight hours in economy hadn't been that bad.

Okay, that was a lie. It had been awful.

She had naively romanticized air travel, imagining soaring through the sky like some 1950s movie heroine, sipping on a cocktail and admiring the view.

The reality? A slow descent into madness.

She'd spent the first hour trying to get comfortable, the second hour regretting ever being born, the third questioning how British Airways could use the term "airline food" to describe their crimes against humanity, and the fourth wishing she could trade seats with literally anyone in first class.

By hour five, her seatmate had finished his second movie. A very large, very sweaty man with elbows the size of Montana, he'd begun snoring like a freight train. She had to fight the urge to shake him awake just to see what he would do about that thick line of drool seeping through his beard.

By hour six, the baby in the row behind her had started recording its latest live Screamo album entitled "The Wailings of Eternity," shrieking like it had personally been betrayed by the gods.

At exactly the seven-hour mark, Amber somehow made peace with it all and entered a state of zen-like calm. Seven hours and two minutes? She acknowledged zen-like calm was a crock and couldn't exist in this universe.

And now? Now she was staring at the damp ring of condensation her forehead had left on the window, wondering how Dani and Ashe had somehow managed to convince an entire city that a domestic gas leak had triggered a detonation powerful enough to erase a row of buildings.

Then again, Ashe could be very convincing when he wanted to be. Despite the legitimacy of the documents supporting his new identity as Ashe Golding—his new "legend," Dani had called it—Ashe had insisted on keeping a low profile, staying on the fringes of the explosion investigation, offering just enough involvement to avoid suspicion but not enough to invite scrutiny.

Dani had agreed, which had surprised Amber at first. Until they had explained who they thought was responsible.

Standish.

Even the name made Amber shudder.

Dani had filled in the gaps for her. Lamentation Standish had left the FBI in disgrace after the data center "incident" in Ashburn, VA. His mishandling of the situation, his unjustifiable appropriation of vast amounts of Bureau resources in his hunt for Ashe, and Owen Spirit's very significant legal threats after the incident had effectively ended the man's career. After that? He had simply disappeared. Vanished like a ghost into a crack in the wall of the world.

But if Ashe was right, then he hadn't just vanished. He had been waiting. Plotting. Dani hadn't disagreed. Standish was something of a bulldog, she had explained, and he remained their most plausible suspect.

Amber shifted in her seat, away from her neighbor's colossal elbow. She pressed her forehead to the cool glass again, eyes flitting over the fading sunset spilling across the British countryside below.

Dani believed Ashe was changing, finally moving forward, that his time living like a ghost, a relic from a war only he remembered, had finally ended. That he was reclaiming parts of himself that had been buried in violence and vengeance for too long.

She had theorized—because Dani loved theorizing—that Ashe's accelerated healing worked faster on muscle and skin but took much longer to repair nerve tissue and brain function. Dani had gone on for way too long talking about medical stuff Amber had no hopes of understanding and couldn't write fast enough to notate in her journal, but that was the basics of it. She thought.

And, in Dani's opinion, the Ashe they were getting to know now, the one who had been buried for so long, was the real Ashe.

Amber wasn't sure if she believed all of that. But she did see that this Ashe, whoever he was, was starting to let go of the past. The fact that he was willing to donate stuff he had spent centuries holding onto was proof of that.

Dani had said that some things, Ashe would never part with. But others?

Ashe had simply mumbled, "They should enrich someone else's life, not mine."

Amber wasn't sure what to make of that. She wasn't sure she would ever understand what it meant to hold something for hundreds of years and then just let it go.

But she wanted to.

The intercom crackled, and the pilot's voice rumbled through the cabin.

"Ladies and gentlemen, we are now beginning our final descent into London Heathrow Airport. The local time is 6:35 p.m. Please ensure your seatbelts are fastened and tray tables are in the upright position."

Amber snapped back to the present, sitting up and stretching the stiffness from her neck.

Finally.

She glanced toward first class, where Ashe and Dani were no doubt already sipping another round of luscious beverages from fine crystal, laughing at the suffering of those crammed into coach.

Amber straightened her back. It was fine. Coach was fine. At least it was over. And she was about to embark on her whirlwind tour through Europe. Her! Amber Olsen. She was here. And whatever happened next?

She was going to write the heck out of it.

"ARE WE LOST?" Amber asked from the back seat.

Dani didn't take her eyes off the road as she adjusted her grip on the steering wheel of the rental, her knuckles tightening slightly to relieve the minor ache in her hands resulting from two hours of driving the English countryside. As spry as she was, getting old still sucked.

"I don't know, Ashe. Are we lost?" she asked, a smirk evident in her voice.

"Southam is... north... of Cheltenham," Ashe muttered, squinting at the map on his phone, as if glaring at it hard enough would make it rearrange itself into something that made sense. "Does that seem right to you?"

Amber, from the backseat, chimed in. "Okay, but serious question: what's a 'cleeve' and why does a bishop have one?"

Ashe groaned. "Here we go."

"I mean, it's right there," Amber continued, tapping on the window as they passed another road sign. "Bishop's Cleeve, 37 kilometers. It sounds like a medieval euphemism. 'Beggin' your pardon, Your Excellency, but your cleeve is showing.'"

Dani chuckled, glancing at Ashe, who looked thoroughly unimpressed.

"Cleeve," Ashe said, his voice the patient tone of a man who had long since resigned himself to these conversations, "is from an Old English word meaning 'cliff' or 'steep hill,' which you might know if you'd ever read a book."

Amber made a thoughtful noise. "Uh-huh. So, what, the local bishop had a nice little hill all to himself?"

"It's the name of a village."

In the mirror, Dani saw Amber sit back, folding her arms.

"I dunno. I like my version better."

Dani grinned, shaking her head as they rolled through yet another stretch of winding countryside road, flanked by hedgerows and rolling farmland. The sun had risen hours ago, casting long, golden streaks over the patchwork fields, but the beauty of the English countryside wasn't helping the very obvious fact that they were, in fact, completely lost.

Dani arched a brow at Ashe. "Remind me again. How did we end up lost in a place you used to live?"

Ashe didn't look up. "I never said I used to live here," he grumbled.

"Yes, you did."

"No, I said I knew the area."

"Did you, in fact, used to live here?" Dani hadn't missed this contrary aspect of Ashe's nature.

"Well... yes, obviously, or we wouldn't be here."

"And yet..." Dani gestured vaguely at the road ahead. "Here we are. Only we don't know where 'here' is."

Ashe grumbled something under his breath, still focused on the map.

Amber leaned forward between the seats. "Okay, so, like, not to pile on or anything—"

"And yet, you're piling on."

"—but if you knew the area, then why are we lost?"

Ashe finally looked up. "Because it's changed."

Dani blinked at him. "Ashe. Places change. It happens."

"Yes," he said evenly. "But it's not like it's been two thousand years. I was here recently."

She gave him a side-eye glance. "How recently?"

Ashe turned his attention back to the window, voice as casual as if he were discussing last week's weather.

"Nineteen-thirties," he said quietly.

Amber snickered in the back seat.

"Ashe," Dani asked, "do you have any idea how the passage of time works?"

☙ • ❧

THE BARN SMELLED of old wood, damp earth, and time. Dani had spent enough years in the Bureau to recognize the kind of places where history lived: not the polished museum halls where the past was curated and controlled, but the makeshift spaces where artifacts sat waiting to be classified, tagged, and cataloged.

It was quiet inside, save for the occasional rustle of a tarp shifting in the breeze from the open door. Stacks of crates lined the walls, labeled in neat block lettering. In the center of the space, a long wooden table was covered in trays of pottery fragments, aged metalwork, and photographs clipped in bundles. Brightly-colored adhesive squares of note paper were everywhere, affixed to the myriad shards of antiquity.

Ashe stood at the edge of it all, staring at the past. His past.

He said nothing, but Dani didn't miss the way his fingers hovered over one of the photographs: a shot of the excavation site, showing the unearthed foundation of what had once been a Roman villa.

His villa.

Dani knew the weight of ghosts. Knew how they pressed in when you walked the ground where things had once mattered.

She wasn't going to press him on it. Not now.

Amber, of course, had no such hesitation.

"Wow," she murmured, picking up a high-resolution image of the three busts together. "They didn't pull any punches, did they?"

Dani glanced at the photograph in Amber's hands. The bust of Appius Aurelius Cinis was carved in almost brutal detail, every line and crease of his face captured with the unflinching realism of Roman portrait sculpture.

"It was a 'warts and all' era of art, I guess" Amber continued. "They wanted people to look old, serious, and, I dunno... historically important?"

"They liked accuracy," Ashe acknowledged, his voice quieter than usual.

Amber tilted her head, studying him. "Still. I don't see you commissioning one of these for yourself."

"I didn't."

Ashe's gaze flicked to the photo, then away again, clearly uncomfortable.

"They were a gift," he said softly. "From Aurelia. To mark the birth of her first child."

Amber's fingers tightened around the edges of the photo.

Dani absorbed that. "You were a grandfather."

Ashe didn't answer.

Before the silence could stretch, the barn door creaked open again, and a man stepped inside, wiping his hands on his canvas jacket.

Dr. Ari McGinnon was lean, sharp-eyed, and perpetually squinting, as if the sun had transformed his face over many years in the field. His mid-fifties frame was wiry but solid, built more for long days of digging than soft academia. His hands, still stained from the soil outside, tucked into his pockets as he stepped forward.

He barely got two paces in before his sharp gaze landed on Ashe and Amber, and he stopped short.

Dani recognized the look. Shock. A slow, creeping disbelief. She felt a moment of passing pity for the man's confusion.

"I—I assume you're here about the theft," McGinnon said finally, his voice carefully measured.

Dani's stomach tightened. She exchanged a glance with Ashe.

"Theft?" she asked.

McGinnon frowned. "You... don't know?"

Amber, ever helpful, said, "We do now."

McGinnon hesitated before stepping closer. "I'm sorry. I thought that was why you were here. Two of the busts were stolen."

Dani exhaled sharply. "Which ones?"

McGinnon rubbed the back of his neck. "The bust of Appius Aurelius Cinis." His gaze flicked to Ashe again, as if he still couldn't quite believe what he was seeing. "The father. And his daughter, Aurelia."

Dani's pulse ticked up; first Ashe's house in Chicago. Now this.

Amber muttered, "Great. That's not weirdly specific or anything."

McGinnon looked between them. "You've had similar thefts?"

"Similar," Dani said flatly.

Ashe's jaw tightened. "Tell us about yours."

McGinnon sighed, arms crossing. The man exhaled through his nose. "It happened about two months ago, shortly after my article was first published. I can't imagine it was anyone other than the last man who visited, and I mentioned that to the authorities. The man was very interested in the busts, and they came up missing some days after I spoke to him."

Dani's gaze sharpened. "You saw him?"

McGinnon nodded. "He came in the afternoon, asking questions about the busts. At first, I assumed he was a collector. That happens sometimes, more than you'd think. Real problem around here. But there was something off about him."

Dani slipped her hands in her pockets. It was a trait she'd noticed about herself when questioning a subject; a habit she was trying to break. She pulled her hands back out into the open. "Describe him."

McGinnon didn't hesitate. "Tall. Gaunt. Pale, but not sickly. Just... severe. Black hair, combed back, unnaturally neat. Dressed in black, like he was going to a funeral."

Amber froze. Dani felt a chill settle in her gut.

McGinnon saw her reaction. "I take it you lot know him?"

Dani exhaled slowly, looking at Ashe. Their suspicions were confirmed.

Lamentation Standish had been here.

Amber muttered, "That's not ominous at all."

Chapter 5 : L'AFFAIRE LINDER

AMBER HAD WANTED to spend more time in England. Like, really wanted to.

Not that she was complaining about being in Paris now, of course. Paris was amazing. But England had felt unfinished, like a book she'd been forced to put down before reaching the last chapter. She'd said as much to Ashe and Dani, but Ashe had just mocked her for making a book reference.

So, England was cut short, and she had to be okay with that. It wasn't her trip. More importantly, it wasn't her money.

She had quickly figured out that the flow of this little adventure had become about not staying in one place any longer than absolutely necessary. It made sense; the whole getting-blown-up thing in Chicago had put a different angle on the schedule.

Still, it would have been nice to linger just a little longer.

At least she'd managed to squeeze in some sightseeing in London before their flight to Paris. Dani had gone off to the American Embassy for some Bureau-related errands, and Ashe, unsurprisingly, had preferred to skulk around in the shadows near the Thames, which had left Amber completely free to play tourist.

She'd hit many of the big stops: Buckingham Palace, Westminster Abbey, the Tower of London, even took a ride on the London Eye, which she'd always wanted to do. She'd made sure to get the full "annoying American in London" experience, which included overpaying for tea, deciding coffee was still better, nearly getting hit by a car when she looked the wrong way crossing a street, and spending way too much time watching emotionless guards with funny hats stand perfectly still.

But, as much as she'd enjoyed seeing places she'd only ever seen in movies, she'd spent more time thinking about something else entirely.

Ashe's daughter, Aurelia, had looked just like her.

Amber still wasn't sure how to process that.

She had spent her whole life being an anomaly, a little too much of everything and never quite fitting into anything. And yet here was proof, carved in marble and preserved for two thousand years, that there had once been someone just like her.

It was unnerving.

But, she supposed, it had also been the thing that had drawn Ashe to her in the first place. Maybe that was why, when she had first met him, he'd actually engaged with her instead of immediately shutting her out.

So... good thing? Maybe. Probably.

Definitely weird, though.

But what part of knowing Ashe wasn't at least a little weird?

At dinner the night before, Dani had slid a small box across the table toward her with a knowing smirk.

"For you," she had said.

Amber had opened it to find a sleek, state-of-the-art voice recorder, the kind of device that looked straight out of a spy movie, with built-in encryption software and biometric security.

Dani had explained that with Ashe's concerns about security, maybe jotting down all their adventures in physical notebooks wasn't the best idea. So, during her meeting with the FBI Legal Attaché in London, she'd pulled a few strings.

Amber had fallen in love with the device instantly. If she had to censor her work for safety reasons, at least she could do it with something that made her feel like a secret agent. She'd spent half the flight to Paris testing out all the features, much to Ashe's visible irritation.

Now, they were in Paris.

Amber had been ecstatic as soon as they'd landed, bouncing off the walls from the moment she set foot on French soil.

She'd wandered the Louvre while Ashe and Dani dealt with museum curators, trying to tune out whatever long-winded discussions were happening about artifact donations. Something about Ashe fulfilling a promise made to some Russian guy who had been dead for ages.

Amber hadn't paid attention, because she was too busy getting lost.

It had taken Museum Security to track her down, much to Dani's mild amusement and Ashe's complete and utter lack of surprise.

Now, as the three of them walked along the Champs-Élysées, the city vibrating around them with golden lights and distant music, Amber could still hardly believe she was here.

She was in Paris.

And not just as a tourist, but as part of something bigger. Something tangled and dangerous, but thrilling all the same.

Dani had convinced Ashe that walking back to the hotel was a good idea, and so far, it had been a beautifully scenic route, taking them through the Jardin des Tuileries, past illuminated gardens, and now toward the Arc de Triomphe.

Amber sighed happily. "This city is unbelievable."

"It's not bad," Dani admitted.

Amber looked at the older woman. "Not bad? Are you serious?"

Dani smirked. "I was here for work last time. Didn't have time for sightseeing."

Amber opened her mouth to respond, then stopped, frowning.

"Victor Hugo," she muttered, reading a street sign as they passed. "That name sounds familiar."

Ashe gave her that look again. "Amber, you're a writer."

"Yeah?"

"Victor Hugo."

Amber stared blankly.

Dani chuckled but didn't respond. Glancing at her, Amber observed that she seemed to have noticed something. She didn't react right away, didn't say anything to Ashe or Amber, but she subtly adjusted her posture, slowing their pace slightly.

Shortly, Dani leaned toward Ashe, voice low. "We have a tail."

Amber perked up immediately. "What, we're being followed?"

"Shhh," Dani shushed.

Ashe's demeanor shifted immediately, his casual stroll turning into something quieter, sharper.

"I'll take care of it," he said.

Dani wasn't thrilled with that idea, but Ashe was already falling behind, letting them move ahead as he peeled off into a side street.

Amber tried to act casual, but she must not have done a great job of it, from the looks Dani shot her way.

A few moments passed. Then a few more.

Dani maintained a steady pace, leading them closer to the hotel, pretending not to notice anything behind them.

They had only made it a few blocks closer to their hotel when Ashe reappeared, slipping back into place beside them as if he had never left at all.

Amber spun toward him. "Well?"

"Gone."

Amber frowned. "Gone as in 'got away'? Or gone as in 'you took care of it'?"

Ashe rolled his eyes and turned to Dani.

Dani studied him. "We need to start assuming we're being watched everywhere we go."

"We already assume that," Ashe replied.

"No," Dani corrected. "You expect it. There's a difference. But now? It's real. We have confirmation. We need to be proactive."

Ashe exhaled slowly, tilting his head slightly as they passed under the glow of a streetlamp, the light cutting sharp shadows across his face. "Hard to do when we don't even know who they are yet. It wasn't Standish."

"Which is exactly why we should be more cautious," Dani shot back. "Whoever was tailing us tonight was good. Professional. You lost them, but it took you a while."

That earned her a withering look.

Dani let out a quiet chuckle. "We should assume this isn't a one-off."

Amber sighed dramatically and pulled out her brand-new voice recorder. She cleared her throat, lifted the mic, and spoke with the grave intensity of a true crime podcaster.

"Day One: As the day draws to a close, the city of light glows softly around us, but danger lurks in the shadows. We are being watched. Followed. A faceless enemy tracks our every step. Who are they? What do they want? Will we survive the night? Only time will tell."

She released the recorder's thumb button, feeling very pleased with herself.

Ashe just shook his head.

☙ • ❧

AMBER STARED OUT the taxi window, watching the streets of Paris slip away as they neared Charles de Gaulle Airport. The early morning light was soft and golden, casting a warm glow on the city she had barely begun to explore.

She sighed. Two days. She had gotten two days in Paris. It wasn't fair. She had been in this city for less than forty-eight hours, just long enough to fall in love with it and not nearly long enough to enjoy it.

With a sigh, she pulled out her encrypted voice recorder and flicked it on.

"Day Two," she intoned in a voice dripping with breathless emotion, not all of it faked. "Paris is slipping away all too soon, ripped from my grasp before I could even begin my whirlwind romance with overpriced pastries and moody intellectuals in tiny cafés. If this trip has a theme, it is this: never get comfortable."

She snapped it off dramatically, glancing over at Ashe. He was unmoved.

Instead, Ashe turned and spoke in fluent French to the driver, confirming their drop-off location. His voice was smooth, effortless, his accent so natural that Amber found herself impressed despite her frustration.

"You speak French?" she asked, raising an eyebrow.

Ashe gave her a look, like the answer should have been obvious. "One would think."

Amber scowled. "Right. Because of course you do."

Dani smirked but didn't comment.

The taxi pulled up to the curb outside the terminal, and Ashe handed over a handful of euros, thanking the driver with a brief nod. They stepped out, carting their modest collection of bags toward the entrance.

Amber grabbed her recorder once again. "Day Two," she said, her tone exaggeratedly tragic. "Paris, my love, I hardly knew you. Ripped from your embrace before I could enjoy a chain-smoking existential crisis or suffer a dramatic break-up on a bridge. I am, once again, a victim of forces beyond my control."

Dani smiled at her. "You're acting like you're never coming back."

Amber huffed. "I'd just like to spend more than five minutes in a city before we go running off again."

Dani simply cast her a sympathetic grin.

They had just stepped onto the sidewalk, heading toward the terminal's glass doors, when Amber's stomach tightened.

Two people, dressed in dark clothing, headed straight for them.

The man was broad-shouldered and thickset, but most notable for his salt-and-pepper hair, cut close. His face was lined with age but not softness, his expression serious but not unkind. He had the look of a man who had spent decades dealing with the worst of humanity and had yet to be impressed by any of it.

Walking beside him was a tall, almost regal woman. She was tall, willowy, with sharp brown eyes that took in everything without giving anything away. Her raven-black hair was pulled into a severe bun, her posture rigid but not stiff. Controlled, precise. There was an air of quiet menace about her, the kind that made Amber immediately decide not to get on her bad side.

Dani slowed her pace just slightly.

Amber caught the change immediately. Dani knew them, she realized. More than that; there was some history there.

Dani stepped forward.

"Harrigan, how are you?"

"Linder," the man said, reaching out to take Dani's extended hand.

Dani's greeting for the woman was less cordial. "Wycliffe. Been a while."

"Not long enough," the dark woman responded as she shook Dani's hand with an air of reluctance. "But we'll save the pleasantries. We've got a problem."

The man gave a small nod. Then, glancing at Ashe and Amber, he asked, "Who are they?" His voice was gravelly, no-nonsense.

Dani introduced the two of them. "Ashe Golding, my PSO. Amber Olsen." Dani's voice was calm but firm, her introduction clipped and professional.

Wycliffe's brows lifted slightly, her expression hovering somewhere between amusement and skepticism as she eyed Ashe from head to toe. "Since when have you ever needed a personal security officer, Linder? And besides, aren't you… what's the word? Oh, right. Retired?"

Dani's lips curved in the kind of smile that Amber had found typically preceded someone else's professional embarrassment. She tilted her head slightly, as if considering the question, then replied smoothly, "Oh, I don't know, Wycliffe, since when have you been proficient at earning your agency's middle initial?" She barely gave Wycliffe time to open her mouth before continuing, "And let's be clear. I'm retired because I chose to be, not because I had to be. You, on the other hand? I bet it keeps you up at night knowing I'll still probably be his first call when things go south."

Amber was more than a little confused, unsure who "he" was, and what Dani figured he might be calling about.

Harrigan, to his credit, didn't even try to hide his amusement. "Alright, you two. If you're done trying to figure out whose is bigger," he said, stepping toward a black SUV nearby. "We've got bigger problems to deal with." He held out a hand, indicating that he'd like the group to enter the vehicle.

"Ms. Olsen," he said politely.

Amber gave her best winning smile. “And you are?” She’d had too many unpleasant surprises being herded into black SUVs to just go along quietly.

Dani turned to her and formalized the introductions. “Al Harrigan, FBI Legal Attaché for Paris. Miriam Wycliffe, CIA Chief of Station.”

Amber’s smile faltered just a bit.

CIA? Amber looked at the tall woman, actually not surprised.

Wycliffe’s gaze, however, was focused entirely on Dani.

“I assume you’ve checked your phone?” Wycliffe asked, her tone cool.

Dani tilted her head slightly. “Not since breakfast. I’m retired. I take it I missed something?”

Wycliffe’s expression didn’t shift, but Amber could feel the tension between them.

“Things went south,” said Harrigan.

“The… President has requested your assistance,” Wycliffe added.

Dani smiled sweetly. “That was hard to say, wasn’t it?”

Al Harrigan interceded before the impending catfight could develop further. “Dani. We need to talk. Now.”

Dani’s jaw tightened, but she didn’t argue. “Lead the way.”

They took the remaining few steps and entered the black SUV, Harrigan opening the door and helping Dani and Amber inside. Ashe climbed in from the other side.

The SUV pulled away from the terminal, winding down a restricted airport access road, heading toward the far edges of the airfield.

Amber kept her mouth shut, wide-eyed, waiting for someone to explain what was going on.

Finally, Wycliffe spoke. “Are they cleared?”

“They’re cleared enough. What did he say about it?” Dani asked.

Wycliffe’s jaw clenched.

“Miriam,” said Dani, “what did POTUS say?”

“He said you were in charge. Like last time.” The woman had to physically force the words out.

“Then it’s settled,” Dani said, waving a hand. “They’re cleared enough. Talk.”

Miriam Wycliffe didn’t take her eyes off Dani as she reached into her bag and produced a computer tablet. A few rapid taps later, the screen displayed a satellite image of Jerusalem, marked with several concentric circles marked as overlays.

“This,” Wycliffe continued, “is our current best estimate for an impending nuclear event.”

Amber’s stomach dropped.

Dani, to her credit, didn't react immediately. She simply stared at the image before speaking.

"How reliable?"

"Reliable enough," Harrigan said. "A terrorist cell operating out of the West Bank has acquired nuclear material. Intelligence suggests an attack on Israeli soil, most likely in Jerusalem."

Amber blinked. Terrorists. Nuclear material. Jerusalem.

Okay. So not a routine airport pickup, then.

Dani exhaled sharply, shaking her head. "I'm retired."

"The President disagrees," Wycliffe said. Not for the first time, there was something pointed in her tone.

Dani turned her head slightly. "Oh?"

Wycliffe's lips pressed into a thin line. "You're the most capable person on the ground in the region."

Amber couldn't help but notice how much Wycliffe hated saying that.

"You'll be leading a team on the ground," Harrigan said. "This needs to be surgical. Quiet. Controlled. You know the players, the risks. And the President trusts you."

Amber saw it then. That was the real problem.

The President had personally asked for Dani. Not Wycliffe. Not anyone in the Agency. Dani. And Wycliffe resented it. Badly.

Dani considered for only a moment before nodding. "I'll go."

"We'll go," Ashe corrected.

Dani shot him a look, but she didn't argue.

Amber felt a familiar sense of unease creeping in. It was only a matter of time before someone remembered she was also sitting in this car. She cleared her throat, deciding to get ahead of it. "And me?"

Harrigan and Wycliffe exchanged a glance.

"You're staying in Paris," Wycliffe said flatly.

Amber frowned. "That's not—"

Dani cut in. "She's right, Amber."

"You're a civilian," Ashe concluded, almost as if he were finishing Dani's sentence for her.

Amber crossed her arms. "Oh, now I'm a civilian? Because a few months ago, I was a 'valuable witness,' and last week I was 'useful to have around.'"

"You still are," Ashe said. "Just not for this."

"No. I want to go."

Dani sighed. "Amber—"

Wycliffe arched a brow. "And do what?" she snapped.

Amber's mouth opened. Then closed.

She hated that she didn't have a good answer. "So I'm just supposed to sit in Paris and wait?" she asked.

Dani softened slightly. "For now. We'll regroup when it's over. You wanted to spend more time here anyway. Harrigan, here, will make sure you're set up in a nice hotel. No cheap hostels."

Amber rolled her eyes. "I wasn't going to stay in a hostel."

Dani smirked faintly. "You would have, just to say you did."

Amber huffed, but didn't argue.

Moments later, the SUV slowed as it approached a remote airfield hangar, where a chartered jet was waiting, the turbines of its engines already spinning. Amber felt a tightness in her chest as she watched Dani and Ashe step into the plane.

Chapter 6 : THE TARGET THAT WASN'T

THE AIR WAS thick with heat and tension from the moment Dani stepped off the plane.

Ben Gurion Airport was a study in controlled chaos, the kind Dani had seen in the aftermath of terrorist threats before. It was atypical to see this type of activity in the prelude to an attack, but she hoped that was a good sign. The usual steady flow of international travelers had turned into something more frantic, a ripple of unease passing through the crowd as the sudden presence of heightened security became impossible to ignore.

Armed police and counterterrorism officers were positioned near every major checkpoint, their eyes scanning every face, every movement, every bag. The overhead departure screens flashed with cancellations and delays, announcements crackling through the PA system in rapid Hebrew, Arabic, and English. A growing number of passengers stood in tight clusters, whispering to each other, glancing at their phones, waiting for someone to explain why their flights weren't leaving.

The airport wasn't shut down, not officially, but Dani could see it moving fast in that direction.

Numerous private security contractors could be seen scattered about, some in tactical gear, others blending in with civilian attire, their earpieces barely noticeable. Some watched the entrances. Others were positioned near the baggage claim, the café areas, the terminal lounges: everywhere a potential threat might try to slip in.

She barely had time to take it all in before a voice called her name.

"Dani."

A man strode toward them. Tall, with the compact build of someone who could dismantle an opponent in seconds and not wrinkle his suit doing it. His beard was neatly trimmed, his dark hair streaked with just enough silver to suggest experience.

Dani had worked with enough field agents over the years to know which ones were all bureaucracy and posturing and which ones were built for the real work—the kind of work that happened in places where diplomacy fell apart.

Nehem was one of those.

His sharp brown eyes took everything in at once, cataloging Ashe, Dani, and the flow of movement around them without ever slowing his stride. There was a coiled energy to him, like someone who never fully relaxed, never stopped evaluating a room. Nehem was a man who had seen things go sideways enough times to know that they always would.

He wasn't smiling. He never smiled.

"Nehem Avraham," Dani greeted, shifting her bag to her other shoulder as he approached.

"You're late," Nehem said. There was no actual reproach in his voice, just fact. His sharp brown eyes flicked briefly to Ashe, assessing him in the way only intelligence officers could.

Dani smiled. "You know I had to stop for coffee."

That, at least, got a twitch out of one corner of his mouth. "You joke, but I would not put it past you."

He extended a hand toward Ashe. "And you must be Ashe Golding."

Ashe's eyes flicked to Dani and back to the taller man. He took the proffered hand. "I must be."

Nehem gave Dani a look. "You have a personal security officer now?"

"They're trending on social media," Dani said dryly. "I figured I'd try one out."

Nehem huffed, shaking his head before gesturing sharply toward the terminal doors. "Come. You can be funny later. Right now, we move."

Dani matched his pace immediately, adjusting to the rhythm of the unfolding crisis. Ashe fell in beside her, silent, watchful, taking everything in. She didn't have time to worry about how he was adjusting to this kind of situation or its environment. The old man would just have to keep up.

Avraham led them through the restricted access corridors, passing through a series of security checks that his credentials breezed them through. Moving rapidly down a flight of stairs, they emerged to a waiting convoy of blacked-out SUVs.

"I assume you've been briefed?" he asked, pulling open the back door for Dani.

"I was briefed on a problem," Dani corrected, sliding inside. "I need the details."

Nehem got in beside her, Ashe taking the seat on the far side as the SUV peeled away from the airport, merging into traffic with precision born of necessity.

Nehem handed Dani a tablet, his jaw tight. "Here's what we know."

Dani tapped the screen, scanning the satellite images, intercepted communications, and intelligence assessments.

Nehem continued as she reviewed the information on the tablet, his voice clipped and precise. "A terrorist cell, an offshoot of an already fragmented organization, has gotten their hands on nuclear material. We don't have confirmation on what form it takes, but what we do know is that they're planning to detonate a device in Jerusalem."

He tapped the tablet screen, bringing up images, names, and organizational flowcharts. "The cell is calling itself Jund al-Fajr: 'Soldiers of the Dawn.' They splintered off from a larger group about eighteen months ago, after a rift over leadership. They aren't backed by any single state or known major faction, but they've been moving quickly, pulling in disillusioned operatives from multiple networks. We've traced financial transactions from donors in the Gulf, equipment sourced from Eastern

Europe, and tactical training likely conducted in the Bekaa Valley. They're organized but decentralized, which makes them difficult to pin down. They operate in cells: small, independent teams that don't always know what the others are doing. That means even if we take out one branch, the others can keep moving."

Dani scanned the intelligence files, her brow furrowing as she recognized certain names from past briefings. Nehem continued, his tone darkening. "Their ideology is less about establishing a state and more about burning everything to the ground. They've made it clear that they don't just want to target Western interests or Israeli security forces. They want to create absolute chaos. They believe that by striking at critical infrastructure, they can collapse governance, disrupt economies, and force nations into overreach and retaliation. Jerusalem isn't just a target, it's a symbol. If they're planning a nuclear event here, then the goal isn't just destruction, it's disruption on a scale we haven't seen before."

Dani absorbed that with no visible reaction. "Any specific targets?"

Nehem's eyes flicked to the tablet in her hands. "There's disagreement on that."

She frowned. "How so?"

"We intercepted communications suggesting an attack on a major civilian target: crowds, casualties, political impact. But then—" He tapped the screen, pulling up a new file. "—we found this."

Dani's brow furrowed as she scanned the new intelligence. It wasn't an embassy, a religious site, or a market square. It was a data center.

She glanced up. "They want to hit a tech facility?"

"That's what it looks like," Nehem confirmed. "Which suggests this isn't just about terror. It's about information."

Dani's mind raced through the possibilities.

She'd seen the projections in dirty bomb drills during her years in counterterrorism: simulations of what would happen if a radiological dispersion device, or RDD, was detonated in a major city. Unlike a nuclear warhead, a dirty bomb wasn't about mass casualties from the initial explosion. It was about what came after. The true weapon was fear, contamination, and the paralysis that followed. Even a small detonation packed with radioactive material could force the evacuation of entire neighborhoods, turning bustling urban centers into ghost towns overnight. Cleanup efforts would take weeks, if not months, and even if the actual radiation levels weren't immediately lethal, the psychological impact on the public—the fear of invisible poison in the air, in the water, on their skin—was enough to make cities grind to a halt. Governments would have to choose between overreacting and creating widespread panic or underreacting and risking an unseen catastrophe. Either way, the terrorist wins.

But the choice of a data center as the target shifted the implications. Traditional dirty bomb targets were symbolic or densely populated: landmarks, financial districts, transit hubs. A high-profile, public space would guarantee maximum fear, media attention, and political fallout. But a tech facility? That suggested something different. If Jund al-Fajr was planning to hit a data storage hub, they weren't just trying to disrupt daily life, they were trying to corrupt information itself. A radiological event would force evacuations, lock down access, and cripple the digital infrastructure housed inside. Critical government data, financial transactions, classified intelligence... all of it could theoretically be compromised, lost, or manipulated under the chaos of a radiation scare. If they planned to pair physical destruction with cyberwarfare, or even just use the explosion as a smokescreen for another operation, then this was something new.

"Who owns the building?" she asked. "What flows through there?"

Nehem's expression darkened. "That's part of the problem. It's leased by multiple international firms. There are servers hosting everything from government databases to corporate financial records."

Dani exhaled sharply, handing the tablet back. "So, we're dealing with a potential nuclear threat, a cyber warfare angle, and an unknown endgame."

"Essentially."

"Perfect," she muttered.

Ashe, who had been quiet up until now, finally spoke.

"How much time do we have?"

Nehem glanced at his watch. "Not enough."

❧ • ❧

THE DRIVE FROM Ben Gurion Airport to the command center in Jerusalem was tense, fast, and devoid of small talk. The convoy of black SUVs wove through traffic with precision, escorted by two police motorcycles that cleared their path through the dense morning congestion.

Dani didn't need a briefing to know how bad things were. Radio chatter, last-minute reports from analysts, secure-line phone calls: all the usual background noise of an intelligence operation in motion had an edge to it, a quiet urgency that said they were all sitting on a live grenade and waiting for the pin to drop.

Ashe sat beside her, silent, watchful, his sharp eyes flicking between Nehem and the shifting scenery outside the tinted windows. He didn't ask questions, not yet, but Dani could tell he was absorbing everything.

She had worked with combat-experienced operatives, intelligence assets, and shadow operatives alike, and Ashe didn't quite fit into any category. He wasn't rattled, wasn't eager to jump into the fight, but he wasn't passive either. He was studying. Calculating.

Nehem, seated across from them, kept his phone in one hand, scrolling through the latest situational feeds. His brow furrowed as an update flashed across his screen.

Dani arched a brow. "Bad news, or just more of the same?"

Nehem didn't look up. "Bad news is more of the same."

They reached their destination minutes later: a nondescript building in an unmarked compound near the western edge of the city. It looked like just another government facility, but the moment they stepped inside, Dani recognized the markings of a counterterrorism response in full swing.

The air hummed with tension as they entered the central operations room. The walls were lined with monitors displaying live satellite feeds, intelligence reports, and tactical maps. A handful of officials crowded around a large touchscreen wall panel.

As soon as Nehem stepped inside, one of the analysts stood to attention and called out.

"Avraham. We've pinpointed the likely target." The young intelligence officer in his early thirties looked at him with sharp, tired eyes and spoke quickly. "We've narrowed it down to this commercial data center. Seventh floor. It houses multiple international firms, cloud storage servers, and financial infrastructure hubs."

"I am aware. What else?"

The technician, derailed by the question, fell silent. In the chaos of the situation, he had no way to know what had been briefed to which levels.

"They're not going after anything stored inside," Ashe said, finally speaking. His voice was low, even.

Dani glanced at him, noting the way his gaze had locked onto the blueprint with absolute certainty.

Nehem frowned. "Explain."

Ashe leaned in slightly, tapping the server rooms marked on the map. "If they wanted to cause panic, they'd go for a market square, a transit hub, an embassy. Instead, they're aiming at a tech firm in a financial corridor. Not a lot of people here to kill or even terrify, and nothing else to gain, either."

Dani and Nehem both looked at Ashe, who shook his head.

"What happens if they blow up the servers? To the data, I mean."

Avraham's eyes remained locked on Ashe's face. "Nothing. Data is... well, it is data. It all lives in the cloud. They recover the data from offsite backup, and only recent transactions are lost."

"So why blow it up at all?" asked Ashe.

Dani exhaled, rolling her shoulders back, feeling the weight of the situation.

No civilians. No demands. Just a tech facility with a nuke wired inside.

Something wasn't adding up.

~ • ~

THE STREETS SURROUNDING the target building were being locked down block by block. Israeli counterterror units moved with practiced efficiency, setting up a wide perimeter around the seven-story structure. Police barricades diverted traffic, while armored SUVs and tactical units positioned themselves at key entry points.

A drone buzzed overhead, feeding live footage back to the command truck where Dani and Ashe stood with Nehem Avraham and a team of intelligence analysts and field commanders.

The data center loomed large in the video feed, its glass-and-steel exterior reflecting the flashing blue and red lights from distant emergency vehicles. A typical modern office building, except for the layers of dread and anticipation.

Dani was frustrated. Something still wasn't adding up. She pulled her headset into place, adjusting the audio feed from the lead tactical team preparing to breach.

"In position," came the clipped voice of Unit Commander Levin, a seasoned operator with over a decade in Israel's counterterror response force. His team of heavily armed specialists stood ready outside the lobby doors, weapons primed, waiting for the final go-ahead.

Dani exhaled sharply. "I don't like this."

Nehem, standing beside her, grunted in agreement. "Neither do I. But we don't have time to proceed slowly. Those men are prepared to die in the attempt to stop this tragedy before it happens."

Ashe, watching the drone feed on one of the monitors, finally spoke.

"If this is a dirty bomb, why haven't they made demands?"

Dani turned toward him.

"No, think about it," he continued, his voice measured. "Where's the spectacle? Why no demands? They want the world to watch. What have we heard from them?"

Ashe had caught Nehem Avraham's attention as well. "Only silence."

Dani crossed her arms. "That means one of two things. Either they don't care about public attention—"

"Or this isn't about terror at all," Ashe finished.

Nehem's expression darkened. "Then what is it about?"

Dani glanced at the live thermal scan of the seventh floor, produced by a stationary camera some fearless soul had placed on the roof of a building across the street. The scan was mostly blue with splotches of pink, yellow, and red moving around. "We know they're there," she said. "But what are they doing?"

The tactical team shifted in their positions. Over comms, Levin gave a whispered update.

"Breaching the bottom floor in thirty seconds."

Dani clenched her jaw. Something was wrong. She didn't know how, or why, but she knew.

Before Levin could voice the final seconds in his countdown, the seventh floor of the office building in downtown Jerusalem erupted in a violent but controlled detonation.

The entire top section of the data center blew outward, glass shattering, metal support beams groaning under the sudden loss of structure. But from where they stood, two blocks away, the force of the blast failed to even rattle the command truck. There was no tremor through the pavement.

Dani's breath caught as she instinctively ducked, shielding her eyes from the blinding flash that didn't come.

For half a second, everything was noise: a roar of distant noise, shrapnel clattering to the ground, sirens wailing.

And then... nothing.

No secondary explosion.

No collapse of the building.

Dani snapped her gaze upward to the thermal scan.

The top floor of the data center was now bright yellow-white, but she could see enough black framing to realize the structure was still intact. The monitor faded quickly back to a placid blue with scattered shots of red and pink, now clearly indicating small fires and not living bodies.

She looked over to the drone feed; it had gone black. The drone had been destroyed in the blast. Instead, Dani rushed over to a window that faced in the direction of the building, forcing her way between Ashe and a female Mossad officer. There was no falling debris beyond the innermost blast radius. No signs of a radiological event. The building was still standing.

Ashe, eyes already fixed on the wreckage, muttered, "That was too small."

Dani's pulse pounded. "That wasn't a dirty bomb. That was something else."

Whatever had just happened up there, whatever this attack was, it wasn't the attack they had expected.

Chapter 7 : THE BOMB THAT DIDN'T

FOR A FEW seconds after the blast, nothing moved.

The blast had been loud, but not deafening. Despite the lack of a violent shockwave to rattle through the streets like an earthquake, all conversation and activity had stopped. In the stunned silence that followed, the world seemed to pause, catching its breath in the moment between disaster and understanding.

Then the room erupted in chaos.

Voices overlapping, panicked shouts in Hebrew and English, calls resuming in those languages plus Farsi and Arabic. The command center's previous hum of controlled activity exploded into full-blown disorder.

Dani heard speakers crackle with frantic chatter as operators on the ground shouted over one another.

"Seven is gone. It's gone! Windows blown out, walls compromised—"

"Perimeter units, report! Where's the secondary? Do we have a second device?!"

"All teams, hold position until we confirm contamination levels!"

Across the room, a young intelligence analyst with a headset pressed to his ear was yelling in rapid-fire Hebrew, trying to get a response from someone in the field. Another man Dani presumed to be his superior—a grizzled man with thick glasses and a five o'clock shadow—was barking at a satellite technician.

"Where is our aerial feed?! I want eyes on that floor!"

A woman in her mid-forties, dressed in a dark blue suit, possibly Israeli Internal Security, shoved her phone against her ear, pacing furiously. "No, tell the Minister we don't have a confirmed detonation, we have an explosion. There is a difference. Until we know if it was radiological, we hold back press statements. No! We hold back everything!"

Across the main bank of monitors, static filled the space where the drone feed had been.

Dani's stomach tightened. They had just lost their best overhead view.

"The drone's down," one of the technicians confirmed needlessly, voice strained as he worked the controls, trying to reconnect. "We lost it in the blast wave; signal's dead."

Dani gritted her teeth. That was a problem. The drone had been their best set of eyes, their clearest view into the aftermath. Now they were flying blind.

To her right, Nehem was barking into his radio, trying to get fresh eyes on the site.

Ashe, however, didn't move.

He stood near the reinforced window at the back of the command center, watching the smoking wreckage of the seventh floor from their vantage point two blocks away. His arms were crossed. He wasn't relaxed, exactly, but neither was he tense. It was as if none of the chaos around him mattered. Only the scene in front of him.

Dani shot him a look. "You're very calm for someone watching a bombing in real-time."

"It's not my first. I'm waiting," Ashe replied.

Dani wasn't sure what exactly that meant, but she didn't have time to question him about it. Behind her, monitors flickered, finally showing new footage: a handheld camera feed, jittery and unsteady. Nehem called her attention to the new images. The lead tactical team on the ground had switched to helmet cams.

On-screen, through a haze of smoke, Dani could make out the exterior of the building, the shattered windows of the seventh floor still raining glass onto the street below.

"Tactical One, report!" Nehem ordered.

The voice that came back was shaken but controlled. "We have no movement in the building. No secondary detonation yet, but we're holding until contamination check."

"Get a reading. Now."

Dani exhaled slowly, flexing her fingers. This was the moment. The dirty bomb threat had been their working assumption. If this explosion, however undersized, had spread radioactive material, every second mattered.

On one of the helmet cam feeds, Dani saw an operative step forward, holding a Geiger counter. The beeping started immediately, faint, but fast and sharp.

Dani's pulse spiked until she realized: it was just the background radiation of the city.

The beeping slowed, then stopped, as the operator adjusted the sensitivity of the device.

The man hesitated. "Uh... Negative for radiation."

Silence stretched over the command center for several seconds.

Then voices exploded all over again.

Nehem was already switching channels on his radio. "Confirm that! Check again! Run secondary diagnostics!"

Dani's head was spinning. A dirty bomb without radiation wasn't a dirty bomb.

She turned toward Ashe, who hadn't moved from his spot at the window. His expression hadn't changed. He was still watching the smoking ruin of the seventh floor, hands in his pockets, as if this had all unfolded exactly as he had expected.

Dani narrowed her eyes. "Still waiting?" she asked, voice low.

Ashe's gaze flicked to her. "Still waiting," he confirmed.

Dani exhaled sharply, looking back at the monitors.

Whatever this had been, it wasn't over.

The commotion in the room steadied over the next several minutes, but the tension had only sharpened. No one was shouting anymore, but there was an urgency to every movement, every clipped response. Confused chatter crackled over the comms, operators speaking over one another, trying to make sense of what had just happened. A low murmur of uncertainty filled the command center, replacing the sharp focus that had driven them only moments before.

Dani stood near the primary monitor bank, arms crossed. On the monitors, the live drone feed had gone dark, caught and destroyed in the initial blast. The only remaining visuals came from helmet cameras and handheld devices, shaky footage bouncing between smoke and debris, flashing emergency lights, and stunned silence.

Across the street from the target building, a thermal imaging scope was still offering the best real-time information they had of the seventh floor.

The heat map showed nothing but cooling embers. She studied the shifting blues and reds on the screen, her frown deepening. The seventh floor had been reduced to charred metal, shattered glass, and bodies that no longer registered heat. No figures were moving through the wreckage, no signs of life or last-minute resistance. The terrorists had all died in the explosion.

Dani exhaled slowly. That raised more questions than it answered. If the goal had been to detonate a dirty bomb, why had they sacrificed themselves in the blast? This wasn't some makeshift suicide vest attack in a crowded marketplace, this was planned, coordinated. A detonation without demands. A target that didn't make sense. And a crew that either hadn't planned to leave or hadn't gotten the chance.

Dani turned slightly to see Ashe standing near the window, his gaze locked on the damaged building two blocks away. His posture was calm, unbothered, his hands resting loosely at his sides.

Dani studied him for a beat before joining him there. "No survivors up there."

Ashe didn't react. "I know."

She lifted a brow. "Still waiting?"

His eyes flicked toward her for the briefest moment before returning to the plume of smoke curling into the sky.

"What's he up to?" Ashe asked her.

Dani looked at Ashe, trying to read the man's face. "You think this was Standish." It was a statement, not a question. She had little doubt herself.

"Not him exactly. He wasn't there. But he wanted us to see it."

Dani couldn't find a reason to disagree. She sighed and turned back toward the monitors. The breach team was nearly ready.

Onscreen, the first wave of operators finished their final gear checks. Their movements were calm, methodical, practiced. Weapons checked, safeties off. Breach charges placed. Protective gear collaboratively secured and re-secured. Their voices were low, even over the comms, professionals doing what they had been trained to do.

Beyond them, in the secured staging area, the HAZMAT specialists ran through final precautions. The full-body suits were bulky, stiff with protective layers, but the men and women inside them moved with smooth efficiency, sealing visors, adjusting oxygen regulators. They spoke in short, clipped exchanges, confirming readiness. Even with no radiation detected, protocol had to be followed. The delay was necessary but felt costly; every second spent in preparation was another second the terrorists could be covering their tracks.

Near to this group, a decontamination tent had been erected, equipped with chemical rinse showers and medical supplies. A team of paramedics and radiation specialists stood at the ready, speaking in small groups as they reviewed emergency procedures.

Dani heard Nehem's voice cut through the radio chatter. "Final check. Do we have an entry point?"

The lead tactical officer responded immediately. "Primary doors are clear. Interior structure is holding. Stairwell access intact. We're moving."

Dani inhaled slowly as the first breach team advanced through the building's entrance, stepping over broken glass and twisted metal.

Now they would get some answers.

Or worse, more questions.

❧ • ❧

THE COMMAND CENTER had fallen silent, every eye fixed on the live feed as the breach team swept through the wreckage of the seventh floor. It was so quiet save for the soft hum of radio chatter and the occasional flicker of static that Dani could hear herself breathing.

Onscreen, the helmet cam feeds flickered as the operatives moved carefully through the devastation left by the blast. The air still hung thick with smoke, but the immediate threat of a secondary detonation had passed. What they had expected to have been a charred, irradiated hell was instead something entirely different: something strange, calculated.

The floor was shredded. Not just burned, but chewed apart, deep gouges and pockmarks covering the surface like enormous claws had raked through it. The furniture had likewise been ripped to shreds, pieces of desks, chairs, and electronics embedded into the walls. The windows had been pushed violently outward, their shattered remnants scattered in the streets below.

And the bodies...

Dani felt her stomach tighten as the camera panned across the fallen terrorists. They weren't just dead. They were ruined.

Their bodies hadn't simply dropped where they stood; they had been hurled outward, shredded by thousands of steel ball bearings ripping through flesh, bone, and fabric alike. The blast pattern was horrific and precise, not the randomized destruction of an improvised bomb, but something methodical and intentional.

One of the operators swore under his breath. "They were shredded where they stood. Ripped apart."

"This is wrong," Nehem muttered.

Dani didn't disagree. The blast had been powerful, but strangely contained and directed: enough to destroy everything fragile but not strong enough to compromise the structure of the building. A device meant for terror should have left the entire floor gutted, if not brought the whole building down.

"Zero radiation, still," came the voice of Levin, the breach team leader, over the comms.

There was a pause, then a collective sigh of relief from several people in the room.

Dani, however, felt no such relief. She would almost have preferred a known threat to this ambiguity and mystery.

"Remove your hoods and see if we can improve the visibility," Nehem ordered, his voice clipped.

On the monitors, the first of the breaching team unclipped their helmets, their visors fogged with sweat, faces set in grim determination. The camera feeds sharpened, no longer clouded by curved lenses and reflections.

Nehem's jaw was tight, his brow furrowed in growing unease. "What was the source? What killed them?"

"Approaching central detonation site."

Levin's voice came back over the comms, even but laced with confusion.

"From the fragment signatures, the patterns? They were taken out by... Claymores."

Nehem blinked, taken aback. "What?"

"Confirming now..." Levin's helmet camera showed his perspective as he stepped over bodies and approached the core device. Facing outward, he surveyed the carnage in all directions as those in the command center watched. "Yes. I'd say M18A1 Claymores. Several of them. All faced outward."

Claymores? Not an IED? Not a dirty bomb. This had been a trap.

Beside her, she felt Ashe's body grow suddenly rigid.

She turned to him, instinct kicking in. "Ashe, what is it?"

He didn't answer.

Instead, he reached forward, grabbing the radio mic from Nehem's hand.

Nehem barely had time to react before Ashe keyed it.

"Confirm that placement," Ashe said, his voice sharp and controlled. Deadly serious. Dani had never seen this part of him; he was suddenly on a battlefield, and perfectly competent in his role there. "Say again; confirm an outward-facing array."

A long pause.

Then Levin's voice, quiet but certain. He was unsure who gave the order, but he responded to its authority: "Affirmative. Mines were set around the core, all facing out."

Nehem moved to grab the mic back, but Dani waved him off. She narrowed her eyes. "Ashe, talk to me."

He just stared at the live feed, his gaze locked on the core of the device sitting in the ruined center of the blast site. Dani followed his line of sight, eyes narrowing as she studied the remains of the detonation chamber.

Even fully destroyed, she could tell the device had been highly engineered, meticulously designed.

The outer casing had been cylindrical, about 1.3 meters in diameter and a little less than that tall, reinforced with heavy steel plating that had mostly peeled back like shrapnel curling away from the reinforced center in all directions. The building's support girders surrounding it had warped outward, laid bare like bones by the device's "skin" of Claymore mines.

"That inner casing's too strong for a conventional explosive," Dani murmured. "That thing was built to survive."

The outer shell had blown outward, revealing an interior compartment still intact, but cracked open by the backblast along what looked like a reinforced seam.

Dani's mind worked fast, calculating.

The blast hadn't been meant to maximize destruction, or even produce terror—though the terrorists had remained unaware of that fact up until their grisly end. The device had been meant to kill everyone standing around it. The bomb's designer had orchestrated the deliberate slaughter of the terrorists handling it. This hadn't been an attack; it had been an execution.

"Ashe. What are we looking at?"

Ashe's expression was intense. Without looking away from the screen, he keyed the microphone.

"Open the box."

Chapter 8 : A GAME OF TWO

THE COMMAND CENTER was still, every operative transfixed by the monitors as the breach team continued their methodical sweep of the seventh floor. Smoke curled lazily around and through the wreckage: slow, eerie ghost witnesses to the sudden, violent force of the explosion and its aftermath. The team worked in tense silence, their gloves slick with sweat inside the heavy HAZMAT suits as they struggled to pry open the reinforced core of the device. The steel casing, warped outward by the Claymore blast, had left the seam twisted and jammed, resisting their attempts to force it open.

"The thing's stuck."

"Bring in the spreaders," ordered Levin.

While Levin and that part of the team focused on the device itself, Nehem had regained his mic. He asked for an update to the broader review of the data center blast site. "Tactical Three, what do you have?"

Another voice came back, steady but tense.

"We've found something unusual. Secured mount. It's a camera housing."

The operative's feed tilted toward a small, reinforced recording device, bearing scorch marks and sporting a cracked lens. A stray ball bearing from one of the Claymores had ripped through it, but the bulk of the hardware was still intact.

"It's not standard building security," said Nehem.

"No, sir. It's hardened. Reinforced case."

Nehem leaned in. "Bag it and tag it. We'll analyze what's left."

Dani exhaled. "Someone wanted to watch?"

Ashe hadn't moved. He was still staring at the monitor, his posture rigid, unreadable.

"Someone wanted to watch," he repeated, but the way he said it was different.

Not a guess. Like Dani, Ashe already knew why the camera was there; he knew who had placed it. And whoever that was, they had been watching until the moment they remotely detonated the blast.

On Levin's feed, a pair of operatives stepped forward, wielding a hydraulic spreader, the kind typically used to extract people from wrecked vehicles. The tool's metal prongs dug into the cracked seam, groaning as it exerted pressure. Every person in the room was on edge, breath held as the armor-grade steel finally gave way with a horrific screech.

"We're in."

No one spoke as the camera panned inside. The view refocused as the operative tilted his helmet-mounted lens toward the core. Inside, nestled within the hollow cavity, was a strange and unsettling collection of objects.

"There's something inside. Looks like... marble?"

The operative reached in carefully, brushing off a layer of fine dust, revealing the shattered remains of a Roman-era bust.

Dani recognized it before the dust had even settled: it was Ashe. His features were instantly recognizable, but the bust had been shattered, the cracks not random, not incidental.

Hammer strikes. Methodical destruction.

Someone had wanted their message to be loud and clear.

And yet, next to it, unblemished, pristine, lay another bust: a woman's face, beautifully carved, perfectly preserved.

Aurelia.

Nehem muttered, "Someone certainly has a love for the theatrical, doesn't he?"

"Why break one and not the other?" one of the operatives muttered.

No one answered.

As if sensing something more, the lead operative reached in again, carefully lifting the busts away. Beneath them, under the film of dust, a brittle, yellowed page lay flat against the steel floor of the armored box.

Even through the grainy camera feed, Dani recognized it instantly. It was a page from the Latin Vulgate. Even before the camera zoomed in, she knew where it had come from. Chicago. Ashe's row house.

She had seen this exact page before, once framed in glass, hanging in Ashe's hidden Chicago lair. It had been one of the few things he'd carried with him across the centuries, a relic from his former life. One that he had never explained to her.

Now, it was here, ripped from its frame. Defaced.

Scrawled across the ancient Latin text were three words.

"I AM WAITING."

The words had been scrawled across the ancient vellum in large, red letters, the ink smeared and uneven. Dani didn't need to ask Ashe who had done this; she already knew.

Standish.

Then it hit her. Her stomach went cold, her fingers curled into fists. Because she suddenly understood the other part of the message. The message wasn't solely for Ashe. It wasn't just a challenge, or a warning. It was a statement of intent, a broadcast of his next move.

Aurelia's bust had been left untouched.

And Dani knew exactly who Standish saw as Aurelia's reflection in the present.

Amber.

Dani's breath left her in a slow, controlled exhale.

She turned toward Ashe.

His expression was still locked, inscrutable, but she knew he had come to the same conclusion.

"We have to call Paris."

DANI'S MIND WAS already ahead of her body, snapping into motion before she even registered reaching for the nearest phone.

"I need a line to Paris, now."

One of the communications techs in the command center, a young guy barely out of his twenties, blinked at her, confused. "Ma'am?"

Dani didn't slow down. "Paris. Hotel Le Roch. Concierge desk."

Nehem was already pulling out his phone, speaking rapidly in Hebrew to one of his intelligence contacts. But Dani wasn't about to wait on the slow grind of international cooperation. He spared a wave at the tech, saving the young man from Dani's impending wrath. The tech scrambled to comply, punching in numbers as Dani snatched up the receiver and held it to her ear.

The line rang twice.

Then a smooth, practiced voice answered in French-accented English.

"Hotel Le Roch, concierge desk. How may I assist you?"

Dani cut straight to the point, stretching the truth slightly. "This is Assistant Director Dani Linder, FBI. I need to speak to Amber Olsen. Now."

There was a pause. Then, in a tone laced with polite confusion—

"I'm sorry, madame. I'm afraid I do not understand."

"You understand fine, and you're going to get me patched through to her room. Now." Dani repeated Amber's name to the man for good measure.

"I'm sorry, madame. We have... There is no guest here under that name."

Dani's grip on the phone tightened. "Yes, there is. She was checked in by the Paris FBI attaché's security detail. Room—look, I don't know what room, but you do. Put me through."

A longer pause.

Finally, the man responded, "I'm afraid I cannot help you."

Dani ground her teeth. "Listen to me, this is a security matter. I don't have time for—"

Ashe, still standing by the monitors, held out a hand.

Without hesitation, she slapped the phone to speaker mode and shoved it toward him.

The moment Ashe started speaking, his voice even, controlled, and fluent in perfect French, the tone on the other end shifted. By the time Ashe's words had started to shift in a more dangerous direction, the man complied.

"Pardon, monsieur, je suis désolé, mais... il y a eu un incident."

Dani's heart slammed in her chest.

"Quel type d'incident?" Ashe asked smoothly, but the steel was unmistakeable beneath his voice.

A reluctant sigh. Then, returning to heavily accented English, the man spoke. He sounded defeated. "Perhaps you should speak to the authorities."

There was a shuffle of movement, muffled voices in the background, and then a new voice entered the conversation: a firm, familiar one.

"Harrigan."

Dani's stomach dropped half an inch in relief. "Harrigan. Tell me you have her."

"She's gone, Dani."

A cold silence stretched across the room.

Dani closed her eyes briefly, exhaling. "Tell me everything."

Harrigan's voice was clipped, professional, but not nearly as calm as he tried to sound. "Abduction occurred sometime in the past two hours. She was last seen entering her hotel suite on security footage. No forced entry. No signs of a struggle. Concierge alerted police when they noticed her room had been left wide open. Staff claims they saw nothing."

"They didn't see anything, or they don't want to admit it?" Dani snapped.

"Both, I'm sure. The French authorities are handling this their own way, but—" Harrigan sighed, rubbing a hand over his jaw. "The security footage showed something else. A man entering through the front door, bold as daybreak. Dani, you already know who we're looking for."

"Standish?" She didn't need to ask.

Harrigan continued, "Yeah. Single male. White. Tall. Dressed in dark clothing. It was him, the Bureau's Lament. Moved like he belonged there. Left with Olsen through the loading docks, and no one was smart enough to think twice about it."

Dani closed her eyes.

❧ • ❧

DANI BARELY HEARD the click of the receiver as the call ended. Her brain was already kicking into high gear, her pulse steady, her movements automatic.

Amber was gone. Standish had taken her. She surmised they had very little time to stop whatever came next.

She turned to Ashe. He was already pulling away from the command center, stepping past the window where he had watched the burning data center just minutes ago. His expression hadn't changed much—still cool, but something was different.

The stillness had changed. It wasn't the patient waiting anymore; it was the calm before the storm. Dani followed, keeping her voice low but firm. "This whole thing, this entire op, was never about a dirty bomb."

Ashe didn't answer right away.

But he didn't need to.

She kept going, working it through aloud. "The explosion, the Claymores, the message. It was all just a distraction."

Still, Ashe said nothing.

Dani exhaled sharply, feeling the anger coil at the base of her spine. "Standish. He had this planned from the start. He knew we'd be here, tied up in all of this, while he took Amber."

Finally, Ashe spoke, quietly but with absolute certainty.

"Yes."

Dani felt her jaw tighten. She could deal with this. She had to. There wasn't time for emotions, for frustration, for anything except action. But something still wasn't lining up.

She turned fully to face him, stopping him with a hand on his arm. "I get the busts. The message was clear. One broken, one intact. But the Bible page? What was that?"

Ashe finally looked at her.

And for the first time since this whole mess had started, Dani saw it. Recognition.

Not surprise. Not confusion. Recognition.

She inhaled slowly. "It meant something specific to you, didn't it? Something I'm not seeing."

Ashe exhaled in sync with her, his gaze flicking toward the monitors one last time. When he spoke, his voice was steady, controlled.

"He's telling me where to find him."

Dani blinked. "The Bible page?"

Ashe nodded. "I don't know how he figured it out, but he did. He wants me to come to him. And I know where."

Dani decided she didn't like this particular game.

She could track movements, decode signals, analyze patterns. But this? This wasn't about any of that. This was personal, a game between two men, and Dani didn't like playing games she didn't control. Ones where she didn't know the rules.

"Where?"

Ashe met her gaze. "Turkey."

Dani swore under her breath. That complicated things.

"The people here aren't going to like that," she muttered, nodding toward the Israeli officials still running cleanup on the high-profile operation behind them. "We're already pushing the limits of their patience. We take off to Turkey, we're on our own. They won't be able to get involved."

Ashe turned back toward the window, looking out at the wreckage of the seventh floor, the fading plumes of black curling into the sky.

When he spoke, his voice was calm, certain, and just a little too quiet.

"That doesn't matter." His gaze remained fixed on the smoking ruins of the data center.

"All he wants is me."

Chapter 9 : CITY OF ASHES

THE PLANE'S WHEELS hit the tarmac at Istanbul Airport with a heavy, rattling thud, jarring Ashe out of his stillness. A tinny voice crackled over the intercom in Turkish, then English, welcoming them to the city, announcing the local time, the weather—as if any of that mattered. The plane taxied slowly to the gate, its engines whining low as it navigated the sprawling network of runways. The glow of the airport lights outside the window did little to dispel the darkness that hung over the city beyond. Over Istanbul.

Istanbul.

Not to him.

To him, it was still Constantinople.

And it was still his personal hell.

He hadn't set foot here in centuries, and yet, the weight of the entire city came crashing back against his chest the moment they touched down.

The city still reeked with the stench of hundreds of thousands of old ghosts.

Dani sat beside him in the first-class cabin, watching him too closely. She hadn't said much since they left Israel, but he knew she'd been tracking his every shift in posture, every flicker of reaction.

She could feel it. She knew him well enough for that, despite their decades apart.

She didn't know what it was, not exactly, but she knew enough to sense the change in him.

"Welcome to Istanbul," she muttered dryly as she stretched in her seat.

Ashe didn't respond. He kept his eyes on the window, watching as the airport terminal loomed closer. The modern architecture, all gleaming glass and steel, felt like an insult to all that had been buried beneath it.

Because he still saw it as it had been. He would never see it another way.

No matter how badly the world had tried to erase the past, gloss over what happened in this thriving city while most of the world was still living in mud huts. The brittle bones of the old empire remained beneath the surface: the shattered remnants of Byzantium, of blood and betrayal, of loss beyond reckoning.

Loss that he himself had caused, blood by the gallons that would always be on his hands.

The worst period in his long and wretched life had been spent here.

He had tried to do good here. He had tried to change. And he had been punished, as had so many around him, for his arrogance.

And now he was back.

They moved through passport control quickly, aided by Dani's diplomatic pull and Ashe's flawless, forged documentation.

"Try not to act like you hate this place so much," Dani murmured under her breath as they stepped into the main concourse, where a wave of commuters, tourists, and business travelers swirled around them in a sea of movement. "People are sensitive."

Ashe didn't answer.

The air in the terminal buzzed with a thousand voices, each layered over the others in an endless cacophony: announcements in Turkish, Arabic, English, the chatter of travelers, the hurried steps of airport staff, the laughs and cries of children.

It all faded away into static as they stepped outside into the city.

The moment he felt the night air, something inside him tightened.

Istanbul was alive, modern, sprawling, restless.

But under it, beneath the lights and the noise and the smog of the twenty-first century, was the city he remembered.

The city of betrayal and violence and decay and hunger and death. The city where he had lost everything. The city that had lost so much of itself, at his own hands.

Dani hailed a cab while Ashe stood at the curb, staring out at the skyline.

It wasn't the same, not remotely.

But he still saw it the way it had been.

The Great Church, standing like a silent guardian of holiness in the distance, had once been the crown jewel of the empire; a jewel he had himself helped to erect for Theodosius after the main basilica of the old structure burnt. Its walls had heard the prayers of countless men long since dust, their voices now swallowed by the centuries.

Now it was just a renamed landmark. The Hagia Sophia. A tourist attraction.

A place where no one remembered the screams that had once echoed as flames consumed its glory again.

Screams Ashe could still hear.

Dani called to him, snapping him out of it.

"Come on, Golding, let's go."

He turned, forcing his mind to the present, and slipped into the taxi after helping Dani into it and closing her door.

The cab smelled of stale cigarettes and worn leather, the kind of scent that never quite leaves a car, no matter how many times it's cleaned. Its driver was young, maybe mid-thirties, but carried himself like a man who had spent a lifetime behind the wheel. He had the sharp, observant gaze of someone who made a living reading the people in his backseat, and a knowing smirk that suggested he'd seen it all before.

He thought.

He met Ashe's eyes in the rearview mirror, then flicked a glance at Dani. "Le Meridien, yes?"

Dani nodded. "Evet."

The driver's grin widened. "Ah! You speak a little. Good! Good. Istanbul is a place you must know to enjoy. A guide is always helpful." He let the suggestion hang in the air as the car pulled away from the airport, but he didn't push his luck. The taxi merged into the heavy late-night traffic, headlights casting long streaks over wet pavement that hadn't seen rain. The driver's hands moved lazily over the wheel, effortless in their control. This was his domain.

"And you, beyefendi?" he asked, addressing Ashe directly. "You are a man who knows this city? Or is this your first time?"

Ashe's jaw tightened, but he said nothing.

The driver didn't seem to notice. Or if he did, he ignored it. "It is a beautiful city, you know. A place of wonders. Perhaps your mother will enjoy it?"

Dani, halfway through checking her phone, froze mid-scroll as the alarms went off.

Ashe tilted his head slightly, staring at the man's reflection in the rearview mirror.

The driver, oblivious to the sudden shift in tension, kept going.

"A good son brings his mother to Istanbul! Takes her to see the Bosphorus, the Blue Mosque, the palaces. It is a good city for family." He tapped the steering wheel, nodding to himself. "Yes, very nice. You will be a good guide for her, beyefendi."

The air in the cab dropped several degrees. Ashe could sense Dani holding her breath. He didn't care.

The driver kept smiling, still completely unaware.

And then Ashe spoke.

"Drive the car." His voice was low, flat, and carried just enough weight that the driver faltered mid-thought.

The smile faltered. "Ah, of course, of course. Just saying, you are—"

"Shut up. No one asked for your opinion."

The words landed sharp and cold, with an edge that sliced the air between them.

The driver's smile froze, then flickered into something smaller, more cautious.

He glanced back at Dani, as if hoping for an ally, but found only her tight-lipped silence.

Then, wisely, he faced forward again.

The road stretched ahead, weaving through the dense sprawl of the city, the neon glow of nightlife blending with the shadows of centuries-old structures.

The only sounds for several minutes were the hum of the engine and the hiss of tires on pavement.

Dani exhaled quietly, then turned slightly toward Ashe, keeping her voice measured.

"It's late."

Ashe didn't respond. He figured she hadn't meant him to.

Instead, she turned her attention back to the window, watching as the aforementioned Bosphorus shimmered in the distance, its dark waters stretching like an unspoken promise.

The driver said nothing else for the rest of the ride.

The streets of Istanbul continued to unfold around and past them, a mixture of old and new, the skeletal remains of ancient structures pressed up against bright neon signs and modern developments.

Ashe felt Dani's eyes drift to him on occasion from the other side of the backseat.

She hadn't asked anything yet. But she would. He knew it.

The silence stretched for a while before she muttered, "You look like you want to burn the whole place down."

Ashe exhaled sharply, but it wasn't a laugh. She wasn't wrong; he hated this place.

Hated it like he had never hated any other place on earth.

Not Rome. Not Jerusalem.

Not even the endless blood-soaked battlefields of Europe.

This was different.

This was personal.

"I'm fine," he finally said.

Dani huffed.

He didn't glorify her doubt with a response.

The cab driver, catching something in their tone, glanced at them in the rearview mirror and put his smile back on, this time without telling his eyes. "Americans?"

Dani, not wanting things to get any worse for the man, nodded. "Yes."

Her tone indicated that it was best for the young man to terminate the conversation, and he was wise enough to comply. Weaving through traffic, they neared the Galata Bridge, spanning the Bosphorus. The waters below shimmered, reflecting the city lights like scattered funeral pyres.

Ashe kept his gaze forward; he had already decided.

Dani didn't know it yet but tonight, he would leave without her. He would go alone. Because whatever game Standish was playing, it wasn't one Ashe would let Dani step into.

This was between the two men.

And Ashe had caused so many deaths in this city, one more would hardly make a difference.

THE HOTEL WAS modern, expensive, and quiet, the kind of place where people with money came to disappear behind soundproofed walls and discreet service. The lobby smelled of polished wood and imported citrus, the air thick with the carefully manufactured calm of a place designed for luxury.

It wasn't Constantinople, not even close. It was just... in it.

Still, Ashe could feel the weight of the city pressing in from the outside, seeping through the glass, whispering beneath the hum of distant traffic.

He didn't want to be here. He didn't want to be anywhere near here. But he didn't have a choice.

Dani checked them in without fuss, her reinstated Bureau credentials ensuring a smooth process. The concierge was polite, efficient, and discreet, handing over their keycards with a warm yet utterly detached smile.

Ashe barely noticed. His mind was elsewhere, already ahead, already moving beyond this place. He stepped into the elevator with Dani, the doors gliding shut with a soft hush, enclosing them in mirrored walls and sterile lighting.

Dani studied his reflection as she spoke.

"You're vibrating."

He didn't look at her. "I'm fine."

"You're not fine. You're barely keeping it together."

Ashe exhaled slowly, clenching and unclenching his fists.

He wasn't nervous. He wasn't afraid. If that was what she thought, she wasn't as smart as he'd given her credit for.

He immediately chastised himself for such a harsh thought. Maybe she was right, at least to a degree. But something inside him was twisting, tightening, winding too tight to hold for much longer.

The elevator chimed softly as they reached their floor.

"You don't have to talk to me, but you do have to stay in one piece, Golding."

Dani's voice was measured, steady, the way she spoke when she knew she was losing ground but refusing to admit it.

Ashe didn't answer.

The suite was exactly what one expected it to be: lavish, impersonal, and sterile.

Floor-to-ceiling windows framed a view of the Bosphorus, its dark waters reflecting the scattered lights of the city. Somewhere out there, ships moved, people walked, life went on as if the ghosts of history weren't clawing at the edges of the world.

Ashe stood near the window, looking at the distant water and not seeing it.

Dani moved through the space with purpose, dropping her bag onto a chair, opening her laptop on the sleek black table near the minibar. She had no intention of rushing into this blind. She was working the problem. Gathering intel. Making calls.

Ashe couldn't care less; he already had all the information he needed.

Time was slipping through his fingers, and every second they wasted here, Standish was getting farther ahead.

"We need to go," he muttered, voice low, almost to himself.

Dani didn't even look up. "We will. After I figure out what we're walking into."

His fingers tightened into fists, looking at Dani's reflection in the large window. "You already know what we're walking into. You saw what he left for me."

Dani exhaled slowly, finally turning toward him. "I saw a challenge. I saw a message. But I also saw a trap. And I don't intend to let you walk into it blind."

Ashe stared at her, the anger in him cool, controlled, simmering just beneath the surface.

"That's not your decision."

"It certainly is."

"Says who?" Ashe knew it sounded childish as soon as the words left his lips.

"Says the president," Dani replied.

Ashe snorted. "He's not my president."

She met his stare head-on, arms crossed, unflinching.

"You think I don't know what you're doing? You think I haven't seen this before? This whole act where you shut down, where you decide to take everything on yourself and walk into combat alone?"

Silence.

Then—

"It's not an act."

The words came out quieter than he intended, but no less certain.

Dani shook her head, pushing forward. "You think you can do this alone, but you can't. You're not some untouchable force of nature, Ashe. You bleed. You break. And I'm not letting you throw yourself into Standish's hands because you think you have to."

Ashe's jaw tightened. She didn't understand. She couldn't. This wasn't about winning. This wasn't about survival. He was way past that.

This was about ending something that had been set in motion long before Dani had ever known his name.

Before Amber. Before Task Industries. Before the country Dani vainly served.

This place had taken everything from him once.

Now, Standish was forcing Ashe to relive it all. But Dani wasn't a part of that. She never could be.

And that meant she wasn't coming.

Time dragged while Dani worked. She made calls, reached out to contacts, gathered information. She was convinced she was making progress.

Ashe let her believe it.

He sat near the window, watching the city shift from evening to the earliest hints of a dark night, the glow of Istanbul never truly fading, only settling into a deeper, quieter hum.

He could feel her eyes on him every so often. Checking. Watching. Waiting for him to unravel unless she could solve the puzzle in time.

But she didn't understand that he had solved it the moment he saw Standish's message. He had all the information he needed. He knew where he was going.

As Standish knew he would.

And he knew that by the time Dani realized it, he would already be gone.

THE AIR INSIDE the suite was stifling. The silence pressed against Ashe's skin like a weight, growing heavier by the second. Beyond the glass walls of the hotel, Istanbul stretched in every direction, its lights shimmering against the river, its streets still alive even in the deep hours of the night. The past clawed at the edges of the city, buried under layers of steel and asphalt, but he could still feel it: the ruins beneath, the ghosts crying for justice.

And he could feel Dani watching him.

She had been watching him since they landed, reading every flicker of his expression, every slight shift in his posture. She wasn't wrong to be suspicious, of course. Ashe had already made up his mind.

He was leaving. Alone.

But Dani wasn't going to let him walk out of the hotel room without a fight.

"Alright, let's get something straight." Dani's voice cut through the quiet like a knife against glass.

Ashe didn't turn from the window. His reflection stared back at him, a ghost in a city of ghosts.

"You're not going in alone."

Ashe finally turned, his expression blank. "I know."

Dani folded her arms. "Do you? Because you're pacing continuously like a caged animal, and you haven't stopped looking at the exit since we checked in."

"It's just a door."

"And you want to walk through it without me."

His silence was answer enough. Dani let out a slow, measured breath, then took a step closer. She placed a palm on his chest. The skin of her palm was warm against his.

"Look, I get it. Standish made this personal. He's pulling you into something bigger than just a kidnapping, bigger than just revenge. But you're acting like you're the only one who can play this game."

He met her eyes then, and the cynicism in his response surprised even him.

"I am the only one who can play this game."

Dani withdrew her hand like it had been burnt. Her jaw tightened. "That's bull."

"No, it's survival. Yours. Amber's. You think Standish doesn't already know exactly how you operate? You think he didn't anticipate you trying to back me up? You follow me, he kills Amber. You stay out of this, she lives."

She shook her head, refusing to accept his logic. "And you just assume he's going to play by those rules? You assume if you walk in there alone, you're in control? That's not how this works, Ashe."

"No, that's exactly how this works."

His voice was low, measured, absolute. "This is between him and me."

Dani took another step forward, not backing down.

"I've seen you pull this before, you know. You're not a martyr, Ashe. You don't get to decide who lives and who doesn't."

His eyes flickered. A tiny shift, barely noticeable, but Dani caught it.

She was pressing into something real now. She'd hit a nerve.

But then, just as quickly, he forced the mask back into place.

"I don't need to be a martyr, Dani. I just need to be the only one in the room when it ends."

Her expression darkened. "That's the dumbest thing I've heard you say, and I've heard you say some stupid stuff."

He let out a slow breath, acting like he was giving in, like she was getting through to him. It was time.

He nodded. "Alright."

Dani's eyes opened wide. "What?"

He gestured toward the laptop she'd left on the table.

"You're right. We should figure out exactly where Standish is before I make a move. We go in smart. Together."

Dani studied him for a moment, as if waiting for the lie to surface. She had once prided herself on her ability to know when he was lying. Ashe was gambling a lot on his ability to circumvent that skill. Her life relied on him selling the lie. Amber's life.

Dani let out a long, slow breath. "Yes, we do. Let's get fueled up and get back to work."

She turned back toward the kitchenette to brew a cup of Turkish coffee in the hotel room's electric cezve.

Moving silently, Ashe was already gone.

•

AS ASHE LEFT The Peninsula Istanbul, the modern city buzzed around him: cars pushing through midnight traffic, neon signs casting artificial light over old stone, the scent of diesel, grilled meat, and the salt of the Bosphorus weaving through the air.

But it felt like a lie. Ashe barely saw Istanbul.

He saw Constantinople.

All Ashe could see was Constantinople, broken and burning and bleeding.

He stepped into the streets, his movements precise, unhurried, vanishing into the night as if he had never been there at all.

The modern city was a falsehood. The trams, the neon lights, the glass-fronted high-rises: they were masks, paper-thin covers stretched over the rotting bones of an empire he had once watched die.

No. Constantinople had not died.

It had suffocated beneath the weight of time, its ruins buried, its people forgotten except for those who had lived through their screams.

Ashe had heard every single one of them. Caused them.

Standish had dragged him back to this place, and it was not by accident.

No. Standish understood. He *knew*.

The cab ride from the hotel had been a long, suffocating exercise in restraint. Dani had watched him too closely, her instincts catching onto something just beneath the surface.

She knew he was about to run. She just didn't know how soon.

By the time she realized he was gone, he would already be deep in the city, too far ahead for her to catch up. And she didn't know where he was going.

The moment he stepped out of the hotel, Ashe ceased to exist.

He ambled along like he belonged there, like he had always been there, like he was nothing worth noticing. He walked these streets as if he had never left.

And in a way, he hadn't.

The city had changed, but its bones were the same.

He followed old paths, buried beneath modern asphalt, his mind moving between the present and the past, layering one over the other, making them indistinguishable.

When he passed the harbor district, he didn't see the glowing storefronts and luxury hotels, he saw the Theodosian Harbor, thick with the stench of tar and fish, dockworkers shouting in Greek and Latin as Egyptian grain and Persian silks changed hands.

When he crossed Eminönü Square, he didn't see trams and markets and tourists, he saw the Forum of Theodosius, the statues of emperors long since crumbled, the mosaics shimmering in torchlight.

And when he walked the path that had once been the Mese, he still heard the roar of the crowd, the cheers of an empire at its height, the procession of legions, of rulers, and death.

The city was still alive, but it was rotting from the inside.

Just like him.

He moved without hesitation, a figure slipping through narrow alleys and wide, modern avenues, unseen despite making no effort to hide. It was a skill that had taken centuries to master. You didn't disappear by sticking to the shadows or by moving too carefully. You disappeared by blending in so perfectly that people never saw you in the first place.

Be nothing. Be no one.

Dani would know he was gone by now.

It didn't matter; she'd never find him.

Ashe merged so fluidly within the crowd that no one would think to remember him. He walked at the right speed, with the right posture, his shoulders loose, his expression blank. He was just another traveler, just another man moving through the night.

No one stopped him.

No one would remember him.

Ashe had spent lifetimes learning how to be a ghost in plain sight.

And tonight, he was one again.

The Great Church—the Hagia Sophia—loomed in the distance, not as a landmark, not as a museum, but as a monument to a world that no longer existed. And with it, a version of himself that had long since perished as well.

He breathed deeply of the place. The air smelled wrong, but he could still imagine it as it had been. Ashe continued along, walking through two cities at once. The past was thick here, suffocating, waiting to drag him under.

And he let it.

Because this was where he had to be.

This was where Standish wanted him to be.

This was where it was going to end.

He slowed as he approached the monastery, the weight of the past pressing heavier with every step. It was here—*here*—that he had tried to become clean. And it was here that he had been punished for it.

The place had once been grand.

Today, it was a husk, a place the modern city cared little about. In an ironic turn of fate, the monastery had become a prison sometime after the Crusades and had lived that life until two short centuries ago. And now, even that life was long forgotten, its secrets buried deep in crumbling corridors and hidden cells.

Stone walls, half-broken, still clung to what little dignity remained, their edges worn by time, by neglect, by the quiet, slow erosion of things that no longer mattered.

Ashe didn't hesitate. He stepped inside, past the threshold of the ruins, into the place where he had once stood before.

He could still feel the weight of it. The past pressed down, thick and relentless, but he didn't stop moving.

Standish had set the stage. And Ashe had walked right onto it.

But Standish had made one mistake; he thought this was a game. He thought Ashe would play by the rules.

But Ashe had been playing this game long before Standish was born.

And he wasn't here to play the game.

He was here to end it.

Chapter 10 : COUNTERPLAY

THE DEEPER ASHE went, the heavier the air became. It was not the weight of stone, nor the grip of darkness, nor even the suffocating crawl of time that choked these corridors. It was something older. Something that did not want him here.

Ashe had no light but his own eyes, and they had long since adapted to darkness sharper than any torch could pierce. He could not only see the outlines of the broken halls, the carved remnants of mosaics that had once told stories of faith and devotion, now fractured beyond recognition. He could remember them.

It felt like a graveyard. Not because it had once been holy, but because it had since been abandoned. There was nothing more haunting than a place where men had prayed for salvation and received only silence.

And yet, Standish had chosen it.

Why?

Because he wanted Ashe to feel the weight of this place again. Because he knew. Somehow, he knew. He knew what had happened here. He knew what it meant. And he wanted Ashe to drown in it.

Ashe followed the subtle signs Standish had left behind. Not deliberately. No, Standish was too smart for that. But even the greatest stealth left traces if you knew where to look. A faint disturbance in the dust, where something heavy had been dragged. A set of shallow footprints, barely visible, leading deeper. The lingering scent of gunpowder and oil and sweat, shining in the stale air like a beacon.

Ashe cataloged them all without thought, without hesitation. Tracking was breathing. Hunting was instinct.

It had been that way since the first time he had pursued a man through dark corridors, blade in hand, blood hot in his veins. And it was that way now.

Standish had not chosen this place to hide. He had chosen it to wait. Ashe could feel the inevitability of the coming conflict settling in his bones.

This was not a fight that would be won or lost in words. Standish had made that clear. This was a fight that would be paid for in blood.

And that suited Ashe just fine. Because the truth was, he was tired of words. The restraint, the quiet calculation, the tactical patience: all of it had been wearing thin since the moment he set foot in this city.

The air itself seemed to press against him, whispering in a voice that he had spent centuries trying to silence.

Standish had taken Amber, an innocent, hostage to serve his own dark purpose.

And Standish had called his name.

Blood called for blood.

Ashe exhaled slowly, rolling his shoulders, feeling the weight of muscle, sinew, and purpose settle into him.

Ashe had become the thing men feared in the dark. His intention to change had been naive, useless. As abandoned now as the prison through which he walked.

The corridor widened, the darkness yawning into something larger, deeper. A chamber. Standish was waiting.

Ashe stepped out into the room.

❧ • ❧

THE CHAMBER WAS dark and damp, the air thick with the scent of cold stone and old iron, tinged with something sharper beneath it: sweat, fear, and the faintest trace of blood.

Amber was here.

Ashe knew it before he saw her.

The chamber was deep beneath the ruins, carved from stone older than the empire that had built this place, an ancient cell repurposed for a prison of another kind. It was too perfectly placed, too deliberately chosen. Standish wanted him to find her.

She was bound but not gagged, her wrists tied with rough, fraying rope, her body slumped against the cold wall of the chamber.

Her hair was tangled, dirt smeared along her cheek, but her eyes were sharp, furious, and burning with unspent defiance. They locked onto him the moment he stepped into the light.

"Ashe."

The way she said his name: it was relief, but tinged with something else, another layer. Ashe knew it was a thinly veiled accusation that he had taken just a little too long.

Her breath was shallow, but she wasn't broken. Not yet, but the fear was there. Not in her face, not in her posture, but in the way she clenched her fists, in the way she tried too hard to sit upright, in the way she blinked too often as if trying to keep tears at bay. It wasn't something he was accustomed to seeing in her.

She was angry. She was terrified. But at least she refused to let either one win.

Ashe crossed the darkness without hesitation, crouching beside her, fingers immediately working at the knotted rope binding her wrists. She hissed slightly as the fibers scraped her raw skin, and Ashe caught the way her hands trembled when he finally pulled them free. But she didn't complain. She just rubbed her wrists, took a slow breath, and turned her full focus on him.

"Where's Standish?" Her voice was hoarse. No preamble. No small talk. Straight to the point.

Ashe didn't answer immediately. His gaze flicked to the walls, the ground, the shadows beyond them. He wasn't looking for Standish. He was looking for the trap.

"You know, you could say 'thank you,'" Ashe muttered absently, scanning the chamber's only exit.

Amber made a noise that might have been a laugh had she not been running on adrenaline.

"Yeah. Sure. Thank you for being an idiot and getting yourself killed for me. He has a bomb, Ashe."

His gaze snapped back to her. She was staring at him now, jaw tight, eyes hard, like she knew exactly what he had already decided. Like she knew he wasn't planning to walk out of here with her.

"Ashe..."

There it was again. His name, but this time laced with everything else she wasn't saying.

He reached out, grasping her arm firmly, pulling her up to her feet. She stumbled slightly. The exhaustion and stress were catching up with her. But she didn't let herself falter.

Amber wasn't fragile. It was one of the things he respected most in her. She had survived things worse than this and come through better for the experience.

That didn't mean she wasn't scared. She was certainly frightened, but fear wouldn't stop her from moving.

She met his gaze, waiting, expectant, pupils dilated with more than just the dark.

"We need to go," she told him, "Now."

He shook his head. "You need to go."

She stiffened, eyes flashing. "You're coming too. Right?"

A beat of silence.

"I will be. I need to make sure the bomb is safe."

Her jaw tightened; she knew it was a lie. She also knew she didn't have time to argue.

Ashe repeated a command he had given her several months ago, one that she had infuriated him by blatantly ignoring.

"Run," he said.

And, in that moment, Amber did something that surprised him.

She ran.

Amber ran without hesitation, her bright red hair a streak of fire against the dim, crumbling corridor, her breath sharp and controlled despite the exhaustion weighing on her limbs. Her sneakers slapped against the stone, kicking up dust, each step taking her closer to the exit, to freedom. Ashe watched, tracking every movement, every shift in her balance, willing her forward even as the air itself seemed to tighten, waiting. Then, just as her silhouette vanished through the far threshold, an explosion ripped through the hallway, obscuring her form in a surge of light, dust, and falling stone.

The hallway collapsed in a sudden, violent roar, stone and fire and dust swallowing the only path out.

Ashe didn't move. His eyes stayed fixed on the smoke-filled corridor, his mind caught between two thoughts: *Did she make it?* and *Of course she made it. This was never about her.*

Because this wasn't a rescue mission.

This was a trap.

And now, all he had to do was wait for Standish to come and gloat so Ashe could spring it.

Chapter 11 : NOT AGAIN

THE DUST WAS still settling, drifting in slow, lazy coils from the now-ruined corridor. It wafted in his lungs, coated the inside of his mouth with the taste of old stone. The explosion still echoed somewhere in the back of Ashe's skull and hummed through his ribs in sympathetic vibration with the bones of the ancient structure holding him.

Ashe leaned back against the cold wall, breath slow, measured. The structure itself was waiting for something. Or someone. As was he.

Amber was gone, or she wasn't. He had no way of knowing at the moment, but he couldn't afford to waste mental energy on speculation. Not now.

Not with the way the air shifted, the way that strange sense of presence flooded the dust-choked room. Ashe was no longer alone.

Then, a clap. Mocking applause, slow and deliberate. The sound cut through the dust, sharp, mocking, spaced out just enough to send a clear message of arrogance.

Then came the voice.

"Greetings, Appius Aurelius Cinis. Salutations, Ashe."

Ashe didn't turn immediately. There was no need to; he knew the voice.

The slow, gravel-edged cadence, dipped in something like amusement but too hollow to sound fully human.

Ashe had been waiting for this reunion since he first saw the message scrawled across the Vulgate page. Hurtling inevitably for it.

Standish made him wait just long enough to twist the knife.

"Where have you been, mister O'Reilly? Or is it Golding now? I still like O'Reilly."

This time, Ashe turned.

He stepped from the shadows and swirling dust, his outline emerging first: lean, sharp angles of a man who had stripped himself down to nothing but purpose.

"Standish," Ashe grinned at him.

His clothes were dark, practical, almost invisible in the dark, but not tactical. Outcast from his previous life, he bore no insignia, no identifying marks. Just black fabric and the air of someone who had already decided how this was going to end.

His face was impossibly leaner than before, the hollows of his cheeks sharper, his skin drawn tight over a body that was past its limits but refused to admit it. But it was his eyes that had changed the most. They were bright, burning with something colder than rage, harder than hatred.

Certainty.

This was a man who had already written the final page of the story in his head.

Ashe had seen that look on men before. He had worn it himself, and done so often.

Standish flicked his eyes to the collapsed hallway, the mess of stone past which Amber had vanished. Then he turned back to Ashe, offering a slight, humorless smile with a gesture at the wall of fresh rubble.

"The last of your Claymores," he said, his voice even, measured, unhurried. "Those things have come in handy."

Ashe inhaled slowly, pressing his shoulders back, pushing off the wall.

His body ached from the repercussions of the blast, but he wasn't finished. He was just getting started.

Standish saw the movement, and his smile tightened, just slightly.

There was no gloating, no grand speech. Just a man setting up a kill.

Ashe's fingers curled into fists. His muscles tensed, bracing. But he didn't charge.

Not yet.

For his part, Standish didn't hesitate.

He lifted his gun and emptied the clip into Ashe's chest.

❧ • ☙

THE FIRST BULLET slammed into Ashe's chest like a hammer, sending a ripple through muscle and bone, a violent, concussive shock that reverberated outward. The second punched through his ribs, tearing flesh, carving a path through his body like red-hot iron.

A third. A fourth. A fifth.

Impact after impact, as fast as Standish's finger could move, the rapid-fire, precise, rhythm of death pounded its staccato in cold steel and gunpowder into Ashe's body. Each shot was a fresh explosion of agony, burrowing into him, tearing through skin, into muscle, ricocheting off bone. The wet percussion of flesh and lead filled the chamber like a drumbeat.

Ashe staggered.

But he didn't fall.

Standish saw it, and something in his face tightened.

The gun clicked empty, the slide locked back.

A heartbeat. A pause.

Standish ejected the magazine, smooth, practiced, already reaching for another.

Ashe took a wavering step forward.

Standish slammed the fresh mag into place before the first had hit the stone floor, racked the slide, and fired again.

The next volley ripped through him. More rounds punched through his torso, digging deeper, splintering ribs, perforating organs that would take days or weeks to heal properly. Ashe didn't have days or weeks.

He kept moving.

Every nerve in his body sang out in agony, every bullet a fresh note in the symphony of fire and blood.

But he didn't stop. The pain was irrelevant; there was only the objective.

Standish's eye twitched as the slide on his automatic locked open once more, smoke rushing out of the hot barrel as the pistol gasped. He had miscalculated.

Too late.

Ashe was already there.

The moment his body hit Standish's, the world collapsed inward. There was no finesse. No controlled strike. This was a force of nature slamming into bone and muscle and breath. Standish had no time to pivot before Ashe drove him backward, slamming into the rough stone, the impact sending a loud crack through the chamber.

Ashe's fingers latched onto Standish's wrist, forcing the gun away, twisting the bone until something popped.

Standish gritted his teeth and let it go, dropping the weapon, because he was already moving.

A knee came up, fast, sharp, slamming into Ashe's ribs—the same ribs that had already been perforated by lead, the same ones that hadn't even begun to knit back together.

Fresh pain exploded through Ashe, but it wasn't enough.

Nothing was enough to stop him now.

Ashe roared, a sound ripped from somewhere deeper than his lungs, and drove his head forward, cracking his forehead against Standish's nose.

A sharp, wet crunch. Blood spattered against dust-covered stone.

Standish snarled, shoving off the wall, trying to break the hold, but Ashe didn't let go.

He drove Standish back again, this time slamming him down onto the uneven stone floor, one hand crushing against the other man's throat. He could feel the rage unfurling, deep and violent and ancient, rage that had been forged in centuries of blood and war and failure.

This was the thing he had spent lifetimes trying to bury.

And now, he unleashed it all.

And yet, somehow, Standish kept fighting.

Ashe felt the shift of his weight a half-second too late.

Standish's thumb hooked into his eye socket, pressing deep—not a clean gouge, not a killing move, just enough to send a burst of searing pain through Ashe's skull. A momentary distraction.

Ashe jerked back instinctively—and Standish used the moment.

He twisted, pivoted, hooked a leg around Ashe's knee, and wrenched them both sideways. They hit the floor together, a tangle of limbs and fury, neither with the upper hand for more than a breath.

Standish rolled, slamming his elbow into Ashe's throat, cutting off his air for a brief second: enough time to get back to his feet.

Ashe was up less than a second later.

Standish spit blood onto the stone, swiping the back of his hand across his face, nose bent at an odd angle, breathing hard.

Ashe smiled.

Standish saw it and for the first time, he hesitated.

Ashe rolled his shoulders, blood still leaking from the gunshot wounds, from the torn flesh across his ribs, from the torn tissue of his lower lip.

He could feel his body valiantly starting to mend itself on the tiniest of levels, even as whatever sense was left in his brain told him his strength would never be restored in time.

And through it all, he felt something else, too. Something he hadn't felt in a long, long time.

Respect.

A lesser man would have been dead already.

But Standish? Standish was still here. Still standing. Still ready.

Ashe couldn't quite decide how he felt about that.

Because if Standish was willing to throw everything away for this vendetta: his career, his sanity, his life? Then maybe, just maybe...

Ashe had underestimated him.

And maybe, just maybe—

That was going to be a problem.

❧ • ❧

THE AIR IN the chamber reeked of blood and dust, thick with tones of sweat and gunpowder. Each breath was a struggle against the cloying heat that clung to the walls like a living thing. The acrid sting of cordite and shattered limestone burned at Ashe's throat, mixed with the iron tang of his blood, pooling somewhere beneath him, seeping into the cracks of the ancient floor. The air itself felt weighted, every inhalation thick with the grit of pulverized rock and the slow, creeping haze of settling debris.

Somewhere in the distance, water dripped, slow and steady, a cruel contrast to the erratic pulse pounding in his ears, the frantic rhythm of a body pushed beyond exhaustion but refusing to fail.

Both men stood staggering but unbroken, their bodies shaking from the effort of staying upright. Muscles screamed, lungs heaved, vision narrowed at the edges. Their skin was slick with sweat and streaked with blood, their breathing deep, ragged pulls of air that barely satisfied their heaving chests.

Time itself had collapsed inward upon them; there was only this moment, this place, this fight. Nothing else existed beyond the shattered stone, the dim glow of flickering torchlight, and the two of them, locked in a war that neither could walk away from.

The world outside the ruins didn't matter anymore.

There was only this place, only this moment.

And neither of them would stop until the other was on the ground.

Ashe's breath came hard and ragged, blood trailing from a dozen open wounds. Some were closing, none of them fast enough.

Standish was no better off. His face was a mask of bruises and fresh gashes, his left eye swollen half-shut, his ribs likely cracked from where Ashe had driven his knee into his side.

His hands trembled, but he didn't drop his guard.

Neither of them spoke now; words were meaningless.

This was just muscle and will, instinct and rage, survival and the rule of violence.

Ashe moved first, launching himself forward, using everything he had left.

His fist drove into Standish's ribs, feeling bone shift beneath the impact.

Standish grunted, pivoted, caught Ashe's arm and twisted, forcing Ashe's body into a vulnerable angle.

Ashe spun with the motion, using the momentum to slam his forehead into Standish's already broken nose.

Standish stumbled, but he didn't fall. Instead, he dropped low, spun on his heel, and drove a fist hard into Ashe's kidney.

Pain ripped through Ashe's side, blinding and sharp.

His vision blurred at the outer fringes, a growing fog creeping in.

Not yet. Not yet.

He snarled, grabbed Standish by the collar, and threw them both to the ground.

They hit the cold stone, rolling, limbs locking in a brutal, struggling knot.

Neither had the strength for precision anymore.

They were two animals, grappling for breath, for purchase, for the last shred of control.

Standish broke away, and then he saw it: something half-buried in the wreckage. A hilt, worn with time, smeared with dust... but unmistakable.

Standish's gaze flicked to it.

Ashe saw the calculation in his eyes.

Standish knew what it was.

So did Ashe.

Standish lunged for it and Ashe reacted, but too late.

Fingers closed around the hilt, pulled it free. The blade gleamed dull in the firelight, its once-pristine steel tarnished but still deadly, still sharp.

A Roman gladius.

Ashe's gladius.

The very blade he had carried when he had been a Legionnaire, marching beneath the Eagle standard, fighting wars for an empire that had long since turned to dust.

The one that Standish had stolen from his row house in Chicago.

Ashe barely had time to process the memory.

Standish was already moving. He feinted left, drawing Ashe's reflexive block.

Then, with the speed of a dying man who had nothing left to lose, he pivoted. Low, brutal, efficient.

The gladius clove deep into the back of Ashe's neck, sliding between vertebrae, severing the spinal column.

White-hot pain exploded through Ashe's body, his every nerve flaring before—

Nothing.

His limbs went dead.

The world tilted.

His body folded, collapsing like a felled tree.

There was only a single thought Ashe could muster as he slammed into the stone floor.

Not again.

Chapter 12 : MADE JUST FOR YOU

THE FLOOR WAS cold stone beneath him, slick with blood. This was a curious thing to Ashe. His body refused to respond, the sharp, wet agony of severed nerves leaving him a prisoner inside his own skin. But he could still feel everything: the slow pulse of pain radiating from his chest, the torn flesh weeping blood down his back, pooling beneath him. The pain was a constant companion, but there was no movement, no control. His body would not obey him.

Standish stood above him, breath heaving, hands trembling, his grip loose on the gladius. The blade dripped red, its steel stained with the blood of centuries and Ashe's own. For a long moment, Standish didn't move. Then he let out a ragged breath, sheathing whatever was left of his pain behind a tenuous smile.

"You just do not quit, do you?"

Ashe said nothing. There was no point. The rage burning inside him was useless, impotent without a body to back it up.

Standish took a step closer, crouching slightly, his face barely illuminated by the dying torchlight, shadows carving deep lines into his skin. The fight had taken everything out of him, the exhaustion pulling at his posture, his voice.

But there was still something dangerous in his eyes. A calm: something that said he had already won. Without ceremony, Standish reached down, his fingers curling into the remnants of Ashe's shredded shirt.

Standish dragged him across the stone. Ashe's boots scraped the ground, his body limp, dead weight. Pain flared, sharp and deep, but it meant nothing now. He was hauled across the ruined chamber, the world tilting around him, until his back was propped against something solid, some metal object.

Cold plastic met his skin. A black case, roughly the size of a large ammo box or a moderately-sized suitcase, the object had been placed strategically in the center of the chamber.

The object? The device.

The device?

There really was no question now. Ashe knew at once what it was.

The real bomb.

Standish let out a slow breath, sinking to his knees in front of him. The man's exhaustion hit all at once, weighing him down, his shoulders sagging.

His breath was uneven, not just from the fight, but from something deeper.

Ashe recognized it; Standish wasn't just hurt, he was dying.

Suddenly, the picture clarified in Ashe's mind. Standish had gotten hold of the radioactive material, as the reports had indicated. But instead of the material—the bomb—being delivered to the terrorist group, he had kept it for himself. For such a time as this.

And as a result, Standish was dying. The gaunt appearance, the sallow eyes, the hollow cheekbones. He was dying, poisoned by the weapon of his own making.

Maybe not now. Maybe not in the next few minutes. But soon. And he knew it.

Which meant he had nothing left to lose.

Standish wiped the blood from the gladius, using Ashe's own ruined clothing as a rag.

He wasn't mocking him, it was just practical, in a strangely meaningless way.

Ashe's breath came slow, uneven, but he forced his eyes to focus. He had to stay present.

Standish was finally going to talk.

"I could have picked any bait, you know," Standish murmured, his voice thick, low, tired. He let the words settle between them, weighted with something that wasn't quite regret. He sank to the ground a couple feet away from Ashe.

Ashe's fingers twitched, a reflex more than a movement.

His body remained useless.

Standish exhaled sharply, shaking his head. "The paintings. The artifacts. None of them would have drawn you the way the Olsen girl did."

Ashe felt his jaw tighten.

Standish leaned back slightly, tilting the gladius, turning it in the dim light, studying the weight, the balance, the history in its steel.

He huffed out a soft, humorless laugh.

"And this?" He lifted the blade slightly, examining the edge. "This is what you are. What you have always been."

His voice was matter-of-fact, not cruel, not gloating.

"You think you can pretend. Hide behind time, behind new names. But this?" He tilted the sword toward Ashe.

"This blade? This was you before anything else."

Standish leaned in, his breath shallow, labored, but steady.

"A soldier. A killer. How many men have you killed, Ashe O'Reilly?"

His grip tightened around the hilt.

"The soldier that would not die."

The torchlight flickered, casting deep shadows across his bruised, bloodied face.

His voice dropped to a whisper.

"You are a thing of evil, Ashe O'Reilly. A thing that does not belong in this world."

THE BLACK METAL box beneath him was cold against his back, its steel exterior seeming to thrum with something unseen. The pain in his body was a dull roar now, not gone, not lessened, just a part of the background. Just another among the countless weights already pressing down on him.

Standish sat, still bleeding, still breathing hard, but there was no hesitation in his movements as he tapped the gladius against the device. The sound rang hollow, a metallic echo that travelled through Ashe's chest.

The blade. That stolen relic from another life, one Standish seemed to think defined him. How wrong could one man be? *Grabbed the wrong hunk of metal, bub.*

Ashe's lip curled, his breath uneven, but his voice still held a sharp edge.

"The gladius?" The words came slow, deliberate, thick with disdain. He managed a shallow breath, tasting dust and copper. "You think that's the weapon that defines me?"

Standish arched a brow, but Ashe shook his head, his voice gritted and full of quiet, burning contempt.

"That just proves you don't know me at all."

Standish didn't react right away. He just stared at Ashe for a beat, then let out a slow, dry chuckle.

"Oh, I know enough," he said, turning the sword lazily in his grip. "I know what matters."

He tapped the metal box again.

"And I know you gave me everything I needed to craft the weapon of your final demise."

Standish knelt slightly, wiping sweat from his brow with the back of his arm, breathing shaky but measured.

"You want to know where I got it? The material in there?" Standish tapped the device lightly with a knuckle, as if knocking on a coffin. "It came from the Los Angeles Exclusion Zone."

The words hit Ashe like a knife between the ribs.

That dead zone, that poisoned ruin, had followed him here.

Standish exhaled, shaking his head slightly. "It is a place you had something to do with making, right?"

The words were casual, but the meaning beneath them was a knife turned slow.

Ashe's jaw locked.

Standish grinned, seeing it.

"And a place that Dani Linder had everything to do with protecting for you."

A pause. Just long enough for the weight of that to settle.

Then Standish continued. "You let me test my theories, one after another. The blast in Jerusalem? That was just a message. But this—"

He patted the surface of the box, fingers drumming lightly against the metal.

"This is the real bomb. The one I built for you."

Ashe looked at Standish with eyes already half dead.

His breath was slow, measured, but the words still came rough, dragged from his throat through the haze of pain.

"You think a bomb is going to kill me?"

Standish smirked. "That, Ashe O'Reilly, is the next theory to test."

He shifted his weight, tilting his head slightly, studying Ashe like a scientist watching a specimen pinned to a tray.

"No, I do not think it will kill you."

He rested his elbow on one knee, leaning forward slightly, voice dropping lower.

"Not a regular bomb."

Ashe's pulse slowed, not because he was calming, but because he could see where this was going.

"But if I blow you into enough pieces," Standish continued, voice almost too casual, too easy, "and those pieces are small enough, and they're soaked in radiation? Mixed with the dust that the fuel rod will turn into?"

He tilted the gladius, watching the blood still splotched along its edge.

Then he met Ashe's gaze and smiled.

"Maybe then, your body cannot put itself back together."

A pause.

"Maybe, just maybe, I can finally erase the thing that should not exist."

Chapter 13 : TELL ME A STORY

THE CHAMBER RANG with silence. Not the kind that came with peace. The kind that came with waiting. Waiting for the final moment, the last breath, the inevitable collapse of everything.

Ashe couldn't move.

He could feel the blood seeping from his body, cooling against his back, pooling beneath him. The severed spinal column left him useless, weightless, a spectator in his own body. The only thing still working was his mind.

And right now, even that wasn't doing him much good. But it had become a waiting game, and Ashe was very good at those.

Because Standish was dying. And he knew it.

Standish's breath came in uneven, rattling pulls, his body swaying slightly where he sat slumped against the stone.

The fight had taken everything that was left out of him.

His shirt was soaked through, the deep wounds across his side and shoulder leaking blood in a steady, unrelenting trickle. His fingers still held the gladius loosely, but there was little strength left in his grip.

Even still, he smirked.

Ashe's eyes narrowed. Standish knew something Ashe didn't. And it was clear he was going to relish every second of revealing it.

The man exhaled sharply, the sound half a cough, half a laugh, and leaned his head back against the stone.

He turned his head just slightly, looking at Ashe now. His eyes were still sharp, still filled with that same certainty. But beneath them, Ashe could see it.

The fatigue. The end creeping in.

Standish sighed, rolling his shoulders, or trying to. One of them barely worked anymore.

"I figure I have minutes left. Maybe more, maybe less."

He shifted, pressing a trembling hand against the worst of his wounds, and let out a quiet chuckle.

"But it is enough."

Ashe's voice was low. Steady. "Enough for what?"

Standish didn't answer immediately.

Instead, he lifted his free hand slightly, letting Ashe see it.

In his fading grip was a small, unremarkable device. One very familiar to Ashe.

An M57 Electrical Firing Device. A claymore clacker.

Standish let it hang there for a moment, then rolled his fingers slightly.

The gesture might not have been intentional, but it was more than adequate to show how unstable his grip was.

"Reverse wired," he said, as if explaining the weather. "Dead man's switch."

Ashe stared.

"The moment I die," Standish said, rolling his head back against the wall, his voice growing lazier, looser, "the moment my hand goes limp and lets go? That is your last moment on earth as well."

Ashe inhaled slowly.

This was not how he had expected this to play out.

Several minutes passed in silence before Standish spoke again.

"I chose this spot for a reason, you know," he continued, exhaling sharply.

His voice was reedy and thin now, but still anchored by something deliberate.

"Under all this stone?" He gestured vaguely to the ceiling, the weight of the ruins above them. "A detonation down here, under feet of rock, under the bones of Constantinople? Not too much harm to the city."

A ragged breath.

"But you?"

He tilted his head, eyes half-lidded now but still locked onto Ashe.

"You get buried forever. Your atoms mixed with powdered rock and radioactive waste for eternity."

He coughed, blood flecking his lips now, his body sagging slightly.

"Isn't that what Aeternus means?"

Another long, dragging silence.

Standish shifted slightly, his legs stretching out in front of him, his hands still loosely cradling the clacker.

Then, softly, the man laughed.

It was a quiet, breathless sound.

He looked down at himself, his blood pooling around him, then shook his head.

"Ironic, isn't it?"

His fingers tensed, his knuckles white against the clacker.

“I sit here, and I will die soon, simply from bleeding out. I sit here and do something you cannot do."

Ashe blinked, his vision still swimming at the edges.

“What are you talking about?” he asked. “I think I’m sittin’ here just fine.”

Standish laughed again, this time deeper, throatier.

Then he coughed a deep, guttural cough, wet with too much blood.

☙ • ❧

THE RASP OF Standish’s labored breathing rattled through the chamber punctuated by the metronome of water dripping somewhere unseen in the ruins. Ashe could do nothing but sit there, his body useless, his mind racing, his pulse a dull throb in his ears, acutely out of time with the dripping water.

Standish sat just a few feet away, propped against a displaced stone watching Ashe, fingers somehow still wrapped tightly around the dead man's switch.

The silence stretched, long and heavy, neither of them speaking for a moment, the weight of what was coming pressing down on them both. Then Standish shifted slightly, reaching into his jacket with his free hand.

Something small, black, and familiar gleamed in the dim light.

Ashe recognized it: a voice recorder.

Amber's voice recorder.

The one Dani had given her in Paris.

Standish held it up between two fingers, turning it slightly, watching the way the faint light glinted off its casing.

Then, without a word, he pressed "play."

A faint click.

Then, her voice.

"I still can't believe they let me come along. I mean, I get it. I'm useful, I'm documenting everything. But at the same time? This is insane!"

Ashe clenched his jaw, his fingers twitching uselessly at his sides.

He knew exactly where this recording had come from.

"On the other hand, I'm stuck here in Paris, while they go off saving the world. Oh, man; I'm probably going to have to read about it to even find out what happened!"

He could picture it perfectly: Amber, sitting somewhere, probably in her hotel room, her feet tucked beneath her, voice brighter than it had any right to be considering what she had gotten tangled up in. Again.

Standish exhaled slowly, watching Ashe as the recording played on.

"I mean, let's be honest, I don't think he's ever actually let me in. He watches everything I do like he's expecting me to do stuff I can't even comprehend. I don't think he trusts me. Not really. But maybe that's fair. Maybe he's right not to. Because the more I see? The more I start to realize... I don't think I'm ready for any of this."

Ashe's chest tightened, a sensation that had little to do with his injuries.

Her voice continued. *"Like they didn't trust me to go along to Israel. Him or Dani. I mean, sure, I'm no trained anti-terror agent, but come on—being told to stay in the car like a little kid? I wouldn't get in the way that bad..."*

Amber's voice trailed off, indicating she was momentarily lost in thought before she spoke again. *"Well, okay, based on my track record, maybe they had a point. Harrigan said that they aren't even in Israel anymore, anyway. I guess things are moving pretty quick wherever they are, but he wouldn't tell me anything about it. Especially after that nasty Wycliffe lady with the rod up her butt jumped all over him for even saying that much. Like I can't keep a secret or something."*

Standish clicked off the device at that point.

"She is an interesting young woman, is she not, Ashe O'Reilly?"

Ashe just glared at the man.

"I truly figured she would be the one to break under interrogation about the Task affair, but she proved me wrong. I commend her for her devotion to you. Tell me, do you suppose she thinks of you as a surrogate father, the way you have adopted her as your replacement for Aurelia?"

Ashe strove at the bonds of his unresponsive flesh, wanting nothing more than to get his hands around Standish's throat and speed up the inevitable.

Standish smiled. "I have touched another nerve, I see. Very well," he said. "We shall talk about something else." He looked around the stone chamber that would be their tomb. "I knew you would find me here, when I used her as bait."

Ashe's head fell back as sweat poured down his face from recent and futile effort.

"Yeah, I knew. What I can't figure out was how you knew. How'd you find out about Constantinople?"

"The darkest years in human history? Where else would you have been but right in the middle of it?"

Ashe stared at him for a moment. "No, that's not it. I don't buy it. You had details, to know about this place. How'd you know I'd been here?"

Standish smiled again, and this time the expression reached his eyes. Ashe realized the man was very proud of his detective skills.

"The Emperor Justinian the First would have loved this recorder, do you not think?" he said. "As it was, his imperial recorder must have had to write furiously to keep up with your last action-filled visit to his palace."

"I see," said Ashe. He managed to keep his voice even.

Standish's smile widened further, and he clicked the voice recorder's button again. Amber's voice once more filled the chamber, ringing off the ancient stone as the water continued to drip in some far-off corner.

"I thought that thing was encrypted."

Standish arched a brow, a slow, knowing smile tugging at the edge of his mouth.

"You know about encryption?" He tilted his head slightly. "You are a fast learner, Appius Aurelius Cinis."

Ashe forced a slow breath through his nose.

"I know enough that you weren't meant to hear any of that."

He flicked his gaze toward the recorder.

"How'd you get into it in the first place?"

Standish grinned in amusement, rolling his head back slightly against the stone. He could see the effect Amber's voice was having on him.

"It's standard FBI issue," he stated.

He turned the recorder over in his palm, as if appreciating it, before meeting Ashe's eyes again.

"I no longer have the Bureau's rotating ciphers, but I was able to call in some favors."

Ashe didn't like that answer. Didn't like what it implied.

Didn't like the idea that Standish had been listening to Amber's private words, dissecting them, pulling them apart like another piece of evidence in whatever twisted case he had built against him.

But there was nothing Ashe could do about it. Not yet.

So he waited.

~ • ~

THE RECORDER CRACKLED noisily during the silent portions of the recording, which Ashe found peculiar. Its tinny speaker was distorted slightly in the still, cavernous air of the chamber, but it didn't crackle when there was a voice breaking through.

Which it did now.

"Okay, so what I don't understand—what I really don't understand—is how this Ming guy fits into all of this. I mean, I know Ashe was in Vietnam, and I know he lost his whole unit in some tank attack, but Ming wasn't even there for that. He was... somewhere else. Doing something else. Something that turned into this thirty-year vendetta with Ashe. But I have no idea what it was."

A pause.

Then, in a thoughtful, musing tone—

"And he doesn't like to talk about it. Ashe is weird like that. He doesn't want to talk, then suddenly, he tells you some story and expects you to figure out what he's talking about. Then, he never mentions it again! I thought old people were supposed to tell and retell stories over and over. That's been my experience, anyway. Part of the fun of being a waitress. But Ashe? No way. Never hear it again. Anyway, I guess the Ming thing was bad. I know it was bad, because it made Ashe spend the next three decades planting more munition caches across the country than Carter has pills."

Another crackly pause.

"Wait a second. Who is this Carter guy? And why does he have so many pills? Like, what kind of pills are we talking about? And why is that even a phrase people say?"

Ming.

The name alone was enough to drag him backward, pulling memories sharp and fresh through the haze of pain.

Amber didn't know.

She didn't know where Ming had been, what he had done, what had set the fire burning in Ashe's gut for thirty years.

It was good she didn't know. It wasn't a story for a girl like Amber. She needed to retain some faith in humanity.

Faith in humanity. Faith inhumanity. Ashe chuckled. One of those terms described him, and it wasn't the first.

A jolt of pain shot down Ashe's leg, though it failed to move in response.

Ashe's jaw clenched against the pain, his voice coming low and edgy.

"Turn that stupid thing off."

Standish didn't react at first.

He just sat there, watching Ashe, his expression hard to read except for the faintest hint of amusement curling at the edge of his lips.

Then, finally, he tilted his head.

"What is it, Appius Aurelius Cinis?" He rolled the name over his tongue like he was tasting it. "You do not care for the prattling sound of your protégé's voice?"

Ashe let out a slow, controlled breath, forcing down the fire that had nowhere to go.

"I like the voice just fine." His words were even, flat. "I just don't want my past to be the last thing I ever hear."

Standish exhaled, shaking his head slightly, as if Ashe was missing the point entirely.

"While I, on the other hand, am eager to hear more..."

And he didn't turn it off. Just sat there, bleeding out, dying slowly, but still in control.

And Amber's voice continued to play on.

❧ • ❧

THE RECORDER FINALLY died. The chamber, which had been filled with the tinny, looping sound of Amber's voice for over two hours, fell into absolute silence.

For the first time in what felt like eternity, there was nothing but the dripping of water, the faint rasp of two men breathing, and the slow, eerie hum of unseen heat rising from the stone.

Ashe exhaled. Not quite relief. Not quite victory. Just a small reprieve from the endless assault of his past played back to him in the voice of someone far too innocent to ever understand him. Someone pure, but tainted by what he was, what he'd shared with her.

Standish sat slumped, his fingers still curled around the dead man's switch. His face was paler now, his breaths coming shorter, sharper. Ashe wasn't sure what was keeping him upright at this point. Pure willpower, most likely.

But for how much longer?

Ashe shifted, or tried to. He couldn't. His body was still unresponsive, still nothing more than dead weight propped against the cold steel bomb that would soon erase him from existence.

But there was something else now. Something different. A creeping, unexpected sensation.

Heat.

It started as a faint pulse, a slow-burning ember in his spine, in his guts, somewhere deeper than the wounds that had been carved into him.

It wasn't just discomfort. And it was rising. Like a fever. Like an inferno. The stone beneath him felt like it was searing his skin, the stagnant air of the chamber growing thicker, heavier, pressing against his ribs like he was breathing fire instead of air.

For a split second, he had a random thought of a middle-aged woman sweating through a menopausal hot flash.

The absurdity of it nearly made him laugh.

Instead, his mind latched onto the strangeness of the thought.

Lucidity.

It was slipping.

Standish saw it. And he smirked.

Ashe forced a slow breath, trying to ignore the fire clawing up his throat.

"Thank goodness that thing finally died," he muttered, nodding toward the dead recorder. His voice was rough, edged with exhaustion.

Then, dryly, "You wouldn't want to disable this bomb thing too, would you?"

Standish huffed a breath, something like amusement, but too thin, too strained.

"Do you want to live that badly, Ashe O'Reilly?"

"Not really," Ashe admitted after a moment, his eyes half-lidded, jaw tight. "But I'm guessing you do. Or at least, you did. Not sure about now."

Standish didn't answer right away.

He shifted slightly, adjusting his grip on the detonator.

"Convince me, then," Standish murmured, voice flat but starting to grow colder. "Convince me that you are not a monster. You do that, and maybe I disable it."

The words settled between them. A challenge, heavy and unmoving.

Ashe exhaled sharply through his nose.

"That's going to be difficult," he said finally, voice low, raspy.

Standish lifted a brow. "And why is that, Ashe O'Reilly?"

Ashe turned his head slightly, looking him in the eye.

"Because I am a monster."

The words didn't so much hang as dropped. Like a stone into a deep well, swallowed into something bottomless and black.

Standish's expression didn't change.

"Is that so?"

Ashe let out a slow breath, his fingers twitching, the heat in his body clawing its way higher.

"I'm cursed," he said simply. No embellishment. Just fact.

Standish tilted his head. "Explain."

Ashe swallowed, forcing down the slow, creeping haze that clawed at his consciousness, trying to drag him under.

"Why?"

Standish sighed, dipping his head nearly to the floor. He adjusted the detonator in his fingers.

"What else shall we do, Ashe O'Reilly? We are both dying."

A pause.

"I'll give you a chance to explain yourself before I release this switch."

Ashe studied him for a moment. Standish was still trying to break him. Still trying to peel him open and see what was inside. But the thing was...

There was nothing inside Ashe but blood and fire and memory.

And if Standish wanted a story? Fine. It would help him stay focused. Though he was running out of reasons to want to do that.

Standish's grip on the detonator remained firm, for the moment. He appeared to have gotten fresh vigor from the idea that had just occurred to him.

"Tell me about the worst horrors you have ever been responsible for, Ashe O'Reilly. Tell me your side of the story. Your 'most heinous act' as your friend, Belisarius, so aptly put it on that day he thought to have killed you. What happened here in these monastery halls, here in the streets of your Constantinople, here in the palace of Justinian?"

His lips curled into something mocking, taunting.

"Maybe you're not a monster after all. How do you know?"

Ashe stared at him. The room still sweltered, suffocating him.

He could barely breathe past the weight of his incapacitated body, the weight of what was coming.

Then, finally, Ashe let out a long, slow, steadying breath.

His voice became quiet. Measured. Timeless.

“Fine,” he declared. "Let’s hear a story..."

Chapter 14 : CONSTANTINOPLE: THE STRIFE

532 AD

MORNING LIGHT FILTERED through sheets of thinly-sliced alabaster set into the wooden frames of the high apse windows of the Church of St. Laurence, casting sparkling jeweled patterns upon worn and venerable stone. The figure walked through the empty church beneath the central dome and exited through the west porch to kneel in the inner courtyard.

Appius Aurelius Cinis resumed his work on a half-hewn oak arch frame for the domus clericorum, his weathered hands gripping an adze with practiced ease. The rhythmic chop-scrape of blade against wood soon barked and whispered through the cool air. Expecting to finish the task later in the day, he smoothed the rough edges of the first of two curved posts destined to replace the weathered support of the bishop's doorway. The scent of sun-dried wood and incense mingled, evoking an allegory of his long, arduous journey—from centuries of death and destruction to these recent years of peace in Constantinople. In these quiet, hopeful moments, the Church was more than wood and stone and mortar; it was his sanctuary, his place of penance and rebirth.

A small, wiry boy darted around a pile of freshly cut stones and, with a burst of youthful exuberance, cried out, "Brother Appius!" The boy's bright eyes briefly lifted Cinis's ancient heart.

"Yes, little one?" he murmured, rising to his feet with a grunt that blended weariness and warmth.

Before the boy could say more, a gaggle of anxious-looking monks herded into the courtyard. Clad in the humble robes of St. Conon's monastery and bearing an unmistakable aura of solemn purpose, they escorted two frantic, trembling men. Cinis knew them at once, despite having never seen either of them before. Clad in rough cloth, both men bore the dark marks of rope burns around their necks. Their eyes flickered with a desperate plea for refuge, hoping the very air of the Church might absolve their sins. Or at the very least, save their lives.

Almost certainly the latter.

The entire city knew of these men, and most of it had doubtless turned out as spectators to their attempted execution earlier in the day. Cinis had heard that two of the seven men from the demes Blue and Green had escaped death through a stroke of fate when they fell not to their deaths, but to the ground beneath the gallows. It was widely presumed that either faulty materials or hasty construction had been the cause. Probably both, Cinis mused.

The seven—four Blues and three Greens—had been arrested by the city prefect for murders they had committed during a post-chariot race riot. Such riots were not unknown at or after chariot races, nor were arson or murder as part of them. It was the way of things, and most of Constantinople would argue that it made the races that much more entertaining. Of course, most of

Constantinople would admit to being allied with either the Blues or the Greens, or the less vocal demes, the Reds and Whites. Cinis could not care less for the chariot races, nor was he aligned with the political posturing or competitive fanaticism of the demes.

And the violence? Cinis was no stranger to violence, but it was in his past, and despite its sheer quantity, it had always been for a purpose, not for sport.

He looked at the two men. Rumors rumbling through the city indicated that the men represented both demes: one a Blue, one a Green. Yet here they were, their opposing views completely obliterated by the shared goal of seeking refuge and survival. Cinis could not help but wonder how long they would remain allies if they received clemency and freedom.

He narrowed his eyes. Not very long, would be his guess.

The monks were instantly put on alert as the clamor of armored boots on cobblestone shattered the serenity of the courtyard. A pair of stern-faced soldiers stormed into the courtyard, their polished cuirasses gleaming in the pale morning. The lead soldier, voice clipped and laced with imperial authority, barked, "Give us those men!"

Cinis stepped forward, his gaze fixed on the two Legionnaires. "These men have invoked sanctuary on Holy ground."

"These men are criminals of the empire! They are sentenced to hang!"

Cinis ran his calloused fingers lightly over the fresh, angry rope burns on the nearest man's neck, turning the man's head this way and that by a firm grip on his chin.

"It would appear they bear the marks of a hanging already," he stated, voice low and laced with bitter irony.

"The scaffolding broke," retorted the second soldier sharply. "They will return with us and be hanged unto death."

Cinis's eyes narrowed, and his expression became as hardened as the stone surrounding him. "It may hap they've already died," he challenged, his tone flat as he regarded the soldiers with an unyielding gaze.

"Have you lost your mind? They have clearly not died! Does a man die and then walk about and breathe, you cretin?"

Cinis allowed a wry smile, his voice calm and even as he replied, "Some have been known to so do, I imagine."

"You blaspheme thus in the house of God?" The soldier snarled, drawing his sword with a metallic whisper that cut through the tense air.

"Less than you know," growled Cinis.

Before the confrontation could escalate further, a commanding presence entered the tumult. General Flavius Belisarius walked with the bearing of a man whose very existence demanded respect. Belisarius was tall and powerfully built, with a chiseled, angular face marked by deep-set, piercing eyes of slate gray. His dark, close-cropped hair framed a visage that was at once noble and stern, and his finely wrought armor bore the scars of recent battles. The general's gaze swept the scene with an intensity that belied his age, and his presence exuded a mixture of regal authority and personal pride.

Belisarius marched in, flanked by another quaternion of soldiers. Cinis didn't see them, but the rest of the detachment was no doubt outside in the street blocking the exits or stationed at key choke points throughout the church. There were likely two or three contubernia—tent groups—between sixteen and twenty-four men in all. Cinis knew he had taught this man that much about securing a building, at least.

"Sheathe your blade, Cornelius! For your own good. That man would kill you before you could decide how to strike."

"Cinis!" Belisarius' voice rang out then in greeting, low and resonant.

Cinis turned slowly, his expression inscrutable for a long moment, having recognized the man's voice before regarding his features—and the sound of his footsteps before that. "Flavius Belisarius," he acknowledged, voice a blend of respect and lingering melancholy.

The general allowed himself a brief, ironic chuckle before a wide smile split his chiseled face. "It is a surprise to see you here in a church, Appius Aurelius! I was once convinced that if you ever entered one, it would fall down around you!" His eyes twinkled with both mirth and memory.

"Then I suppose surprise to be the order of the day, my friend. I hear you are no longer magister militum per Orientem."

Belisarius' face darkened. "Much is whispered in a church, it seems. But yes. Justinian has deemed give that position to another. Mundus, the barbarian," he said. The name appeared to go sour on his tongue, and he spat on the earth at his feet.

"There was a time when you Thracians were outside the empire, Flavius."

"You speak as one who remembers a time before our fathers, Cinis. We Thracians have served the empire as citizens for hundreds of years."

"I speak as one who remembers you as a munifex, with wetness still evident behind your great, flopping ears."

"And yet, here I am in a general's cloak and you in a builder's apron."

"Perhaps we've both found our callings."

"Perhaps, but of a truth, I fear you have abandoned yours," Belisarius smiled ruefully at Cinis. "And working in a church, no less!"

For a few moments, they exchanged quiet, measured words: a fleeting respite amid the clamor. The gentle cadence of old comrades spoke of numerous past glories and regrets. More the former on the part of the general, the latter for the penitent carpenter.

The fragile peace was soon broken by duty as Belisarius' tone grew firm. "These men must return with us. Justinian has ordered it."

"That doesn't make it right. They will remain here." Cinis replied sharply.

"Right? What difference does 'right' make? Justinian's word makes it law," retorted the general, his laugh cold and dismissive as he recalled the inescapable rigidity of imperial decree.

Cinis's eyes flashed with quiet indignation as he intoned, "Est via quae videtur homini iusta novissima autem eius deducunt ad mortem."

There is a way that seems right to a man, but its end is the way of death.

Belisarius laughed, a sound that mixed derision with mirth as he quoted the next passage from the Proverb in rebuttal. "Risus dolore miscebitur et extrema gaudii luctus occupat."

Even in laughter, the heart is sorrowful, and the end of that mirth is heaviness.

The general gave as well as he received, it seemed. His gaze softened momentarily as he regarded Cinis. "You used to be so much more fun, my friend. We are *soldiers*, Appius Aurelius! The right way *is* the way of death!" He shook his head, as though this—like the Proverb—was a truth Cinis should already know by heart.

Silence reigned within the courtyard as the two men reached an impasse and sized each other up. Belisarius, though almost a head taller and backed by ten armed guards, appeared to be remembering days gone by, serving with a very different Appius Aurelius Cinis. He decided discretion might be the better part of valor.

After a long, weighted pause, Belisarius relented. "Very well, I will leave the criminals here for now. But only under guard, so that they cannot escape."

Then, with a flourish that sought to diffuse the ominous gravity of the moment, he clapped Cinis on the shoulder.

"Dine with me tomorrow at midday, friend Cinis! We shall discuss this then, as we relive past glories."

❧ • ❧

THE MESE BUSTLED under the brilliant midday sun, its ancient marble paving worn smooth by countless footsteps. The bustling clamor of the Augustaion filled the open-air dining area in the shadow of the Milion's double triumphal arch and dome. Constantinople thrummed with life: a mosaic of shouting vendors, clattering carts, and the soft, persistent strains of a distant lyre. The air was heady with the aromas of spiced lamb, freshly baked bread, and the tang of sea salt carried on the warm breeze from the Bosphorus.

Merchants hawked their wares and the clink of coins and laughter mingled with the distant hum of chariots and the rhythmic tolling of church bells. Before Cinis to the north, the magnificent dome of the Great Church rose in the near distance, a symbol of both divine splendor and human ambition. Behind him to the southwest, but every bit as present in the conscience of the city, stretched the long structure of the Hippodrome, a reminder of current unrest and conflict.

At a weathered wooden table beneath a striped awning, Cinis sat facing the church. His plate overflowed with a hearty stew of spiced lamb and fresh flatbread. He ate with the voracity of a man who had known famine, gobbling down morsels while gulping deep, cleansing mouthfuls of water from a clay jug. In stark contrast, General Belisarius delicately swirled a hammered goblet of the finest local wine, its rich color reflecting his refined taste and his pride of station despite his recent career setback.

Belisarius broke the silence, expressing again how strange he found it that a man like Cinis should find himself working in a house of peace and refuge. Cinis' eyes grew dark with unspoken memories and flickered to the dome of the massive church edifice before him. He shrugged.

"I find deep fulfillment in building things, Flavius. Of course, St. Laurence is no Great Church. That great structure—its arches, its dome—it sings to me from here," he replied softly. His tone was deep with admiration and hidden memory. He had helped rebuild Constantius' older structure long before the birth of Belisarius' father.

The general shook his head with a half-amused scowl, mock panic in his voice. "Stop, stop! I'm telling you, don't even think of the place! You will curse it. No, stay away from there completely! The Great Church itself will burn to the ground if you ever step foot on its grounds." His laugh, mocking yet genuine, cut through the ambient din of the bustling street.

Cinis allowed a slight smile, humoring the general's theatrics. "Perhaps, but you know one cannot help what the heart desires," he murmured, his voice carrying the weight of centuries past. He leaned back, eyes still fixed on the distant silhouette of the Great Church, and added, "I have even considered entering holy service."

Belisarius nearly choked on his wine. "You cannot! If you were ever to try and become a holy man, the sun itself would hide its face from us! It is thusly written, I swear it! You? The 'architect of death' as a holy man? Please do not even speak of it. If you did, men would simply die by the millions. We'd have to carry them out of the city walls in wagons."

After a brief pause, the conversation shifted. Belisarius' tone became serious. "I want those men back, Cinis."

Cinis' eyes turn to steel. "And yet, you know you will not get them while they are under my protection, and that of the church."

At his tone, a couple of Belisarius' guards moved forward instinctively, hands sliding toward their swords. With a dismissive wave, the general quelled them. "Back, back! I don't need to lose any guards this day," he said quietly. Then, his expression softened as he exclaimed, "There he is! There is the Cinis I remember."

For a moment, memories of shared battles and hard-won glories passed between them in low, measured words. The general then grinned and teased, "Come be a biscuit eater again, Cinis! We both know how you love to eat!"

Cinis shook his head, understanding that the general's jibe about "biscuit eaters" was an overt invitation to join the bucellarii, Belisarius' elite guards.

Belisarius continued, his voice low and earnest. "A Roman Legionnaire of your standing is never truly retired. You're always on reserve, forever ready to be called back to serve the empire."

Cinis shook his head slowly, his tone reflective. "Perhaps I wasn't myself then, and perhaps I am not myself now. But it is a truth that I am not the same man I was, Flavius."

The general's eyes softened further. After a contemplative pause, he said, "Very well. The fugitives shall remain under your protection there at the church for one more day, until a decision can be made. Justinian will decree their fate during the next races at the Hippodrome."

Then, a mischievous glint returned to the general's eyes as Belisarius leaned forward. "Come with me to the chariot races on the morrow, Cinis. We shall discuss this then, and perhaps relive some of our past glories."

❧ • ❧

THE CROWD WAS a seething mass before him and the other occupants of the kathisma at the eastern end of the track. From the elevated safety of the emperor's box in the Hippodrome of Constantinople, the Emperor Justinian I, his general Belisarius and a special guest surveyed the oval expanse below. The sun, high and unyielding, cast long shadows across the spina: a central barrier flanked by towering monuments, including the proud obelisk and scattered statues that bore silent witness to centuries of triumph and turmoil. The air pulsed with a cacophony of voices: the roar of chariots clattering over worn cobblestones, the mingled chants and jeers of thousands upon thousands of spectators, and the distant, rhythmic beat of drums that set hearts pounding in unison.

As Cinis had entered with Belisarius, the Mese outside was teeming with activity. Merchants hawked their wares at every turn, men, women, and children moved about in a flurry of humanity pouring into the stadium. The emperor and his empress, Theodora, had entered the kathisma via their private passage directly from the Great Palace and had been waiting when Belisarius arrived and introduced his guest.

Cinis was grateful that the topic of the fugitives at the church did not immediately press its way to the fore. He was content to leave that discussion with the emperor for a later time, if possible.

Inside the kathisma, beneath a canopy of richly embroidered cloth, Emperor Justinian sat rigidly watching the crowd, not the chariots. Justinian's face was etched with quiet severity as he listened to the growing murmur emanating from below. The political atmosphere was taut with tension, as if the very air might ignite.

At first, the demands were low and subtle: a quiet if insistent murmur from every corner of the Hippodrome urging that the two fugitives, sheltered at the Church of St. Laurence, be released. "They must be set free!" eventually came the chant, echoing from the multitude of voices from all four demes, not just the Blues and Greens. Each voice formed a single note blending into the growing chorus of revolt. But Justinian's gaze remained fixed on some far-off point, his jaw set in unyielding determination.

Belisarius leaned in, his voice low and measured. "Cinis, they call for those men still held in sanctuary." His eyes flicked to the emperor, then to Cinis, as if seeking reassurance in the old warrior's steady presence.

The emperor finally spoke, his voice echoing in the air of the kathisma. "Ignore these clamors. Order is law, and my decree stands." His tone grew sterner as the day progressed and the unrest festered below.

As the races advanced—chariot after chariot thundering around the spina—a new chant arose, rippling through the crowd like a rising tide: "Long live the merciful Blues and Greens!" The cry, at first a single, defiant note, soon swelled into a chorus that vibrated with both hope and ire. Justinian's agitation became palpable; his eyes flashed with mounting anger as he gripped the arms of his gilded seat.

By the time the twentieth race concluded, the atmosphere shifted. The once-celebratory shouts gave way to an incantation of fury: "Nika! Nika! Victory! Victory!" The crowd, emboldened, was no longer crying out for their charioteers, but pointed directly at the emperor. Their voices rose in unison to a crescendo of defiance.

"This is an outrage!" Justinian bellowed, his voice slicing through the rising tumult. "Guards, remove me and the Empress to the palace at once!" His command was swift and imperious, leaving no room for negotiation, but Cinis saw the abject terror in the man's face, hidden behind a mask of anger.

Belisarius immediately signaled to his troops, who advanced with disciplined urgency to ensure passage for the emperor's guard. The imperial guard, faces grim and determined, moved to form a protective barrier around the emperor as he and Theodora were bundled out of the kathisma. In the ensuing chaos, Belisarius' men charged into the unruly mob. A small but fierce melee broke out on the field, the ringing of swords and the shouts of angry civilians blending with the roar of chariots.

Caught in the surge of violent protest, Cinis found himself swept into the crossfire. Amid the chaotic melee, he spotted Belisarius momentarily overpowered by a half-dozen enraged citizens. Without a thought, Cinis lunged forward, his battle-hardened instincts taking over. With a measured, yet forceful thrust of his arm, he deflected a swinging fist aimed at the general, his intervention echoing with the certainty of a soldier who had long since mastered the art of combat. Within scant moments, Cinis had dispelled the small group of untrained but angry fanatics.

Belisarius's eyes met Cinis' in that fleeting moment: an unspoken acknowledgment of respect and gratitude, forged from shared past glories and rekindled by bitter circumstance. The clash raged around them, but for a heartbeat, their mutual understanding cut through the turmoil.

As the emperor's guards disappeared and the crowd's chants morphed into a horrendous mix of protest and violence, the Hippodrome became a seething cauldron of political anger and raw, unbridled violence, a stage where destiny would soon be irrevocably altered.

❧ • ❧

THE EVENING AIR outside the Church of St. Laurence had taken on a bitter chill as twilight deepened over Constantinople. Lanterns flickered along narrow alleys, and the murmurs of the gathering crowd faded into an uneasy silence, pierced often by screams, shouts of "Nika!" and the clashing sounds of metal and wood upon wood and metal and flesh.

Cinis stood on the front stairs of the church, watching the violence engulf the city where he had come to find peace. His heart fell as he caught sight of a contingent of three contubernia of Legionnaires bearing Belisarius' colors. The soldiers were headed directly for him, and he knew at once why they had come.

He was wrong.

"Cinis, the emperor has spoken. You are to return to service at once," the lead man announced, eyes glinting with the fervor of duty and the precariousness of his exposed position on the streets.

Climbing the stairs to the church's stone threshold, the stern-faced officer of the bucellarii approached Cinis. His voice was low and urgent as he relayed the news: through Belisarius' urging, and at Emperor Justinian's command, Cinis had been reinstated as tribunus bucellariorum. The officer's words were clipped as official authority barely won out over professional jealousy.

Cinis scowled, his expression hardening as he crossed his arms. Tribunus bucellariorum—senior centurion over the first cohort of the bucellarii—primus pilus, he still thought of it. "Go pound sand. I have no desire to take part in Justinian's disaster," he replied, his tone weary and final.

Before the officer could press further, another officer—a gaunt, determined soldier with scars etched deep into his face—stepped forward. "Sir, you must accompany us. Belisarius convinced the emperor that your skill is indispensable. The city trembles with unrest; our orders demand your presence."

With palpable inner turmoil, Cinis weighed the call. Before he could respond, a sudden roar erupted from the street. A band of roughly a dozen soldiers wearing the colors of General Mundos, beleaguered and separated from their commander, found themselves besieged by screaming rioters. The clamor was deafening: shouts, the crash of hurled stones, and the clanging of weapons overlaid the acrid scent of smoke pouring forth from distant fires.

As the melee reached the grounds of St. Laurence's, chaos ruled as the group sent for him surged forth into the fray. Cinis's seasoned eyes imagined the mass of rioters being savagely overwhelmed by his men. With controlled anger, he stepped forward and shouted to all involved, "Hold your blows. These are Roman citizens such as yourselves, not beasts to be slaughtered!" His intervention, firm and resolute, halted his soldiers' lethal advance, a brief mercy amid the fervor of uprising. The civilians, equally cowed by this strange man in carpenter's garb who commanded Legionnaires, stepped aside to allow the besieged soldiers to go hurriedly on their way.

Yet, as the violence continued to surge across the city, Cinis sensed the inevitable: the presence of his company, swarming with armed men, would continue to draw the wrath of the masses like honey drew flies. The very church that had offered him refuge now trembled under the weight of mounting strife, and he would not make it a target of destruction. Reluctantly, Cinis agreed to leave its hallowed walls behind, for its defense. "I will go with you," he declared, voice low but resolute, "if it means sparing this holy ground from bloodshed."

Under a bruised sky, the group of soldiers, with their new leader-in-captivity Cinis reluctantly in tow, began their grim journey through the city. Repeated ambushes by enraged civilians punctuated their passage: a thrown stone here, a wild shout there. Each attack was a brutal reminder of the city's position on the brink of chaos. They pressed on until they reached the Praetorium, now a blazing tableau of devastation. Flames licked the walls, and thick, acrid smoke choked the air as the building, once a symbol of imperial order, burned in a furious inferno.

Then came the ultimate test, the event Cinis had hoped against and known would come. A massive band of wild-eyed rioters, savage, impassioned, and vastly outnumbering his company, descended upon them. With no hope of retreat, and as his men began to falter, Cinis felt something awaken deep within: a primal fury honed over centuries of warfare.

He went berserk. In a storm of slashing limbs and furious cries, he fought like a rabid and cornered animal. Too long had he been removed from the order of controlled battle; he fought as a single combatant against anything that moved.

Friend and foe alike were scattered in the wake of his wrath. The clash of steel, the shouts of injured men, and the roiling chaos blended into a frenzied symphony, and when at last the carnage subsided, just over half of his soldiers remained, trembling and bloodied, regarding him with both awe and terror. In the chaos, there had been no way for them to tell what was happening. They knew only that their group had been beset by a far superior force, and that superior force and much of their own now lay bloodied and broken on reddened paving stones. And that their new commander still stood, gasping and triumphant.

It was the test Cinis had expected, and he had failed, just as he knew he would.

As the dust settled, Cinis staggered forward, his heart pounding with a mix of adrenaline and desolation as he realized where he now stood. Slowly, his eyes were drawn upward. There, between him and the ruin of the smoldering Praetorium, the great silhouette of the Great Church loomed against the darkening sky, engulfed in raging flames. The sight struck him like a blow; in that terrible, burning moment, the culmination of his life's hopes and regrets was laid bare before him.

❧ • ❧

AT DAWN ON the day after the chariot races, Cinis, newly recommissioned as primus pilus, donned his military accoutrements with reluctant resolve to again attend the races. Justinian had insisted the races continue, ever trying to placate the mobs, despite being urged to the contrary by his advisors. The Hippodrome was a living, seething arena of light and chaos.

In the imperial kathisma, the emperor's face had been grim as the crowd's defiant chants swelled into a roar. Now, below in the arena, the day's chariot races unfolded with frenzied abandon, but the usual pomp was marred by discord. As the race neared its climax, the north end of the stadium erupted in flames: hot tongues of fire licking ancient stone. The emperor and Belisarius were hurried from the box by Cinis and his men, their retreat echoing against the clamor of an enraged mob. The chaos spilled again beyond the Hippodrome; a furious throng advanced toward the imperial bathhouse, shattering its marble serenity as they marched relentlessly toward the palace. In the tumult, united voices of the Greens and Blues demanded the ouster of corrupt officials: the city prefect Eudaimon, the praetor John the Cappodocian, and even Justinian's wisest and most trusted jurist, Trebonian. Their slogans were laced with declarations of political treachery.

The emperor, visibly spooked by these insidious demands, capitulated in silence and removed the three men from power as Belisarius' bucellarii and Mundus' men pressed close around the palace like a living shield.

The following day, the Augustaion became a blood-stained battleground. Belisarius led a contingent into fierce combat with rioters whose numbers swelled like a tidal wave. The clash was brutal and methodical; professional soldiers, their blades singing in unison, met a rabble too vast to subdue completely. Despite their skill, Belisarius eventually ordered a withdrawal, a decision that fanned the flames of public fury.

Throughout the city, buildings succumbed to fire, and the clergy's fervent prayers for order seemed to vanish amid the acrid smoke. The weary priest of the Church of St. Laurence approached Cinis with pleading eyes, his voice quavering as he recounted the city's cries for help. "Brother, we must calm these raging hearts," the priest implored. But Cinis, burdened by the searing memory of the conflagration of the Great Church and the guilt of his past wrath, listened in silence, his expression hidden beneath the weight of his remorse.

By Friday, the city's spirit had all but withered. The mob, insatiable in its hunger for retribution, set the praetorian quarters ablaze—again—while the Baths of Alexander and the Ecclesia Antiqua were reduced to smoldering ruins. Constantinople's once-bustling marketplaces fell eerily silent; shops shuttered their windows, and only a few stray souls wandered the deserted streets like ghosts, seeking refuge from the relentless, destructive fire. The city, normally vibrant under the sun's gaze, now resembled a forsaken tomb: a landscape where life had fled, leaving only charred remnants of its former glory.

On Saturday, reinforcements arrived by boat, their hulls cutting through the darkened waters as they carried fresh troops to bolster Belisarius' ranks. Yet, as these new soldiers stepped onto the cinder-strewn streets, the fighting escalated anew. The rioters, emboldened and desperate, clashed violently with the reinforced ranks of the guards, and the city's fires spread unchecked, consuming treasured relics and sacred churches alike. The palace itself, besieged by an unyielding horde, became a fortress of chaos. In a final, desperate move, Emperor Justinian, his voice tinged with both fury and resignation, ejected the Senators from his inner sanctum, convinced they were complicit in stoking the unrest. Amid this maelstrom of clashing steel, roaring flames, and the anguished cries of a city in ruin, Cinis stumbled like a man lost between duty and despair, his every step a heavy echo of the wars he had so wished to leave behind. He was now forced to participate in the terrible unraveling of a once-great empire.

ON SUNDAY, THE Hippodrome was again an inferno of discontent. From the elevated kathisma, Emperor Justinian stood watching the roiling mass of over a hundred thousand souls. The arena's ancient marble and stonework, bathed in the last glimmers of twilight, seemed to tremble beneath the weight of the crowd's fury. The air was thick with the clamor of impassioned voices, the metallic tang of dried blood, and the bitter aroma of smoldering wood that no incense could mask. In the distance, the charred husk of the once-mighty Great

Church loomed, a silent witness to the chaos that had gripped the city.

Raising his voice above the tumult, Justinian fumed to those in the box, "Not since Pilate has a man been called on to make so impossible a decision. I have no choice here. If I let them go, I declare my own law to be null and void!" His words, harsh and desperate, failed to move past the walls of the kathisma.

Cinis, standing nearby with his new cohort of soldiers, felt his heart twist at the emperor's pride. Unable to hold his tongue, he spoke without thinking, "Pilate had no power. You have a choice." The bold remark cut through the din, drawing startled murmurs from the assembled guards.

Justinian's eyes narrowed as he fixed his gaze on Cinis. "Explain yourself!" he demanded, his voice a mix of incredulity and imperial command.

Cinis's voice rang clear, defiant even in the face of sovereign wrath. "Pilate was caught between an angry mob and Caesar; he had no power and faced reprisal in either direction. What man is there on earth above you? You hold the power to show mercy, and you will be judged only by the lives you spare. Give the people what they ask. Show mercy!"

For a long, breathless moment, a hush fell over the kathisma. Then, with a theatrical sweep, Justinian stepped forward onto the box, raising a leather-bound copy of the Gospels high for all to see. "I swear by these sacred words," he vowed, "an amnesty shall be granted for any crime committed in this last week, and I shall hear your demands."

But the crowd's response was a thunderous rejection. "Liar!" they roared, voices swelling into a cacophony of contempt. Soon, a new chant erupted from the sea of dissent: "Long live Hypatius!" The people, in their fervor, had chosen a puppet; a reluctant Hypatius now paraded before them as their champion in an attempt to replace Justinian.

Within moments, Justinian's face twisted with mounting frustration. The imperial box became a stage of chaos as the emperor exited in disgrace, his eyes darting nervously, and headed back to the palace. Once there, Cinis was barred from entering the imperial chambers, but heard whispers that the emperor contemplated fleeing by boat. News came that any notion of retreat and exile was squelched by the sharp rebuke of Empress Theodora, whose voice, tinged with both authority and shame, had convinced Justinian to remain.

Following this decision, a new order was imposed. The city was tearing itself apart, and Justinian had ordered Belisarius to fix it, at any cost.

Belisarius, ever the clever one, whispered to Cinis, "You wanted to be an architect? Here is your chance to rebuild this great city." He explained that Justinian's eunuch, Narses, had been sent to bribe the Blues so that they would not hinder the emperor's command.

Belisarius, however, had formulated a bold plan to storm the kathisma and seize the puppet emperor, Hypatius, directly, but the attempt had failed amid the tumult. Now, he proposed a second route: climbing over the rubble on the West side of the Hippodrome.

"No," Cinis countered sharply. "If we take that route, our backs will be to the mob. We will be trapped in a kill box." He urged the general to reconsider and simply wait out the political fiasco, but Belisarius, frustrated and out of options, scanned the arena. On the far side, he caught sight of Mundus, his chief rival, closing ranks and marching in with his large contingent of soldiers toward a throng of 30,000 to 50,000 unarmed civilians packed onto the arena floor.

Belisarius steeled himself, called orders to his men, and began to close ranks, intent on trapping the rioters between his men and those of Mundus. In that charged moment, Cinis felt a chill of dread: a deep, inescapable knowledge of the carnage that was about to unfold, and of his role, powerless to stop it.

UNDER A PURPLE sky bruised red and black, the Hippodrome became a field of unspeakable horror. Cinis stood at the edge of the carnage, his heart pounding as it rent itself between duty and revulsion. At first, he had marched forward—however reluctantly—as a loyal defender of the empire, determined to help restore order. But as the massacre unfolded before his eyes, he realized with dawning terror that both Mundus' and Belisarius' soldiers were locked in a vicious contest, a competition to inflict the worst atrocities upon the unarmed, panicked crowd. Belisarius' disciplined ranks advanced in grim formation, methodically cutting down civilians as though reaping a harvest of human lives, while their counterparts, wild and unrestrained, laughed and jeered as they unleashed brutal, indiscriminate violence from the other side of the trap.

The air was choked with the cries of the dying and the clash of steel, mingling with the coppery tang of blood and the stench of flesh trodden underfoot. In numbers of thousands and tens of thousands the rioters, unarmed and desperate, were trampled and hacked down like wheat before a scythe. Cinis found his voice strangled by horror. He screamed orders for his men to hold their blades, to spare the innocent, but his pleas were swallowed by the tumult; the soldiers, consumed by their bloodlust and rivalry, had forsaken all restraint.

As the two factions descended on the mass of unarmed civilians, the frenzied melee was all that existed. Belisarius' recently-reinforced bucellarii and Mundus' army, each seeking to prove their savage supremacy, attacked indiscriminately.

No longer could Cinis justify his role as protector when the very forces he had once commanded lay waste to the people he had sworn to serve. Driven by a desperate need to halt the slaughter, he plunged into the chaos, swinging his blade in a futile attempt to separate friend from foe. But the tide of violence was relentless, and his efforts were drowned in the relentless, methodical reaping of lives.

The ground transformed into a crimson morass; bodies lay strewn and piled, their anguished faces frozen in masks of eternal anguish. Amid the roar of the frenzied soldiers and the incessant cries of the dying, the Hippodrome was unrecognizable, a vast graveyard where imperial order had crumbled under the weight of anarchy.

Cinis could scarcely bear the sight, his soul wracked with the bitter realization that he had been complicit in unleashing this massacre.

When at last the legionnaires began their withdrawal, leaving behind a ruined field saturated with blood and despair, Cinis sank to his knees. The cooling, viscous blood seeped into his boots, and his tears mingled with the stains on the earth. In that silent, final moment, overwhelmed by the enormity of loss and his crushing guilt, he wept amidst the knee-deep wash of blood, haunted by the unending, relentless echo of his failures and the tragic price of empire.

AS THE ECHOES of the day's violence faded along with the last rays of the sun, Belisarius stood before his assembled legionnaires outside the ruins of the Hippodrome. His voice, proud and resonant, boasted, "Today, we have triumphed. Our courage has tamed the chaos, and our discipline has restored order to Justinian's reign." His men, exhausted by effort and the early blooms of disgust, murmured their assent. Many eyes shone with hard-earned pride, and many more with numb despair.

Cinis strode forward with grim purpose, armor bathed red with blood. The assembled ranks parted before him like a wave.

"Your victory is nothing!" Cinis declared, his voice rough with disillusionment. "It was nothing but slaughter! You speak of order, yet you enforce it with cold steel and drain the blood of unarmed men. Of Roman citizens!"

An uneasy ripple passed through the ranks. Belisarius' gaze fell upon Cinis in a mixture of confusion and shock and anger. "Appius Aurelius, do you dare challenge my command in front of your comrades?" he bellowed.

"Dare I? I dare," Cinis spat, his eyes blazing.

"Enforce your conscription on me if you think you can," he shouted as a challenge, loosing the buckles of his cuirass and letting it fall to the ground. His sword had been abandoned in the arena, he had nothing else to relinquish. "Show me that your sword can bind my fate as mine once did yours. Enforce my conscription. I dare you!"

For a long, heavy moment, the two men stood locked in a silent combat of wills before the assembled Legion. Belisarius searched Cinis' eyes and saw there only the cold specter of death: a reflection of a past soaked in bloodshed to which that in the Hippodrome was just the latest chapter. Moreover, he saw the inevitability of his death at the bare hands of his past mentor, for that was the only thing on Cinis' mind.

With a slow shake of his head, Belisarius relented. "Go, Appius Aurelius Cinis. Your service is no longer required," he muttered.

Chapter 15 : CONSTANTINOPLE: THE DARKNESS

537 AD

ALONE, HE DUG the grave in the dark of day.

Under the leaden, pallid sky, the once-bright city lay muted beneath the relentless grip of the shamed sun, still hiding its face in shame after more than a year. Famine's shadow stretched long across the land, its sorrowful quiet punctuated by the distant, forlorn murmurs of a starving populace. In a hole on a windswept hillside copse overlooking the monastery walls, the monk hitched up the hem of his threadbare robe.

His weathered hands labored at the grave he carved into the frozen earth. The hole was meticulously measured: six pedes deep, eight long, and four wide, its corners true and square. His attention to detail in the measurements was a somber testament to the harsh arithmetic of death in a time of despair. As he dug, the sound of his spade striking the soil, hardened by cold even late in summer, echoed like a solitary drumbeat in the stillness. Each clump of earth he heaved away carried with it a silent prayer for a lost city.

He paused to wipe sweat from his brow, dripping from it despite the coolness of the air. His thoughts drifted like the thin, grey mist that hung over the distant city. The thoughts were tempered by an aching, deliberate hope, a hope found in the humble task of shaping the earth, in the ritual of preparing a final resting place for a man that had given him refuge.

The bitter scent of damp earth and cold stone mingled with the faint aroma of smoke wafting from some remote corner of Constantinople. In that silent moment, as he labored under the weight of a failing sun and a starving world, Appius Aurelius Cinis—now just Brother Appius—allowed himself a quiet reflection: though the days ahead would be dark and unyielding, here in the deep, sorrowful embrace of the earth, he found a strange comfort. For in the act of digging his friend and sponsor's grave, he was, in some small measure, reclaiming his purpose amidst the chaos.

❧ • ❧

CINIS HAD WALKED as Brother Appius for some time now, and in the quiet solitude of the monastery he had reflected on the events that had transformed his life. He had joined the order in 532, emerging like the city from the ashes of the Nika Riots with a desperate hope for redemption. In those years he had risen swiftly, from an Oblate to a Postulate, then a Novice, and finally a Laybrother. His unwavering quest for absolution had not gone unnoticed; Brother Mitus, the gentle and revered Abbot, whose calm devotion had endured even after being stricken with apoplexy, had taken him under his wing. It had been Brother Mitus who had personally endorsed him to the Hegumen, and it had been then that Appius had been granted the honor of becoming a scribe, tasked with copying pages from the Latin Vulgate. Each careful stroke of his quill on vellum had been both an act of devotion and an expression of his deep-seated hope that recording sacred wisdom might, somehow, cleanse the sins of his long and violent past.

He had sat hunched over the ancient wooden desk in the monastery's scriptorium, where the rich scent of ink and parchment had mingled with the soft, lingering fragrance of myrrh. The dim light that filtered through colored alabaster windows would cast fragmented patterns of ruby and sapphire upon his work, and he had felt, for a fleeting moment, that his heart might be mended by these hallowed words. In his mind, he had recalled the centuries of aimless wandering and relentless warfare that had once defined him. He had remembered with painful clarity the loss of his family in Roman Britain, the endless battles fought with ruthless abandon, and that fateful moment beneath the Cross when his very soul had been marked by a curse. And yet, amid the sacred routine of copying the holy texts, he had dared to believe that he might become something greater than the sum of his past transgressions.

But even as he penned the words, the sun had died.

That great celestial orb's rays had grown weak and appeared a bluish color. Men's shadows had fled from the ground, as had the heat of the sun from the air. A dense, dry fog had overtaken the moon rendering it empty of splendor.

Then had followed a winter without storms, a spring without mildness, and a summer without heat, all of which had culminated in a prolonged frost and unseasonable drought. The seasons, all jumbled up together, could not be told one from the other, and alien elements had bound themselves to the very clouds, stretched like a hide across the sky.

For well past a year had the true colors of the sun and moon refrained from being seen, and the sun's warmth had grown ever farther from man. The very earth had seemed to mourn for the loss of its dying crops.

An ominous reckoning had descended upon Appius. On the fateful evening of that first day of darkness, as Appius had carefully set aside his quill and gazed out over the monastery's hillside, he had watched the light that had sustained the world being blotted out, as if a colossal hand were sweeping across the heavens to snuff the sun. In that moment, he had been crushed from within by the cruel certainty that his hubris had invoked divine retribution.

He had stood at the window as the departing sun cast judgment upon his pride, heart pounding in his hollow chest. The spectacle had been a clear sign that his curse was now being laid bare for all to see. And in that shrouded moment, Brother Appius had understood that his vain quest for redemption had carried a price far greater than he had ever dared to imagine.

❧ • ❧

AS THE SECOND year of the famine had begun, the sun had been hidden behind a pall for nearly fifteen months. The constant, oppressive gloom had leeched all color from the world. The once-bright city had turned a dull, ashen gray, and the fields around it had withered into barren expanses of dust.

Relentless hunger and failing crops had begun to bring death even within the sacred cloisters. Yet, what had cut him deepest were the murmurs and sidelong glances of his fellow monks. They had begun, almost imperceptibly at first, to cast disparaging looks his way, as if realizing he alone were the cause of the darkened sun and the barren earth. In hushed whispers, they had murmured that his old nickname, stating that the "architect of death" had, through his pride and his past deeds, invited divine retribution upon them all.

One bitter afternoon, as he had stubbornly continued his work of scribing passages from the Holy Word, an old brother had leaned in close and removed any lingering doubt he may have had regarding their thoughts. "It is the shadow of your sins that darkens our skies, Appius. The blood on your hands has blotted out the sun for us all." The words had seared his heart, leaving him to conclude that his quest for redemption had been nothing more than a curse in disguise.

Even the long, silent processions through the monastery's cold corridors had seemed to echo with discontent in the rustle of pious robes. The failing crops in the surrounding countryside had only deepened the suspicion of his brothers. It was as if every withered vine and barren field bore testament to his misdeeds: a living reminder that his very presence had become a portent of doom.

In every whispered conversation, in every reproachful glance cast in the quiet hours of dawn, Appius had felt the chill of alienation, as if the darkness above had seeped into the very souls of the faithful.

And so, in the faded light of that long-dimmed day, as he climbed out of a hole only he among the monks had been strong enough to dig for his mentor and friend, Brother Appius came to understand that redemption was a fragile dream indeed.

THE DAY FOR Brother Mitus' burial had come, unadorned by any festal decoration or pomp: a stark, bare ritual. What should have been a celebration of a life spent in service to the Most High was shrouded in the unforgiving vestments of loss. In the cold light of dawn, the hillside copse stood in silent, uncaring anticipation. On the hill was the solemn, unmarked grave: a deep, gaping pit hewn by Appius himself, precisely measured and similarly devoid of any elaborate embellishment. Over this void in the earth, Appius had constructed a simple scaffolding and rigged a block-and-tackle system. Although the framework was a modest contrivance of olive wood and oak whose only purpose was the lowering a body into the earth's unfeeling bosom, Appius had taken great care in its design and construction. He regretted not being able to stain the surface of the wood with oil, as there was no oil to be had in the famine-ravaged land.

A heavy, oppressive melancholy had settled over the monastery that morning, its weight palpable in every slow, measured step as the monks ascended the hill in somber procession. Their faces were drawn and quiet, eyes cast downward in a collective display of grief. Normally, the body of a revered brother such as Mitus, wrapped in nothing more than a plain shroud, would have been borne aloft by several brethren, a shared burden that expressed communal honor and solidarity. Yet, in this time of desolation and famine, only Appius had the strength to bear his dead friend's lifeless form. Each laborious step he took was marked by determination, the act of carrying the body an agonizing homage to the man he carried.

The murmurs began almost as soon as the procession set out for the hill. The other monks exchanged sallow, accusing glances, their eyes darkened by hunger and grief. In hushed, disapproving whispers, they cast furtive looks at Appius, knowing him to be the sole root of their collective misfortune. They whispered of his hubris, thinking of his storied past that had led the heavens to withdraw their light, leaving the crops to fail and the people to suffer. Their voices, barely audible over the crunch of their sandals on ancient stones, carried a resigned judgment that clung to the air like a tangible mist of despair.

As the procession wound its way upward, the strain of the relentless famine weighed heavily on Appius. His once steadfast frame had weakened as had theirs. He now moved with a weary determination, every step a battle against his lessened strength. At one point, he stumbled over a stray rock jutting from the path: a simple, unyielding obstacle. For a heart-stopping moment, the other brothers paused in their solemn march, but not one extended a hand to steady him. With a grimace of effort and the quiet resilience of one used to hardship, Appius regained his footing and continued onward with the still, heavy burden of Brother Mitus, the echo of his stumble fading into the murmurs of silent reproach.

Appius wrestled not just with the wrapped body but also with a torrent of conflicting emotions. He could not deny the harsh truth that the departure of the sun and the resulting famine had ravaged the city and claimed the lives of many, including the beloved Abbot, nor did he refute his responsibility for it. Yet, amid the quiet, disdainful glances and whispered accusations of his peers, he held onto one unyielding conviction: that his devotion to the monastery and his brothers had never wavered. He had borne the heaviest burdens, working tirelessly day and night to do not only his work but theirs as well, and he believed that no one could question the depth of his commitment. In a time when so many had been reduced to feeble shadows of themselves by hunger, he alone had managed to keep the sacred flame of duty alive, even though he bore the blame for the darkness that had necessitated his unflagging efforts.

Appius moved with measured care as he approached the scaffolding. Every beam and post had been measured and joined with meticulous care by his rough and weary hands, and the ropes he had strung were taut and unblemished. It was a temporary structure crafted with the utmost precision, a small monument to the esteem in which he held his departed mentor.

In his heart, Appius cared not that many of the brethren resented him. None could despise him more greatly than he despised himself. With solemn reverence, he lifted Brother Mitus' body—wrapped in a simple shroud—and gingerly eased it into the waiting cradle. Every motion was deliberate, each adjustment a quiet prayer of farewell, as his tired eyes met the silent, accusing stares of his brethren gathered in the chill morning light.

Above them on the hill, the Hegumen stood apart, a tall, thin figure distinguished by the less threadbare nature of his robes. The man's hawklike gaze was fixed on Appius, and his face was carved in lines of disdain and sorrow, as if he knew Appius bore the weight of every unspoken reproach, not just the weight of the Abbott. The Hegumen's gaunt features, set in a rigid, sepulchral expression, betrayed neither warmth nor pity as he prepared to deliver the eulogy for Brother Mitus. His thin lips pressed into a hard line, and his eyes, cold and unyielding, flickered over Appius with a quiet judgment that cut deeper than could any harsh word.

As Appius lowered the body into the waiting bosom of the earth, the murmurs of the assembled monks faded into an oppressive silence. The Hegumen stepped forward, his voice low and measured as he began to speak. His words, laced with ritual solemnity yet edged with poorly concealed contempt, filled the air with an aura of finality. In that moment, every creak of the old wood and every sigh of the wind bore witness to the burden of guilt that Appius would carry long after the echoes of the Hegumen's words had died away.

After the Hegumen's somber eulogy faded, a low murmur of discontent began to swell among the brethren. In hushed voices and with sidelong, accusing glances, they whispered that Appius had been seen gathering extra provisions: a secret stash of food that explained, in their eyes, why his strength had not waned while theirs faltered.

The Hegumen, his face a mask of austere authority, stepped forward and declared with cold finality, "The sacrament shall be denied to Brother Appius, for his actions betray a secret indulgence in sustaining his own strength, even as our bodies wither in famine."

For a long, harrowing moment, Appius stood mute, the weight of their judgment settling upon him like a shroud. Inside, he knew the truth: his strength came not from some clandestine hoard of food. No, he had always been able to endure, to persevere. He was an anomaly among men who succumbed around him to hunger.

Yet that very ability, a remnant of his unnatural nature, was now his burden as much as his salvation. He felt that he deserved the censure now imposed upon him, a penance for the sins of his past. And to speak a word in defense would risk unveiling the truth of his extraordinary abilities: a truth he had guarded for centuries, hidden beneath the veneer of frailty common to all mortals.

As the words of condemnation echoed around him, Appius swallowed his protest. His heart, heavy with remorse and resignation, pounded in a hollow chest. He did not flinch when the Hegumen's gaze, sharp as a hawk's, bore into him. In that penetrating look, he recognized not only the weight of collective sorrow but the bitter sting of envy and fear from his brothers. They had grown weak, starved by the unyielding famine, while he, despite his suffering, continued to endure. Every whispered accusation, every sidelong glance of disdain, was a reminder of the solitude of his burden. A burden that would remain unspoken.

Appius chose silence over defiance. He understood that tacit in his silence lay an acceptance of their judgment in order to conceal the secret strength that had long set him apart. And so, with eyes lowered and heart full of unshed tears, he allowed himself to be cast from the sanctity of the ceremony and from the monastery itself.

Appius Aurelius Cinis, no longer Brother Appius, walked down the hill, leaving the monastery and the accusations of his brethren behind. The hidden sun watched unconcerned, through the shroud of a leaden sky.

Chapter 16 : CONSTANTINOPLE: THE DEATH

542 AD

THE STREET STRETCHED as a bridge across a pool of human neglect and decay. The once-proud thoroughfare, long empty of clamor, was coated in a fine layer of dust and cinder that sparkled with false gaiety in the sullen light of afternoon. Sharp growls punctured the silence as two stray dogs tussled fiercely over a rare bone still flecked with a scrap of raw flesh.

At one side of the street stood a large villa, once evidence of some family's wealth. Its alabaster windows were now nothing more than jagged scars on the facade. The white stone, sliced into translucent panes by skilled craftsmen, had been smashed out by looters. Crude wooden boards had been hastily nailed in place and served as a feeble substitute for its former radiance. The heavy wooden door, its bottom hinge missing and its frame scarred by the violence of invaders, swung precariously on its single remaining top hinge, creaking mournfully with every shift of the dry breeze that whispered through the narrow lane.

On the wall facing the street, its surface exposed by carefully-cultivated ivy having been ripped from the brick, someone had scrawled the inscription "manes intus." The phrase, meaning "ghosts inside," was a grim omen, one seen far too frequently throughout the city. The inscription served as the last testament to those lost souls whose memory still lingered in the silence of the ruined estate. The atmosphere was heavy with the scent of burnt wood and decaying plaster, mingling with a sharper odor of stale blood and worse that seemed to seep from the very stones.

Without warning, the door exploded outward, kicked violently from the inside. The upper hinge gave way under the sudden impact, sending a burst of splintered wood into the open air. From the threshold emerged a gaunt, haggard Appius Aurelius Cinis, draped in a simple, dark robe that seemed as weathered as the ruined building. He staggered forward. He carried two diseased corpses, one over each shoulder. Wealthy men now reduced to decaying husks, their pallid skin mottled and marred by the ravages of illness.

The stench of decay mingled with the troubled dust, creating an acrid perfume that clung to the air. His thin, powerful arms strained under the weight of the bodies, and each labored step left faint impressions on the dusty ground.

A short distance away, a simple, wheeled cart waited, its wooden frame meticulously repaired just the day before by Cinis himself. Modest in design, the cart was built for a singular, grim purpose: to carry the dead away from this forsaken place. Cinis hauled the diseased corpses towards it, his bare, calloused hands leaving streaks of sweat that mixed with the dirt on his weathered skin. The corpses would join the lifeless bodies already piled high, erecting a grim monument to the city's recent tragedy.

He set each corpse atop the grim pile, ensuring that every motion was measured and respectful. His care was the only ceremony these men would receive. His eyes, though shadowed by sorrow, flickered with a steely determination as he inspected the arrangement. The cart had been restored to function with a fresh, oaken drawbar affixed to sturdy manubria whereby to grab and handle the cart. The wood was rough and already heavily stained, but each component was as neat and carefully maintained as Cinis could achieve under the circumstances.

With the bodies in place among those of their neighbors, Cinis turned his attention to the drawbar. He gripped it firmly, the hand-carved wood fitting perfectly into the calloused palm of his hand. He then set his jaw, drawing on every reserve of muscle and sinew. As he began to pull, the raw physicality of his effort was on display; sinews rippled in concert beneath his skin, and his powerful legs heaved against the weight. The sound of creaking wood and the soft thud of the cart wheels on the uneven pavers of the street punctuated the oppressive silence of the deserted lane.

ON ANOTHER DESERTED stretch of Constantinopolitan street, beneath a pallid sky, Cinis sat on the worn doorstep of another once-grand villa now marked with another somber inscription of "manes intus." The quiet of the afternoon was broken only by the whisper of dust devils and the distant murmur of a city struggling against its fate. Nearby, his cart stood empty: a silent, waiting witness to his grim labors. Its sturdy wooden frame, bearing the wear of recent use, promised readiness for the next burden.

Cinis leaned against the cool stone of the doorstep and unwrapped a hunk of moldy bread and a modest portion of withered lamb sausage salvaged from the abandoned dwelling. The aroma of greasy meat and stale bread mingled with the earthy scent of dust, the stench of his own sweat, and the scents of putrefaction.

Cinis ripped a bite from the bread and chewed. It was a small, meager repast that he accepted as both sustenance and token payment for the unending work he performed. No one had hired him for this task; he had taken it up because it needed to be done. Early on, when he had taken time to dig graves for the dead he carried out of the city, his labor had been rewarded with a few coins and earnest thanks. Over time, however, the payments had dwindled to hollow words and then to nothing at all. The graves he had excavated had grown ever more hasty and shallow. These had been replaced ultimately by giant mounds of the dead, deposited with a whispered prayer and little else to mark their passing.

Often, as he sat thus in quiet solitude, Cinis recalled another plague that had ravaged the outposts near Hadrian's Wall, a time when he had returned to his villa and witnessed a tableau of death not unlike this one. Then, the graves he had dug had been deep and deliberate, a lasting testament to the ghosts of his own lost family, a memory scrawled as indelibly across his soul as the words now on the walls around him.

Lost in his quiet reflections and the meager comfort of his repast, Cinis barely acknowledged the clatter of approaching footsteps until he slowly lifted his gaze. There, emerging from the dusty thoroughfare and flanked by three contubernia of legionnaires, was General Belisarius. The general's expression flickered with brief surprise and indignation.

Cinis's weathered face registered no such response. He felt nothing, only the steady numbness of a man long accustomed to loss and the thankless nature of his work.

Belisarius strode forward, his voice rigid with authority as he barked, "Appius Aurelius! You live? I had heard you died with the rest of the brothers at Stoudious."

That elicited a response. Cinis mouthed the words, "They are dead?" as his stomach fell into a pit.

"Every one. We burnt the hall ourselves. I guess you cannot cart out every one of the dead, can you?" the general sneered.

Cinis pushed the emotion down. Even if he allowed himself to feel the sorrow, it would do nothing to comfort the dead.

"Appius, rise. You will come with us to answer for your crimes."

Four of Belisarius' bucellarii strode forth, interpreting their commander's intent immediately.

Cinis, unmoved, brought a cracked clay jug of water to his lips and swallowed slowly, then casually wiped his dripping mouth with his forearm, his dark eyes unflinching and cold. In that quiet, indifferent moment, Cinis felt no shock, no lingering memory of past battles or unfulfilled destinies, only the relentless weight of a life that had already borne too much. His apathetic acceptance spoke louder than any plea, a silent testament to the weariness that had long settled into his bones.

Belisarius's tone grew accusatory as his men seized Cinis' arms, harsh tones meant for all to hear. "You bear responsibility for this city's malady, for the hunger and the darkness that have beset Constantinople! The Emperor will have your head for this," he declared, his voice echoing against the ancient stones.

Without a word of protest, Cinis allowed himself to be taken into custody. His silent resignation and the steady resolve in his eyes betrayed nothing of the tumult churning within him, only a profound, unspoken acceptance that the burdens he carried were now to be exposed to the eyes of men. As the legionnaires surrounded him and led him away from the deserted doorstep, the silent villa and its faded inscription, "manes intus," watched on, bearing witness to the departure of another ghost.

• • •

THE BUCELLARII LED Cinis through the silent halls of the Great Palace, his chains dragging against the polished marble floor, the sound echoing through the cavernous corridors like the faint tolling of a distant funeral bell. The once-vibrant heart of the empire now lay shrouded in an oppressive hush, broken only by the occasional rasping breath of a fevered servant or the shuffle of a half-starved eunuch who had outlasted his master. The air was thick with the cloying scent of burning myrrh and vinegar, a desperate attempt to cleanse the plague's unseen corruption, yet it could not mask the deeper stench of sickness, of rot and putrefaction that had seeped into the very stones of the imperial residence.

The guards flanking him remained silent, their faces sunken, their once-proud bearing reduced to something weary and mechanical. These were not the robust soldiers of the empire's glory but men who had returned from the re-conquest of Rome to then spend weeks fighting off the same death that had hollowed out the city. Whether they had survived by fate, by strength, or by imperial privilege, Cinis neither knew nor cared. Their hands were firm on his arms, though not unkind; perhaps they, too, had begun to wonder why they were bothering to enforce the will of an emperor who might not outlive the night.

As the great doors to the imperial chamber were pulled open, the flickering torchlight illuminated a scene that would have been unthinkable only a year before.

Justinian, once the most powerful man in the empire, a ruler who had stood against the face of riots and war, was a wretched husk of himself. He lay propped up against a mountain of silken cushions, his imperial robes hanging loosely on his wasting frame. His skin, once golden with the vitality of a man who had commanded armies and built empires, was now mottled with dark, oozing buboes: swollen tumors of the plague that clung to his throat, his arms, even his face. The emperor's lips, cracked and darkened, trembled slightly as he drew a shallow, rattling breath. The skin on his hands had turned black at the fingertips, necrotic flesh peeling away from beneath his once-pristine nails.

Cinis had seen death in all its forms. He had waded through battlefields where the wounded lay screaming for water, their intestines spilling from their bodies. He had walked through villages where famine had shriveled mothers into husks, their arms still wrapped around the corpses of the children they could not save. But this? This was a different kind of death. This was the slow, merciless grip of disease, the grinding inevitability of nature's cruelty, against which no blade or shield could defend.

Yet, against all odds, Justinian still lived.

Belisarius stood at the emperor's side, his posture rigid. He had endured the plague as well—though, unlike Justinian, he had survived with his body largely intact. The faint, pale scars of old swellings marred his otherwise hardened features, his skin taut from weeks of illness, but his strength had returned. The weight of armor sat naturally upon his frame, polished and gleaming even in the dim light. In the end, he had suffered, but he had not starved. He had not been left to rot.

Cinis took this in with quiet detachment. He had expected it. Those who lived behind the palace walls always found a way to outlast the ones beyond them. Still, a slow, smoldering fury stirred in his chest, a heat that had not burned in him for some time.

For a long moment, no one spoke. Then Justinian exhaled sharply, his voice a dry rasp, like wind scraping against stone. "You will answer," he wheezed. "You will answer for what you have done."

Cinis lifted his gaze to the emperor and then, as if the emperor meant nothing, turned it upon Belisarius.

"What I have done?" His voice was hoarse, not from fear, but from exhaustion. From days and nights spent walking the streets for the dead, from dragging carts of rotting corpses through alleys choked with filth, from breathing in the air thick with decay. "You sit here, rotting, while your people die in the streets," he said, his voice gaining strength, his words cutting through the room like a blade. "You lock yourselves away, hoarding grain and wine while children starve in the shadow of your palace. Your soldiers burn the homes of the dying rather than tend to them."

His chains rattled as he took a step forward, the guards gripping his arms more tightly, but Cinis did not fight them. He simply met Belisarius' eyes, the weight of his fury bearing down upon the general like the pressure of a storm.

"You've abandoned them," he said flatly.

Belisarius spoke sharply, his face darkening as he stepped forward. "And what of you, Appius Aurelius?" he snarled, his voice dripping with accusation. "How have you dwelt so among the dead and not been afflicted yourself? What force protects you?"

The room fell into a deeper silence. The guards shifted uncomfortably. Even Justinian, fevered and on the brink of death, stirred slightly at the implication.

Cinis did not answer. He did not flinch.

He had heard the whispers in the streets. He'd heard the murmurs of those who had seen him walk among the corpses, who had watched him haul the bodies of the diseased out to the mass graves, untouched by the plague that had stolen so many others. It was not the first time he had outlived a sickness that should have taken him. It would not be the last.

But he would not explain.

He simply held Belisarius' gaze, silent and unyielding. The truth, the terrible, inescapable truth of his existence, was something he would not utter. Not here. Not to them.

And so he said nothing.

❧ • ☙

THE BUCELLARII FORCED Cinis to his knees before Justinian, his chains rattling against the cold marble floor as the heavy grip of legionnaires pressed down on his shoulders. The emperor watched through fever-glazed eyes, his ravaged body stirring beneath the drapery of his robes. Even in his illness, even in the throes of this death that threatened to take him, Justinian clung to his throne as if it were an extension of his being: something owed and something eternal.

Beside him, Belisarius stood, his armor polished, his scars visible in the dim light of flickering braziers. He looked every bit the soldier, every bit the victor, even as his master's empire rotted around him. His gaze bore into Cinis with the satisfaction of a man who had finally cornered a beast he had long hunted.

"This is all your fault," Belisarius declared coldly, his voice cutting through the silence like a blade against stone.

Cinis remained still, unmoved. He had heard the accusation before, whispered in the streets, murmured in the shadows of the monastery, scrawled in the eyes of every man who had lived long enough to see his world collapse.

He had uttered the accusation to himself as well.

"The deaths at the Hippodrome? That was your doing," Belisarius continued, warming to his topic. He stepped forward. "You led my men into a trap. You gave them no recourse but wholesale slaughter. You stood amidst the carnage you helped to create. And you dared to weep as though the blame belonged to someone else."

Cinis' jaw tensed, but he said nothing.

"The darkness," Belisarius pressed on, his voice rising, filled with righteous venom. "That, too, was your doing. I spoke to the brothers at Stoudios. I know what happened. You. You dared to write the words of God, and the sun went dark. You claimed a holy life for yourself, and for that arrogance, the crops failed and the earth starved."

He leaned in closer, his breath hot with conviction. "And now this plague. Your plague. Your pride has brought this sickness upon us. You, who walked among the dead without falling. You, who should have died long before now."

Cinis exhaled slowly, his hands balling into fists within the confines of his chains. The words washed over him, and though he might not have disagreed, a slow, seething anger began to rise within him.

He lifted his gaze, first to Belisarius, then to Justinian, his eyes locking onto the untouched platter of food on the emperor's table: fresh bread, dates, a goblet of undiluted wine. How many had starved while their ruler feasted? How many had died beyond these walls while the imperial court languished in its self-imposed quarantine?

"And who are you to judge?" Cinis' voice was low, almost conversational, but it cut through the chamber like a blade. "You, who slaughtered the unarmed in the Hippodrome and stood victorious over a city of corpses? And you—" his gaze flicked to Justinian "—who watches from a throne of rot while your people eat the dead?"

Belisarius took a step forward, anger flashing in his eyes, but Cinis turned his gaze back to him. Something in the general's words had just connected in his mind.

"You spoke to the brothers at Stoudios," Cinis said, his voice tight. It was not a question.

"Yes," Belisarius replied.

The realization dawned like an ember catching in dry kindling. "Then they weren't all dead," Cinis said, his voice suddenly hoarse.

Belisarius tilted his head. "Not when I arrived."

The truth struck with the force of a hammer. The monastery had been a death trap, a nest of plague-ridden corpses. Belisarius had done what he always did; he had solved the problem. Not with care, not with mercy, but with fire.

"You burned them," Cinis breathed.

Belisarius nodded. "I did what had to be done. Just as I will now."

The cold finality of his words sent a tremor through Cinis' hands. He lunged, but the weight of his chains and the sheer number of legionnaires pressing down on him stopped him short. He struggled, but they held firm, and Justinian let out a ragged chuckle from his sickbed.

"The sentence is death," the emperor rasped. "For your crimes against the empire and your blasphemies against heaven."

There was no ceremony to it, no feigned deliberation. Only the question of how.

Justinian turned to Belisarius. "How shall he die?"

Belisarius' lips pressed into a thin line. "A hanging would be too merciful."

"A beheading?" a voice offered from the shadows.

Justinian scoffed. "Hardly fitting for a man who has defied heaven itself."

The general let out another slow breath. "Had Constantine not abolished crucifixion..."

The words barely left his mouth before Cinis moved.

Something in him snapped: a primal, unbidden, centuries-old rage that roared to life like a fire catching a gust of wind. He wrenched his arms forward, the heavy chains twisting like whips in his grasp, and with a sudden, violent pull, he tore free from the nearest guards. The sound of breaking bone followed as one legionnaire crumpled, his skull split by the weight of the iron.

Cinis did not stop. He could not. He surged forward, his chains lashing out like serpents, snapping ribs, crushing throats. The air filled with the panicked cries of soldiers caught unprepared, with the wet, percussive sounds of flesh giving way beneath steel and iron. The world blurred in red and silver. He was moving inexorably toward Belisarius, toward the man who had burned his home, who had spoken of his execution like it was a simple affair. Who had dared utter such blasphemy in his presence.

But he never reached him.

The edges of a dozen swords found him at once.

Blades plunged into his flesh: his ribs, his back, his gut. The pain was immediate, searing, but distant, as though his body had become something separate from himself. More swords followed, hacking, cutting, and stabbing until he could no longer move. He fell to his knees, his vision swimming, the cold bite of iron burning in his flesh.

He exhaled, his breath ragged and heavy.

Then everything went black.

CINIS AWOKE TO the stench of rot.

It filled his nostrils, thick and cloying, the putrid perfume of death pressing into the back of his throat. His body ached, fever searing through his limbs like fire licking at dry timber, but the pain was distant, muted beneath the weight of exhaustion. His fingers twitched against something slick and cold, and as his blurred vision cleared, he found himself staring into a face he recognized.

It was the baker's wife. He had carried her from the Mese himself only days ago, her body wasted and pale, her lips cracked from thirst. Like so many thousands of others, he had laid her on the pile, whispered a prayer, and turned away.

Now she stared back at him with vacant, filmy eyes, her mouth slightly agape, as if caught mid-sentence.

Cinis exhaled sharply, his breath shallow.

He was among them.

As his senses returned in fractured waves, he realized he was lying atop the very bodies he had hauled from the city. They stretched out around him in grotesque stillness, limbs tangled in death, faces frozen in agony or peace. Some he had known in life: men and women he had pulled from abandoned homes, from plague-ridden hovels, from doorsteps where they had collapsed, clutching at their empty stomachs.

He belonged here. This was his home now, among the dead.

The fever in his blood burned like judgment, the weight of his sins pressing down upon him as heavily as the corpses beneath his broken body. This, he thought, was justice.

Belisarius had not been wrong on that score.

The massacre at the Hippodrome, the darkness that swallowed the sun, the famine that had starved an empire, the plague that rotted its people from the inside. He had no answer to any of it but his own existence. He had fought to leave war behind, and yet war had followed him. He had sought sanctuary in the Church, and the sky itself had turned black. He had tried to serve the dying, and in return, death had claimed everything in its path but him.

A wretched laugh rasped from his throat, but it caught in his chest, curling into something closer to a sob.

He pressed his hands against the shifting, bloated mass beneath him and dragged himself forward. The bodies shifted under his weight, rolling like waves beneath his palms. His muscles screamed in protest, the wounds inflicted by Belisarius' men tearing anew, hot and wet. Still, he crawled, grasping, pulling, feeling the dead pull back with their cold, silent grip.

The slope of the pile gave way beneath him, and he tumbled, rolling down the mound of rotting flesh, tumbling past sightless faces and exposed ribs, slipping through the filth and blood until he hit the ground below with a dull, wet thud.

He lay there, chest heaving, his fevered body drenched in the filth of the departed.

He had been a fool.

A fool to think he could find peace, a fool to think Constantinople could be his sanctuary. He had come seeking redemption, and he had delivered to the city only ruin.

The city had refused to give him the peace he craved, and he had repaid it in kind.

He had nothing more to give the city.

And it had nothing left to give him.

Chapter 17 : VANITY OF VANITIES

THE SILENCE BETWEEN them stretched, thick and suffocating. The air in the chamber was still, weighted with the exposed ghosts of words too long buried, secrets too long guarded. Ashe felt raw, the confession of his darkest sins clawing at his insides like something living. It should have been a moment of reckoning, a solemnity shared between two dying men. But instead?

Laughter.

Low at first, a dry rasp from a throat thick with blood. Then stronger, a broken chuckle turning into a full-bodied laugh that echoed through the chamber, bouncing off the cold stone.

Ashe's hands tried and failed to clench into useless fists, simply twitching against his lap. His body refused to move, his spine severed and his legs dead weight beneath him, but his mind was still razor-sharp. He burned with fury, humiliation. Standish had asked, had pushed him to lay bare his greatest failures, and now—

Standish was laughing.

Ashe ground his teeth, biting down against the flood of rage rising in his throat. "What's so funny?" he growled.

Standish wiped at his mouth with the back of his hand, smearing blood across his stubbled chin. He was still grinning, eyes bright with amusement. No, something else. Something triumphant.

"I have spent weeks," Standish said, voice hoarse, "months trying to piece you together. Trying to figure out which one of the deadly sins would be the one to finally unravel the great and terrible Ashe O'Reilly."

His smile widened, feral and cruel.

"As it turns out, I was overcomplicating the question." He coughed, wincing as he pressed a hand to his side. "Greed? No, you hoard things, of course, but only sentimental rubbish. You do not keep just for the sake of keeping."

He began counting on his fingers, ticking off sins one by one.

"Wrath? An obvious contender. But your rage is not wild, not really. It is always focused. Always controlled. Even when you lose control, there is intent behind it."

Standish's gaze flicked toward the bloody remnants of their battle, to the ruined state of his own body, to the way Ashe, paralyzed and broken, still looked like he was waiting for a chance to kill him.

"No," Standish mused. "Not wrath."

He waggled his third and fourth fingers. "Envy? Lust? You've lived long enough to grow past both, I suppose." He exhaled, shaking his head as if disappointed. "Sloth? Well..." He gestured vaguely at Ashe's useless legs, at his ruined form. "The only time I have ever seen you lazy is, well... right now."

Ashe glared. Standish chuckled again, then straightened his shoulders, as if the revelation he was about to bestow was something grand.

"No, no, no. It is Pride." He gave a half-smile, shaking his head in faux amazement. "The sheer hubris of you, Ashe O'Reilly. To imagine yourself as the sole cause of catastrophic events of global proportion... That is some next-level narcissism."

Ashe's jaw locked, but he didn't look away.

Standish continued, voice rich with mockery. "To think that the heavens darkened because of you. That famine, war, plague—all of it was some divine reckoning for your sins. That you, some lowborn soldier with an interesting medical condition, brought ruin upon an empire." He let out a sharp, painful breath. "It is hilarious, Ashe O'Reilly."

Standish raised a brow. "Although I have seen you eat, so we both know Gluttony is a close runner-up."

For some reason, maybe the tension in the situation, the absurdity of it all, the profuse loss of blood, something shifted in Ashe's gut. A crack. A break. Not anger, not fury. Something else entirely.

A laugh bubbled up from deep within his chest, unexpected, unbidden. A bitter, dry sound that rasped against his raw throat.

Standish blinked in surprise, then gave a sharp bark of amusement.

And suddenly, they were laughing.

It was absurd. Completely, utterly absurd.

Here they were, sitting in a half-buried tomb beneath Istanbul, both dying, both exhausted, both knowing neither one would walk out of here whole. Ashe, a man who had lived too long, and Standish, a man who would not live much longer.

Their laughter echoed through the chamber, ragged and sharp-edged. It wasn't the laughter of camaraderie, not exactly. It was the laughter of two men who had been through too much, had bled too much, and had been driven to the same breaking point.

Ashe shook his head, breath still unsteady. "Stop." His voice was hoarse, barely above a whisper. "You'll let go of that clacker and kill half of Constantinople."

Standish smirked, but he settled, slumping against the floor once more.

The moment passed. The laughter died.

"Life is just a few days," mused Standish.

Ashe shook his head. "Life is so many days I lost count a dozen lifetimes ago."

"That's not the only thing you've lost count of, is it?"

"What do you mean?"

Standish strained to raise his head and looked at Ashe. "How many men have you killed?" he asked. "How many women? Children?"

Ashe made no reply. Small consolation that the latter questions could be answered in clear conscience; the answer to the first was exactly what Standish thought it was. Ashe had lost count. He would be hard-pressed to count the number of wars he had fought in for the conquest of lands that would never be seen by the emperor that wanted them, for the capricious whims of a litany of forgotten kings, the fleeting glory of some general. Ashe had once told himself he would only fight for causes he believed in, that he would always find a way to contribute to good rather than evil, but how many times had he been swept along with the tides of history, cemented into the zeitgeist of whatever place he found himself in at the time? Russia was that, surely: that runt of a French emperor was hardly the first Ashe had seen outreach his grasp, though he was the first and only one that Ashe had fought for instead of against. Or was he? Ashe had spent most of the reigns of the bad emperors in some Roman prison or other and strove to build rather than destroy in those early days.

But there was still no shortage of bloodshed. It followed him.

Despite all of that—despite his good intentions, what passed for morals in the ages-old concretion of his beliefs and actions and resultant self-loathing—despite all of that, Ashe knew he had lost count. Or maybe he had never bothered to count at all.

And what about the more recent decades? When the zeitgeist of the time and place supported his vendetta against Ming and the drug empire he was trying to create? Boil it down, and despite all his illusions of fighting for "justice" or protecting the weak, Ashe knew he had gone from principled soldier to nothing more than a vigilante, killing for personal vengeance. And though he had only taken the lives of those who preyed on others (and that, only in open combat, never from the shadows) the fact that came crashing into Ashe was that those battles had brought with them their fair share of collateral damage. He could push that thought away all he wanted, but it was always there waiting, nonetheless.

Standish interrupted Ashe's reverie. "You are—" he coughed, "—an abomination."

Ashe could not find words to disagree.

Standish coughed again, and bright red blood spattered his lips and chin.

"Few days? Seems like your life is just a few minutes, bub."

Standish smiled that creepy Ichabod smile of his. "So, then, Ashe O'Reilly, we will die together."

"Not if you wanna disarm that clacker before you check out."

"So now you want to live."

Ashe stared at the man on the floor. "Sometimes. Not often," he replied.

Silence settled between them again, but now, it was different.

Standish stared back at Ashe, considering him in a new light. His expression was no longer quite as sharp, his voice less venomous when he finally spoke. "You are still vain enough to think it is all about you," he said, voice quiet now. "And you are clearly evil."

"Then kill me already. We both know it's what I deserve."

Standish seemed to want to agree. Instead, he stated, "You are the spawn and creation of evil."

Ashe exhaled slowly. "Creation of evil? Hardly."

Standish scoffed. "Then explain it to me. If you are not some demon, or created by one, what are you?"

Ashe met his gaze, steady now. "I wasn't spawned by evil," he murmured. "Exactly the opposite. I was created—cursed, if you want to call it that—by the only good this world ever had."

Standish's face twitched, a flicker of curiosity there before he masked it.

"Go on," he said, voice quieter now. "I'm listening."

Chapter 18 : THE BEGINNING AND THE END

28 AD

THE ROAD WAS little more than a narrow strip of dirt and loose stones winding along the western banks of the Sea of Galilee. To the east, the land sloped steeply toward the water, where reeds rustled against the lapping tide. To the west, the terrain was uneven: rolling hills scattered with olive trees, their gnarled trunks twisting up toward the dim light of a crescent moon. The scent of the sea mingled with the warm, dry air of summer, carrying with it the distant croaks of frogs and the occasional rustling of unseen creatures moving through the brush.

Appius Aurelius Cinis walked at the head of his quaternion, his short, sturdy frame moving with practiced ease over the uneven ground. The three men behind him—Junius, Marcellus, and Gnaius—were relaxed but alert, their hands resting lightly on the pommels of their gladii, not from any immediate sense of danger but from ingrained habit. They had been stationed in this province for years, long enough to know that while these roads were mostly safe, trouble was never far away.

They were returning to Capernaum from Gennesaret after delivering orders to a small Roman outpost along the coast. It was neither a taxing duty nor an urgent one. The pace was leisurely, and the road ahead was quiet.

Until it wasn't.

A sound split the night. A high, wavering cry: thin, reedy, and panicked. Cinis slowed, frowning. At first, it sounded like a goat caught in a snare. Then the words had formed, shrill and desperate.

"Help! Help me, someone!"

The rest of Cinis' quaternion exchanged glances before he motioned for them to follow.

They moved swiftly, slipping off the road toward the sound. The commotion came from a dry ravine just beyond the bend, where the land dipped away from the road. As they crested the ridge, the scene below became clear.

A corpulent man in rich, sweat-stained robes lay sprawled on the ground, his arms flailing as he struggled to scoot backward with his considerable bulk. His assistant lay a few feet away, moaning as he clutched a bloody gash on his forehead. Three figures surrounded them, lean men in simple tunics, their hands gripping crude but deadly weapons: curved blades and wooden clubs wrapped in iron.

Cinis recognized them for what they were before a word was spoken.

Zealots.

The Fourth Philosophy, as they called themselves, was no mere bandit faction. They were fanatics, men whose hatred for Rome burned like the desert sun, whose mission was not wealth or survival but rebellion. They had no interest in looting; they were not here for the man's silver or gold. They were here to strike at Rome in whatever way they could, to make the empire bleed, even if it was only one tax collector at a time.

The eldest among them, a man with a streaked gray beard and a face lined with sun and hardship, turned at the sound of approaching footsteps. His eyes, dark and burning with purpose, landed on Cinis and his men.

"You'll not stop us," the man said, voice low and even. "Turn back."

The second of the zealots, younger but just as hardened, tightened his grip on his weapon. "You Romans are dogs," he spat. "And we will drive you from our land, as David drove out the Philistines."

Cinis exhaled. He had no direct quarrel with these men. The tax collector, if anything, looked like he would only benefit from a bit of rough handling. But he also knew that if he and his men let this stand, if word spread that a Roman officer had let open rebellion go unchecked, there would be dire consequences. He waved his men forward.

Junius and Marcellus stepped forward, gladii flashing in the moonlight. The two older zealots met them in a quick but brutal clash, steel ringing against steel. But discipline and training won out over passion and zeal, and within moments, the zealots lay dead in the dust, their lifeblood seeping into the pale dirt.

Cinis barely registered their deaths. His attention had fixed on the last of the Zealots.

The boy.

Seventeen, maybe younger. His limbs were wiry, his stance unsure but determined. He gripped his knife before him, his knuckles white, his chest heaving. He had the look of a starved wolf, desperate, determined, but utterly outmatched.

Cinis had seen boys like him before: young men who so believed their cause they believed their rage could make up for inexperience. The kind of boys who threw themselves into battle with nothing but conviction and fire in their hearts, only to be mowed down before they had ever truly lived.

He thought back to his youth, to the first time he had taken a life, his hands trembling over the body of a man who had been fighting for his own home against the will of Rome. He thought of how long it had taken for the trembling in his hands to stop.

Thirty years later, there was no more trembling.

Cinis stepped forward, not raising his blade. He held up an outstretched palm in a placating gesture.

The boy attacked then, rushing at him with a furious cry, his curved blade swinging wild. It was the strike of someone who had never faced a real soldier. Cinis sidestepped the blow, knocking the boy's weapon aside with a quick rap of his empty fist against the back of the boy's hand.

The blade tumbled from the boy's grasp, clattering onto the dirt. He fell to his knees, panting, his hands clenched into fists.

"Go," Cinis told the boy.

The boy's head snapped up, his eyes blazing.

"Get out of here," Cinis repeated, his voice firm but not unkind. "Before you die for nothing."

"Kill him!"

The tax assessor, red-faced and livid, pushed himself up from the dirt. "Kill him, Legionnaire! I demand it!"

Cinis clenched his jaw. The thought of striking the fat bureaucrat across the face was far more appealing than executing a defeated child.

The boy, his face twisted with rage, suddenly reached into his belt.

Another dagger, a smaller one.

Cinis responded out of instinct to the movement even before it was fully executed, before the boy's muscles had finished tensing.

The boy burst from the ground in Cinis' direction.

Cinis' blade slipped easily between the boy's ribs. A clean thrust, precise and practiced, stopping just short of the heart but deep enough to leave no doubt.

The boy gasped, his eyes wide with disbelief.

Cinis caught him as he fell, lowering him to the ground with a care that only a career soldier understood. The boy's breath was ragged, shallow. His fingers clutched weakly at Cinis' tunic, his lips moving soundlessly.

Cinis exhaled. "You should have run."

The boy shuddered once, then lay still.

For a long moment, Cinis did not move.

The tax assessor was still shrieking about his brush with death, still cursing the zealots. He spat upon their fallen bodies, spewing venom about how this land needed to be tamed. Cinis barely heard him.

A taste like ash filled his mouth.

With a weary sigh, he reached down, pried the dagger from the boy's stiffening fingers, and cast it aside on the dusty road.

❧ • ❧

CINIS WALKED TOGETHER with Gaius Milonius toward Capernaum's open market, their sandals kicking up small clouds of dust from the well-worn road. The town was already bustling with activity: the rhythmic creak of carts laden with fresh fish from the sea, the scent of warm bread and salted meats drifting from vendors' stalls, the murmur of traders haggling over goods.

Cinis took little notice of the commotion surrounding them. His mind was elsewhere.

"Thank you for asking, old friend, but no, I did not sleep well last night," he said, his voice low, as if crushed under the press of his words. "That boy, the zealot." He shook his head. "He weighs heavily upon me."

Gaius sighed, folding his arms across his chest as they walked. "It's a shame, Appius. A shame about the boy, a shame about the Zealots altogether. I wish there was a way for this land to know peace, for them to see that we aren't here to harm them." His voice was earnest, but his, too, rode on an undercurrent of frustration. "Rome could do so much for these people: better roads, better aqueducts, protection from bandits. And yet, they refuse to see it."

Cinis exhaled through his nose, glancing at the man. "Not everyone has your perspective, Gaius." His tone was not unkind, but there was an edge of weary realism to it. "The Jews of Capernaum like you because you built them a temple. Not every town in Judaea is as fond of their prefect."

Gaius chuckled dryly. "Perhaps not. But that doesn't mean I cannot hope."

The two men walked in silence for a few moments, the sounds of the town filling the gaps between words. Cinis glanced around at the bustling streets, the low stone buildings with their shaded courtyards, the olive trees rustling in the breeze. Capernaum was a town of fishermen and tradesmen, a place where life, despite the tensions of Roman occupation, carried on with a certain resilience. It was not like Jerusalem, where rebellion bubbled beneath the surface, nor like Caesarea, where Rome's grip was heavy and unyielding. Here, one could see an uneasy truce of sorts.

Cinis turned to Gaius. "It's unusual to see you walking to market yourself. Where is your manservant, Irenaeus?"

Gaius' expression darkened, the humor draining from his face. "Irenaeus is very ill," he said quietly. "Paralyzed. He grows weaker by the day. I don't think he has much time left."

Cinis frowned. He had known Irenaeus for years: an old Greek, loyal and diligent, always at Gaius' side, overseeing his household with quiet efficiency. "I'm sorry, Gaius," he said sincerely. "He has served you well."

Gaius nodded, his jaw rigid. "Yes. And now I can do nothing but watch as he slips away."

There was no response Cinis could make. He had seen death in every form, but that never seemed to lessen in its cruelty. And to waste away slowly? That was not a thought a man like Cinis even wanted to contemplate.

After a lengthy pause, he changed the subject. "I'll be leaving Capernaum for Tiberius today. A short diversion for a few days. Herod Antipas has called for a consultation on a water project; he wishes to divert waters from the springs northward to a new bathhouse."

Gaius gave a short laugh. "A Roman engineer's work is never done."

Cinis smirked. "Apparently not. But I'll look forward to dining with you when I return."

As they turned a corner into the market, the air shifted. The smell of fresh produce and salted fish was overshadowed by the acrid scent of sweat and perfume: an unmistakable sign of a man who used wealth as a shield against filth.

Ahead of them, a familiar voice cut through the hum of morning commerce.

"Do you know who I am?"

Cinis knew at once, even if the target of the man's ire did not. The tax assessor.

The corpulent bureaucrat stood in the middle of the street, his thick fingers wadded into the front of a merchant's tunic, shaking the man like a misbehaving child. The merchant, a thin, graying man, looked down, his lips pressed together in silent suffering.

"You think you can withhold from me?" the assessor spat, his jowls quivering with rage. "I represent Rome, you wretch! Do you want to see your stall burned to the ground? Your grain confiscated? Your sons taken into slavery as collateral?"

A small crowd had gathered, but no one dared to intervene.

Cinis and Gaius slowed their steps, both watching the scene unfold with unreadable expressions.

The merchant, voice barely above a whisper, said, "I have paid what was owed. My family—"

The tax assessor roared. Gone was his goat-like shriek from the night before. "You owe more! The grain tax has been reassessed; I have increased your obligation in accordance. Be grateful I do not demand double!"

The merchant swallowed hard, his hands trembling as he reached into the folds of his tunic, pulling out a small pouch of coins. The assessor snatched it greedily, weighing it in his palm before tucking it into his robes. He shoved the hapless merchant away.

Cinis exhaled through his nose. He had no love for the Zealots, but standing there, watching the exchange, he understood how they had come to exist.

Gaius' face was impassive, but Cinis could sense the tension in his jaw, the way his fingers curled slightly at his side. But they did nothing. They could do nothing.

Cinis and Gaius turned and walked on.

After another long silence, Cinis muttered, almost to himself, "Rome is supposed to light the darkness of the world."

Gaius sighed. "It still can."

Cinis looked around the market of Capernaum, at the streets lined with merchants trying to survive under the ever-increasing weight of taxation, at the hungry faces of children clinging to their mothers' robes, at the fat goat-man waddling away with his ill-gotten wealth.

"I used to believe that, Gaius," Cinis responded quietly. He was unsure if he had changed, or if the Empire itself had. But where he had once seen justice, order, and governance, he now saw only corruption and oppression.

⁂

CINIS AWOKE WITH a start, his breath sharp and uneven in the cool pre-dawn air. Sweat slicked his back, dampening the rough linen of his tunic, though the morning carried a lingering chill. He sat up abruptly, rubbing a hand across his face as his heart thudded dully in his chest.

The boy's face had haunted him in his sleep again. Every night for nearly a week, he had seen those burning eyes, filled with reckless defiance, only to watch them dim as his blade found its mark and the boy's blood poured from his body like a punctured wineskin.

With a weary sigh, he swung his legs off his cot, his feet meeting the packed dirt of his tent floor. He reached for his tunic and belt, his movements slow but efficient, dressing in silence. The camp outside was already stirring: legionnaires tending to morning duties, the low murmur of idle conversation, the clatter of weapons being inspected and straps being fastened. Cinis could have chosen to sleep in comfort within the walls of Capernaum, but he would not—could not—leave his men behind while he lay on a feathered bed.

Still troubled by the dream, he pulled on his boots and strode out into the open air. The dawn painted the sky in soft hues of orange and violet, the first light of morning creeping over the distant hills. But to Cinis, it was just another day, another cycle of duty. With a shake of his head, he made his way toward the city, seeking breakfast and (if he was honest with himself) some companionship to distract him from the boy's ghost and the sleepless nights it caused.

The streets of Capernaum were already bustling by the time he arrived at Gaius Milonius' villa. The smell of baking bread and salted fish carried on the air, mingling with the sharper tang of the sea. The town was waking, merchants setting up their stalls, fishermen hauling in their morning catch, children darting through alleyways.

Cinis knocked on the heavy wooden door of the villa and waited. The latch clicked, and to his surprise, the door was opened not by some young house servant but by Irenaeus himself.

The man who had been at death's door only days before stood before him, healthy, whole, and looking as spry as a man half his age. His eyes were clear, his skin was not pallid with sickness, and he moved with a vitality that defied everything Cinis knew about the progression of disease.

Cinis frowned. "Irenaeus?"

The servant smiled and inclined his head. "Master builder. It is good to see you again."

Cinis hesitated. "You were—" He caught himself, glancing past the man into the villa. "I was told you were near death."

Irenaeus chuckled, stepping aside to let Cinis enter. "That was true then; it is not today. My master will explain. I must see to your repast."

Cinis stepped into the atrium, where the scent of roasted meat and fresh bread filled the air. Gaius Milonius sat at a modest table, already breaking his fast, and he grinned as Cinis approached.

"Appius! Just in time. Come, sit, eat."

Cinis lowered himself onto the cushioned bench, but his mind was still on Irenaeus. The man had retreated to another chamber, but his presence lingered like an unspoken question.

Cinis turned to Gaius, cutting to the heart of the matter. "Your servant. I saw him with my own eyes before I left. He was dying."

Gaius smiled, his expression full of wonder. "He was."

Cinis frowned. "And now he is not. Mind me, I am grateful for the circumstance, but..."

Gaius leaned forward, setting down his cup of wine. "While you were in Tiberias, a man came through Capernaum. A teacher, a healer. His name is Jesus of Nazareth."

Cinis gave a slow nod, considering. He had heard whispers of the name before, murmured in Judean markets and spoken with reverence among the common people.

Gaius continued, "I went to him. I had heard stories—wild stories, mind you—that he had healed the sick with only a word, that he cast out demons, that he commanded disease itself to depart."

Cinis arched a skeptical brow, but Gaius pressed on, his voice steady, certain. "I told him of Irenaeus, told him that my servant was at the brink of death. I asked him to heal him, but do you know what he said?"

Cinis shook his head.

"He said, 'I will come and heal him.' But I felt odd. I told him I was not worthy to have him under my roof. I asked him only say the word, and I knew Irenaeus would be healed.'"

Cinis remained silent, unsure how to respond to the sincerity, the conviction in Gaius' voice. His old friend continued.

"And when I returned home, Irenaeus was already standing. Whole. Healed." Gaius spread his hands, eyes wide as if seeing it again for the first time. "The fever was gone. The paralysis had left him. He was as you saw him just now: stronger than ever."

Cinis leaned back, thoughtful. He had no love for superstition, no patience for whispered miracles. But Gaius had seen this with his own eyes.

Gaius studied him. "You're quiet."

Cinis exhaled, staring into his cup. He took a deep draught of the cool wine before speaking. "Maybe that's exactly what's needed."

Gaius tilted his head. "What do you mean?"

"A man willing to show compassion," Cinis said. "A man who doesn't care if the sick are Jew or Roman, rich or poor." He met Gaius' gaze. "Maybe if men like this Jesus were more common, there wouldn't be so much needless strife."

Gaius smiled, shaking his head in wonder. "You have always been a man of war, Cinis. It is amazing, this change that has come over you. Perhaps a miracle itself! What was the cause?"

Cinis exhaled, tracing a hand along the rim of his cup, smearing a purple-red drop around the endless circle. "You and I, Gaius... we have served Rome from our youth. Once, I believed in the order, the discipline, the greatness of the Empire. But now?" He shook his head. "Now, thirty years on, the wars just flow into one another like liquid. Every campaign, every rebellion, every conquest... it all comes to the same cycle. Expansion, resistance, suppression, unrest... and another war."

He sighed. "I once thought I was building something that would last. Now, I wonder if I've only built graves."

Gaius was silent for a long moment.

Finally, he reached for the wine, steadied Cinis' hand, and refilled his cup.

"Well then," Gaius said, a small smile tugging at the corner of his mouth. "Let's drink to something that lasts."

Cinis picked up the cup and drank with his friend. He didn't believe in miracles. But for the first time in years, he wanted to.

After a breakfast the likes of which he'd not get in camp with his men, Cinis left Gaius' home and stepped out onto the sunlit street, his thoughts still pondering the conversation they had shared. The warm breeze carried the rising murmur of the waking city. The streets of Capernaum stirred with morning activity: merchants arranging their goods, fishermen hauling in their catch, traders calling out prices as the new day began. As the cycle continued.

His mind was restless. The name Jesus of Nazareth repeated itself in his thoughts like an insistent drumbeat. The story of Gaius' servant should have been dismissed outright as fable or coincidence, and yet, Cinis had seen the truth with his own eyes. A man dying one day, restored to full strength the next. It made no sense.

He turned a corner at the end of the street, walking with the deliberate and distant pace of a man deep in thought, when he collided with someone.

Cinis felt it before he saw it: a solid, sudden impact, quick footsteps stumbling backward, the rush of displaced air between them. His gaze snapped down, locking onto the face of a young man, dark-haired, sharp-eyed, gaunt but alive.

His breath stopped.

It was him.

The boy.

The one he had killed.

Alive. Whole.

Cinis' stomach lurched violently, his entire body tensing as the weight of what he saw crashed down on him like a blow. Recognition flared in the boy's eyes as well—eyes widening in fear, in shock.

The boy bolted.

Cinis was moving before he could think, his instincts acting on their own, demanding he give chase. He had to understand.

He pursued the boy down the street, past startled onlookers, his boots slamming against the packed earth.

"Wait!" Cinis called, but the boy ran like a man who had escaped death and no intent to let it catch him again.

They barreled into the marketplace, where the foot traffic was already thick, and the smell of fresh fish and crushed herbs mixed with the earthy scent of livestock and packed bodies. The boy twisted between stalls, knocking over a basket of pomegranates in his desperation.

Cinis was faster, his skill at seeing pathways and openings honed by long years of combat. He cut through the chaos, catching glimpses of the boy weaving through the crowd. He lunged, reaching—

The boy slammed into a merchant's cart, overturning it in a loud crash of splintering wood and rolling vegetables. Cinis was upon him in an instant, grabbing his tunic.

"Wait!" Cinis barked, holding tight even as the boy scrabbled to escape. "I'll not hurt you!"

A woman's voice cut through the confusion, sharp and trembling.

"Oded? Oded, what are you doing?"

Cinis turned his head toward the source of the voice.

An old woman, frail but upright, stood at the edge of the commotion. Her worn hands clutched at her chest as she hurried forward, her dark eyes wild with panic. She reached for the boy—Oded—pulling at him, shielding him, striving to press herself between the boy and the Roman soldier who had seized him.

She wailed, loud and broken, her voice shaking with grief that had not yet healed. "Please! Please do not kill my only son again! I have already lost him once, and the Master is not here to give him back to me a second time! Please!"

Cinis stood frozen, still gripping the boy's tunic, though he could feel the strength fading from his grip.

The Master?

Oded turned then, pressing his hands against his mother's back as though he were the one protecting her. His breath was ragged from the chase, but when he spoke, his voice was steady. "I have abandoned the way of the Zealots," he said. "I swear it. I am no threat to you."

Cinis' grip loosened. His mind was stumbling over itself in a tangle of disbelief. "I don't want to hurt you," he said, his voice quieter now. "I only want to understand. How is it that you are alive?"

The widow turned to him, her sorrow-filled face shining with something between fear and reverence. "He was brought home to me in Nain," she said. "They carried his body—my son's body—and I followed, wailing, mourning the only child I had. Everyone in the city was there. They had come to bury him."

Her fingers trembled where they clutched Oded's tunic. She shook with the fear that she might lose him again.

"But then," she whispered, "Jesus of Nazareth came."

The name struck Cinis like a hammer.

The widow's voice was thick with emotion. "The crowd just... parted. Like the Red Sea. He walked through them, through all of us, until he stood before my son's coffin. And then—" her voice caught, her fingers tightening over Oded's arms, "—he said, 'Young man, I say to you, arise.'"

Cinis' throat felt dry as dust. He looked to the boy.

Oded swallowed hard. "I opened my eyes, and I was... alive. Whole."

Cinis could barely breathe. He had killed this boy. Had watched him die, had seen the life leave his body as he lay in the dust of the road. Yet here he was.

The widow wiped at her eyes with her sleeve and looked up at Cinis with disbelief. "How have you not heard about this?" she asked. "The report has spread through all of Judea!"

Cinis had no words.

He had spent his whole life shaping the world with his own hands: building roads and fortifications, sieging cities to tear them down, rebuilding them in victory from wood and stone and iron. That order of things suddenly meant nothing. Who can raise the dead so they walked again?

The old woman grasped Oded's hand and began to pull him away, casting one last wary glance at the Roman soldier who had once struck her son down.

Cinis let them go. He watched as they disappeared into the crowd, the murmurs of the market swallowing them up. He did not pursue them, did not call out.

Instead, he stood in the Capernaum street, lost in the mazes of his own mind.

For the first time in years, Cinis knew that he must seek something other than Rome's glory.

He had to find Jesus of Nazareth.

Chapter 19 : CHASING THE NAZARENE

28 AD

A MONTH LATER, Cinis' duties led him back through Capernaum. The thick air in the marketplace carried the mingled scents of fresh bread, dried fish, and the sharp tang of citrus fruit. The streets bustled with merchants and traders, voices raised in bartering and haggling as they competed to be heard one over the other. The noise formed a familiar backdrop of life and routine for Cinis. He had not intended to linger long in the market; he had come only to purchase some bread and dried figs before departing the city. But as he turned a corner near the pottery stalls, the familiar sound of grumbling reached his ears.

Pharisees.

A small group of them huddled near a spice vendor's stall, their arms crossed over their flowing robes, their expressions dark with irritation. Though their words were hushed, their intensity made them stand out amidst the ordinary market chatter.

Cinis slowed his pace, pausing near a display of woven baskets, casually examining them as he listened.

"...a blasphemer, I tell you."

"A deceiver."

"He corrupts the people—"

Cinis put on his best law-enforcer smile and approached. "Is there a problem, friends?"

The Pharisees turned sharply, their gazes landing on him with varying degrees of suspicion and disdain.

One of them, a thin man with a sharp nose and deep-set eyes, sneered. "A Roman has no business in the matters of the faithful."

Cinis shrugged. "Probably not. But then, you're discussing this in the middle of a marketplace, loud enough for that deaf beggar to overhear." To Cinis' surprise, the beggar's eyes flicked in his direction before looking away. "If you wanted to keep it between yourselves, perhaps a quieter setting might suit you better."

The group bristled, but before any could rebuke him further, one of their number, a slightly older man with graying hair, tilted his head. "Wait... I know you. You're the friend of Centurion Milonius."

Cinis inclined his head slightly. "I am."

The older Pharisee stroked his beard. "Milonius built the synagogue here."

Cinis offered a dry smile. "So I'm told."

The other Pharisees seemed to relax, if only marginally. Cinis pressed his advantage. "Tell me, then, what distresses you so?"

The sharp-nosed man scoffed. "An upstart, a blasphemer, that's what! Stirring the people with lies and false teachings."

Cinis frowned, pretending ignorance. "And who might this upstart and blasphemer be?"

They all spoke at once. "The Nazarene."

Cinis crossed his arms, tilting his head slightly. "I was hoping for a name. By 'Nazarene,' do you mean Jesus of Nazareth?"

The sharp-nosed Pharisee scowled. "Do not speak his name near us. He is not a teacher of the Law. He is a false teacher, misleading the people, turning them against the traditions of our fathers!"

Cinis scratched his chin. "Interesting. How did one man upend generations of your revered traditions? What exactly did he do?"

The shortest and roundest of the Pharisees snorted, brushing his deep bluish robe away from his rotund stomach. Cinis thought he looked like a sour grape. "What didn't he do?" the man demanded. "He was in a house in the low quarter just the other day, blaspheming openly, spreading lies."

Cinis lifted an eyebrow at the man. "And what lies were those?"

The group hesitated.

"Well, we didn't hear it ourselves," one admitted.

Cinis bit the inside of his cheek and managed not to grin. "Ah. So, you weren't actually there."

"We were told what he said," another Pharisee interjected quickly. "He spoke from the prophets, but falsely."

Cinis nodded slowly. "And what exactly did he say that was false?"

The Pharisees exchanged glances.

"Well... we don't have proof it was false, but—"

Cinis rubbed the bridge of his nose. "So, you don't know what he taught, and you don't have proof that what he taught was false."

The sharp-nosed Pharisee cleared his throat, his irritation growing. "That's beside the point! It's what happened after that was the real offense!"

"Oh, good. I am eager to hear. What happened after?"

The older Pharisee sighed heavily, as though the memory itself pained him. "Some men—fools, all of them—tore open the roof of the house he was in and lowered a crippled man down to him."

Cinis blinked. "They did what?"

"Tore. Open. The. Roof." The Pharisee enunciated each word with indignation. "Can you imagine the damage? The destruction?"

"And this was... your house?"

The Pharisee reared back in indignation that he would dwell in that quarter of the city. "My house? Of course not."

"I see. So, then the owner of the house is the one who complained of the damage."

The Pharisee looked at his feet, then back to Cinis. "No, I don't know that there was a complaint made. But that is not the point!"

Cinis waved a hand. "Right, right. Of course. I completely understand. But then what happened?"

The older Pharisee's scowl deepened. "He stopped his false teachings long enough to tell the crippled man that his sins were forgiven. He spoke as if he had the power to do so!"

Cinis stared at him for a moment. "And that upsets you?"

"Of course it upsets us!"

Cinis raised a hand. "Um. Forgive me. You are saying that your chief complaint is that he forgave someone."

"No! That's not—"

"And after that?"

Another Pharisee, clearly agitated, spoke up. "He claimed to have the authority of God Himself to heal the man's legs!"

Cinis folded his arms. "And did he?"

"No! Of course not! No man could have such authority—"

"I mean, did he heal his legs?"

The Pharisees stopped.

Cinis arched a brow. "Was the man healed?" he repeated.

The older Pharisee's lips pressed into a thin line. "Well... yes. He stood up and walked."

Cinis stared at them. "So... let me see if I fully comprehend the magnitude of this crime. A man spoke in a private residence, quoting your own prophets. You don't know what he said, nor do you know if it was false. If it were from your prophets, we can only hope that it would not have been false. But you know it had to have been false, because he is a false teacher. Then, when the roof was opened, causing no complaint by the homeowner, and a crippled man was brought before him, he said something you didn't like, and then healed the lame man."

The Pharisees fell silent.

Cinis spread his hands. "Now, I understand."

The sharp-nosed Pharisee bristled. "He is a false teacher."

"But what he taught wasn't false."

"That's not—"

Cinis continued, feigning confusion. "So, he was only false in what he did?"

"Yes!" The man's eyes lit up, as if he had won the argument.

Cinis nodded gravely. "And what he did... was heal a crippled man." He let the words settle before adding, "Sounds horrible. He perpetrated a similar crime on the servant of my friend, Gaius Milonius."

The Pharisees stood frozen, glaring at him wide-eyed like fish, their mouths opening but no words coming forth.

❧ • ❧

AND SO, AS the Nazarene traveled across Israel and Samaria, growing in both fame and notoriety, leading Jewish and Roman authorities alike in a merry chase, Cinis undertook his pursuit of the man, such as his duties would allow.

He had no orders to seek Jesus of Nazareth. No mission, no edict from Rome, no command from a superior officer. And yet, when his work was done, when he had marked out plans for aqueducts and fortifications, when his hands had shaped the foundations of new buildings, he found himself listening.

Listening to the murmurs in the streets. Listening to the fishermen in the taverns, the traders on the road, the women at the wells. His name surfaced everywhere now: Jesus of Nazareth, the healer, the rabbi, the miracle worker. And always, there was something else in their voices when they spoke of him. Some strange mixture of hope and division, of wonder and fear.

Appius Aurelius Cinis was thankful many nights that his duties to the empire leaned heavily toward the architectural, to the building of things rather than the taking of lives. Of his two skills, he would far rather create than destroy.

And yet, the dreams continued.

And yet, the void within him grew.

Three months had passed since Cinis had walked the markets of Capernaum, verbally tying the Pharisees into knots over their grievances against the Nazarene. Now, he stood on a windswept hill in Gadara, a city of Syria, surveying the land beneath the heavy, unforgiving sun.

Before him stretched the vast countryside that rolled down toward the Sea of Galilee, a rugged landscape dotted with dry grass and scattered groves. His mission here had nothing to do with Jesus of Nazareth, nothing to do with men performing miracles or forgiving sins. No, he was here at the behest of Herod Antipas, consulting on an ambitious infrastructure project, a vast network of aqueduct tunnels that would bring fresh water to the cities of the Decapolis.

Cinis had spent weeks drafting plans, walking the hills, and marking potential shafts that would cut deep into the rock. The aqueduct system he envisioned would be one of the most significant engineering feats of his career: almost a hundred miles of tunnels, connecting Gadara and surrounding cities to natural springs in southern Syria. The aqueduct would maintain a decline of a foot per mile, supplying a vastly improved water supply to the region. He had even envisioned the construction of an artificial lake, a reservoir that would ensure a steady supply even in the driest seasons. It was a bold plan, requiring thousands of access shafts to be cut into the rock, an undertaking that would take decades to complete. He knew he would not live to see its final stone set.

Of course, it was an audacious plan. A bold one. And knowing the fickle nature of kings, he strongly suspected that Herod would never approve it.

Still, the work was good. It kept his mind occupied. And for a man who had spent years tearing things down, building something—anything—was a comfort.

Herod was hesitant, of course. The expense was staggering, and Cinis could see the doubt in the man's eyes when they met to discuss it. For now, all Cinis could do was continue the surveys and prime the pump for what could be one of the greatest engineering feats of his career.

And, in the meantime, he had to feed his men.

Cinis had been told that a local pig herder had some of the finest swine in the region: enough to feed a construction crew for weeks. And so, after finishing his survey of the heights, he sought out the man.

He found him standing outside a small stone house, glaring into the distance as though the horizon itself had wronged him. He was a wiry man, sunbaked, with a face that looked as though it had been permanently twisted into an expression of exasperation.

Cinis approached, offering the usual pleasantries, and got straight to the point.

"I was told you had pigs," Cinis said. "That the hills here would be teeming with them. And yet—" he gestured around at the conspicuous absence of swine, "you have no pigs."

The pig farmer scowled and threw his hands in the air. "I *had* pigs!" he exclaimed. "Hundreds of them! The finest, fattest swine this side of the Sea! Dozens of them were prize winners!"

Cinis blinked. "I'm... not sure I want to know what kind of competition you have around here that can be won by a hog."

The man threw up his hands again. "Oh, sure! Mock the poor pig farmer! As if my life isn't already a living disaster!"

Cinis rubbed the bridge of his nose, already regretting this conversation. "Look," he said, voice steady, "where—where are the pigs now?"

The man looked at him, aghast. "Weren't you listening?! They're in the Sea!"

Cinis looked to his men. His men looked back at him. They had heard no mention of the Sea being their location, either.

"...The Sea?"

"Yes, the Sea!" The pig farmer gestured wildly toward the distant water, as if expecting Cinis to see hundreds of drowned pigs bobbing on the waves like so many corks.

Cinis folded his arms. "How, exactly, does an entire herd of pigs end up in the Sea?"

The pig farmer sighed dramatically, as though he had been forced to tell this tragic tale far too many times already.

"It was Jesus!" he wailed.

Cinis straightened slightly at the name. "Jesus of Nazareth?"

"Yes! What other Jesus is there?"

"I'm told it is a fairly common name in some parts."

"Well, what other Jesus throws pigs into the Sea?"

Cinis was clearly not keeping up. "He... threw your pigs into the Sea. Jesus did."

The man gestured wildly again, as if the very sound of the name made him relive the disaster. "No! He came here. He encountered Legion!"

Cinis exchanged another look with his men before turning back to the farmer. "...And you have encountered the Legion, as well, have you not?"

"No, no, not you!" the pig farmer practically shrieked. "Not *the* Legion! *The* Legion!" The man shook his head, almost as if he was starting to understand how little sense he was making. He shrugged the feeling off.

"Legion," he said, simply.

Cinis remained baffled. "Yes, I heard you. Legion, but not *the* Legion. Not me. What is Legion?"

The pig farmer took a deep breath, clearly offended that Cinis did not already know every detail of his misfortune.

"Legion? Legion was a man!" he declared. "A madman! He had been out of his mind for weeks—no, months! The people of the town tried everything to stop him. They bound him in ropes, in chains, but he tore through them like they were nothing! He lived up there—" the farmer pointed toward the craggy hills, "—in the tombs, among the dead!"

Cinis looked off in the direction indicated by the man's crooked finger. A white bunny hopped among the rocks at the mouth of a small opening in the rock face.

Cinis looked back at the farmer. He arched a brow. "And this Legion chased off your pigs?"

"No!" the pig farmer's voice cracked. "You're not hearing me!" He took a deep breath, trying to summon from an inner store of patience before continuing. "Jesus came. And when he saw Legion, he called the demons out of him. Out of Legion. There were probably thousands of demons in that man!"

Cinis had no immediate response to that.

"Get it? Thousands of demons? Legion." It was a statement of fact.

The pig farmer, caught in the throes of his tragic retelling, did not seem to notice Cinis' stunned silence. He continued at a rattling pace.

"The demons begged Jesus, pleaded with him not to cast them into the abyss." The man wiped his brow as though he were reliving the horror firsthand. "And so, he sent them into my pigs."

There was another long silence.

"My pigs!"

Cinis stared at the man. His men stared at the man. The man stared back.

Finally, one of Cinis' soldiers, Junius, cleared his throat. "And... the pigs?"

The farmer threw his hands into the air. "They ran into the Sea! Every last one of them, to get away from the demons!"

Cinis exhaled. "So let me summarize." He pinched the bridge of his nose and took a deep breath. "Jesus cast the demons out of a possessed man."

"Yes."

"The demons asked to be sent into your pigs."

"Yes!"

"The pigs then ran into the Sea."

"Yes! You're finally listening!"

Cinis was silent for a long moment.

Then he heaved a sigh.

"...Well," he said. "That's unfortunate."

The pig farmer let out a wail of frustration, throwing up his arms again. "You think?!"

The man continued for some time, lamenting the tragic loss of his beloved hogs, but Cinis had stopped listening.

There was only one thought in his mind now.

Jesus cast out demons.

EIGHTEEN MONTHS HAD passed since Cinis had stood on a windy hillside in Gadara, listening to a pig farmer wail about a Nazarene who had driven an entire herd of swine into the sea.

Eighteen months since Cinis had made listening his first priority.

And what he had heard since that day had changed him.

It had started with a woman.

Cinis had been in a crowded street in a bustling Galilean town, no different from a hundred other towns he had passed through in his years of service. Merchants had called out their wares, children had darted between stalls, but over it all, the name of Jesus had been whispered from person to person like a flame catching on dry reeds.

A woman had been there, speaking animatedly to a small gathering, her hands trembling—not with fear, but with awe. Cinis had stepped closer, listening. She had been healed, she said. Healed with a touch.

Not the touch of Jesus himself. No, *she* had touched *him*. Touched his garments, nothing more. And in that instant, after twelve years of affliction—an affliction she had only vaguely alluded to, though from her hesitation and the knowing murmurs of the women surrounding her, Cinis understood it had been... well, something womanly—she had been restored.

Cinis had looked at her, standing there, strong and vibrant, speaking with fervor. And he had believed her.

But what had struck him most was what she had said next.

"I was in a great crowd," she had told them, her voice thick with reverence. "Hundreds pressed around him, all jostling, all reaching. And yet, he knew." She swallowed hard. "He knew that I had touched him. And when he turned, and his eyes met mine... it was as if there was no one else in all the world."

The weight of her words had settled somehow in Cinis' chest, an ache he could not name.

That same day, Cinis had heard another story, one about a ruler in the local synagogue named Jairus. The details had been far harder to track, lost in the frenzy of conflicting reports. Some said the man's daughter had been sick. Others said she had already died. Still others claimed that she had merely appeared dead, that perhaps the Nazarene had known some hidden trick of medicine.

The one thing they all agreed upon was this: Jesus had gone to the official's house.

And when he had left, the girl had walked out behind him. She had been well and walking, munching on a piece of bread—though others said it was fruit. Whatever the details were, Jairus and the girl had been charged to not noise the miracle about. So of course, they had immediately done so.

The same pattern had been repeated over and over. Jesus would do something impossible: raise the dead, restore sight to the blind, command the sick to stand and walk as though their bones had never known suffering.

And then, he would insist they tell no one.

But they did.

Of course they did. How could they not?

Cinis had followed these accounts, walking in their wake, hearing them from those who had lived them.

A leper, who had been untouchable one day, clean and whole the next.

A child, who had been cast into fire by the demons that plagued him, made well with only a word.

A blind beggar, whose first sight was of the sky, clear and endless, and the face of the man who had restored him.

And they had all been charged not to speak.

But they could not stop.

Cinis could not blame them. If it had been him… he would not have stopped either.

The miracles had grown in scale.

For a time, it had seemed to Cinis that the Nazarene's compassion had been directed toward the individual. A single man or woman, plucked from the masses, restored with a word, with a touch.

But then… Then there had been the feeding of five thousand.

Not one man. Not ten. Not a hundred.

Five thousand.

And that was only the men.

He had fed them all with five loaves. Five loaves and two dried fish.

Cinis had heard the report from dozens of eyewitnesses. They had been there. They had seen the meager meal multiply in his hands. They had eaten, and eaten, and eaten, and when all were satisfied, baskets of bread had remained.

And then he had done it again.

Another place. Another crowd. Thousands more fed by what amounted to nothing.

Cinis had tried, tried desperately, to track these events in some orderly manner. He had met too many people, heard too many stories. The events all tumbled over each other in frantic, fervent detail. The facts blurred at times, the accounts slightly at odds. But through the cloud of disorder, two truths emerged.

First, everything Jesus did angered someone.

Most often, it was his own people. The Pharisees. The priests. The ones who called themselves keepers of the Law. Every time Jesus opened his mouth, every time he laid his hands on the suffering, they were there, watching, condemning.

Why?

Cinis could not understand it.

The Nazarene had done nothing to challenge Roman authority, had raised no army, had given no commands to drive out the legions. And yet, every town, every village, every city, the religious leaders whispered and plotted, muttering of blasphemy, heresy, and threats. It was madness. What kind of man would see the crippled walk, the blind regain sight, the dead return to life, and call it evil? But that was what they did, and Cinis could not fathom it.

Second, Cinis knew that he could not stop until he had found Jesus himself.

Every step he took, every new town, every conversation... he was chasing the man's shadow.

He had followed reports across the breadth of Judea and Galilee, over the hills of Samaria, throughout the cities of Syria. He had heard the name from beggars and nobles, from merchants and fishermen, from Roman officials and temple servants alike.

But he had never found him, never spoken to him.

Cinis had no idea what he would say if he did find the man.

He did not even know what question he wanted to ask.

He only knew that he must ask it.

Chapter 20 : THE MAN ON THE CROSS

30 AD

JERUSALEM NEVER SLEPT.

Even in the depths of the night, the city pulsed with life beneath the cool silver glow of the moon. The narrow streets twisted like veins, lined with stone buildings that bore the weight of centuries. Torches flickered along the walls of the great Temple, casting long shadows over its towering pillars and high courts. The scent of burning oil and perfumed incense drifted from the upper quarters, where the wealthy reclined in their cool courtyards, insulated from the dust and turmoil below.

But Cinis had little interest in the comforts of the privileged.

He was here in service to Rome, overseeing the repair of the water system commissioned by the prefect. Jerusalem's streets were choked with people, its growth unchecked, and its aqueducts, though impressive, strained under the weight of the population. Cinis had been sent to inspect the latest expansions, to survey new routes, and to consult on a project that could modernize the city's crumbling infrastructure.

But tonight, he was not thinking of Rome's future.

Tonight, as he walked through the winding streets, past the towering walls and bustling alleys, his mind was once again consumed by the man he had never met: Jesus of Nazareth.

The reports of his miracles had only grown in the past weeks: a blind man healed in Jerusalem, a man raised from the tomb: four days dead, restored to life.

And always, the mounting fury of the priests.

The tensions in the city were high. The Passover of the Jews was at hand, and Cinis had seen the shift in the air, the quiet way people spoke in whispers, the watchful eyes of Pharisees gathering in corners. Rome had its own watchful eyes, its spies listening in the Temple courts. There had been talk of something brewing, of plots forming in the shadows.

He had been preparing to return to camp for the night when he heard the commotion.

Cinis slowed his steps as the noise filtered through the streets: the heavy clank of armor, the murmurs of men speaking in hushed but urgent tones. As he turned a corner, the flickering glow of torches and lanterns illuminated a detachment of Roman soldiers mixed with temple officers, their faces set in grim determination.

"We are seeking Jesus of Nazareth," said the leader of the group loudly to penetrate the din.

Cinis' breath caught. He was not alone, for the noise of the crowd faded to nothing.

And then, a single voice, calm, clear, without fear.

"I am he."

Cinis' gaze snapped forward, his pulse pounding.

At the edge of a small garden, near an olive grove, stood a man.

He was unremarkable in appearance, dressed in the same simple garments as those around him. Yet something about him, something indefinable, drew the eye. He stood with an air of absolute calm, his presence like a still lake amidst a storm.

Cinis had spent his entire life among soldiers, men who had faced death and war. He had seen warriors stand unflinching before executioners, men fight to the last breath in hopeless battles. But this was different.

Jesus had no posture of resistance. He didn't cast his gaze about in search of an escape route. He merely stood.

Unnerved by this, the temple officers moved forward hesitantly, as if some unseen force held them back.

Cinis' heart pounded. He had imagined a hundred different ways this moment might happen: meeting Jesus in some village, watching him heal another cripple, perhaps even speaking to him as Gaius had. But not this. He'd never imagined a scenario like this. Not here, in the middle of the night, under the flickering torchlight of an arresting mob.

Then, chaos.

A sudden flash of silver: a sword drawn.

One of the men with Jesus—a fisherman, from the look of him, wild-eyed, tense—lunged forward with a cry, his blade swinging fast and finding flesh.

A yelp of pain.

A man staggered back, clutching at his head. Blood poured between his fingers.

The man's ear was gone.

The garden erupted into movement, the soldiers readying their weapons, the officers lunging to subdue the attack.

Cinis moved forward on instinct, his hand falling to the hilt of his sword, though he did not yet draw. His mind was racing. Jesus' followers were armed? Would this be a fight? Had Rome been wrong about him all along?

But then that voice spoke again. Calm. Unshaken.

"Peter, put your sword into its sheath."

The fisherman froze. Tension hung in the air like a blade poised to strike. No one on either side seemed to know what to make of the command.

Jesus stepped forward, his gaze falling on the wounded man: the one who had been struck. His breath came in panicked gasps, his hand still pressed to the place where his ear had been.

Jesus reached out.

And just like that, the blood stopped.

Cinis had no words for what he saw. One moment, there was an open wound, and the next, there was none. A full ear. No pain. No scar.

The soldiers around Cinis hesitated; even they had seen. And like Cinis, they had no explanation for what had just happened.

Jesus could have simply walked away at that point, so dumbfounded was the crowd. Yet he did not flee. He simply turned back to the commander of the temple officers and offered himself.

And like that, the moment passed.

The soldiers moved in, the shackles were fastened, and the detachment of troops and the officers of the Jews arrested and bound the object of Cinis' quest.

Cinis stood frozen, watching.

Watching as Jesus of Nazareth was taken into custody like a common criminal, bound in iron, and led away into the night.

That night, Cinis' sleep was disturbed once more, plagued with images that refused to leave him.

•

THE FIRST LIGHT of dawn spilled over the rooftops of Jerusalem, casting long shadows through the narrow streets. The city was already stirring, though not in its usual rhythm of merchants preparing their stalls and priests making their way to the Temple. Today, the movement was different: hurried, charged with tension.

Cinis moved quickly through the streets. His steps were purposeful, his mind racing. He had told his men he had matters to attend to in the city, and though they had asked no questions, he knew they had wondered at his restlessness.

For eighteen months, he had sought the man called Jesus of Nazareth. And now, at the end of his quest, he had watched the man be arrested.

Cinis had spent the restless hours of the night wrestling with the images burned into his mind: the calm surrender in the garden, the miracle of the servant's ear, the unshaken expression of a man who could have fled but did not.

And so he had come, following the murmurs of the crowd, seeking out where they had taken him.

He found himself at the Praetorium, the fortress of the Roman governor.

It was a place normally filled with soldiers, Roman officials, the occasional petitioner seeking favor or judgment. But today, as Cinis entered the outer hall, he was struck by the sheer number of Jews who filled the space: a rare occurrence in the house of the governor, made more rare by the early hour.

The chief priests were there in force, along with scribes and Pharisees. Their robes swirled as they moved through the crowd, their faces set with determination. The clamor of voices filled the vast hall, a cacophony of accusation, each man seemingly eager to be heard first, to be loudest.

They wanted this man condemned.

Cinis lingered at the edge of the throng, pressing forward as much as he could without drawing attention to himself. He strained to hear above the rising din as Pontius Pilate stood at the center of the judgment hall, his gaze falling upon the man they had brought before him.

Cinis' breath caught in his throat.

There he stood: Jesus of Nazareth.

Bound, his hands tied, yet standing with the same calm Cinis had seen in the garden. The same quiet power that had held even the armed soldiers in check.

The expectant murmurs of the crowd filled the room as Pilate studied the prisoner before him. Cinis had seen Pilate pass judgment before, had watched him weigh the lives of men with the detached calculation of a man who held power but cared little for those subject to it.

But this was different; Pilate hesitated. And then, after a long moment, he spoke.

"Are you the King of the Jews?"

Cinis narrowed his eyes. Pilate was no fool. He had undoubtedly heard the same rumors Cinis had heard over the past year and a half. Perhaps the governor was merely indulging the accusations of the priests. And if Jesus spoke to confirm those rumors, he would be speaking his own death sentence.

But Jesus did not answer with a simple confirmation or denial. Instead, he met the governor's gaze and replied with a question of his own.

"Are you asking this for your own interest, or is it what others have told you about me?"

The murmurs in the room swelled. Pilate's expression shifted slightly, his lips pressing together.

"Do I look like a Jew?" Pilate scoffed. "You know who your accusers are. They surround you." He gestured to the seething throng of priests and elders, their faces contorted with self-righteous indignation. "I want you to tell me: what have you done to merit their accusations?"

Jesus said nothing.

The silence stretched.

Pilate exhaled, clearly irritated at being met with neither defense nor pleading. His patience thinning, he repeated the question, louder now.

"Are you the King of the Jews?"

And then, Jesus spoke.

"You have said it."

Cinis barely had time to process the words before the room exploded. A cacophony of rage surged from the crowd, voices shouting over one another. Priests stepped forward, their faces twisted in fury. The surge of movement displaced Cinis, forcing him back as the sheer press of bodies overwhelmed the outer edges of the hall. He struggled to hold his position, to hear, to see. But the chaos was too great, the cries against the Nazarene growing in volume and number.

Then, above the shouting, Pilate's voice resounded.

"I find no fault in this man."

The words rang in Cinis' ears. The one thing he had most wanted to hear, the thing he had thought himself alone in believing, had just been spoken by the Roman governor himself. Pilate, the man who held the power of life and death in this province, the man who had been Rome's hand of justice, had seen this man, heard his words… and found no fault in him.

The masses surged forward, their fury spilling into the courtyard, their hatred greater than their reason.

Cinis found himself pushed back, away from the hall as the tide of bodies moved without care for those it displaced. He barely managed to stay on his feet as he was forced from the edges of the judgment court and out into the open streets.

And as he steadied himself, the last thing he saw before he lost sight of Jesus was the look on the man's face. He was calm, unshaken. As though none of this surprised him.

And that baffled Cinis more than anything he had seen.

❧ • ❧

IT HAD TAKEN Cinis several minutes to work his way through the press of bodies, jostled and shoved as he sought a fresh vantage point. The crowd had grown larger, a swarming, writhing mass that pulsed with fervor. He had missed part of what had transpired inside the Praetorium, but as he finally managed to position himself near a raised platform overlooking the courtyard, he stared in disbelief at what he now saw.

Pilate had given in.

Despite the words Cinis had heard with his own ears—"I find no fault in this man"—the governor had bent the knee to the demands of the priests and Pharisees, and Jesus of Nazareth had been sentenced to death.

Cinis' fists clenched at his sides. His breath came slow and steady, but inside, he seethed. He had seen injustice before (Rome was not built on mercy) but this? This was something else.

Unlike Cinis, the crowd was exultant. It was not just satisfaction; it was far uglier: a bloodlust Cinis had rarely seen outside the gladiator pits. The same wild hunger for death that he had witnessed in the faces of spectators as they bayed for the slaughter of gladiators now shone in the faces of this crowd.

He felt sick.

The Jews had even roared their approval when Pilate, in a final mockery of justice, had released Barabbas, a murderer, instead of Jesus. The irony was lost on them.

Cinis shifted his focus to Pilate himself. The governor's face was a study of resentment. He did not like this. He did not want this. But Cinis could see the moment his resistance had faltered: when the priests had invoked the name of Caesar. That had been the turning point.

Pilate, already under scrutiny from Rome for his mishandling of previous disturbances, had no choice. If he acted against the wishes of these priests, they would report him, and Tiberius would not take kindly to a governor too weak to control his subjects.

So Pilate had given them what they wanted. And, in a bit of bitter theatrics, as was his way, the governor had a servant bring a bowl of water.

Cinis watched in disgust as Pilate, seated above the seething throng, dipped his hands into the basin. His face was set in a mockery of sorrow.

"I am innocent of this man's blood," he declared, lifting his dripping fingers, and letting the water slide down his forearms. "See to it yourselves."

Cinis saw the sneer in Pilate's eyes, the contempt he held for the people below him.

Pilate did not believe this Jesus to be guilty. But he let them have him anyway.

The soldiers dragged Jesus to a stone pillar, yanking his arms forward, and stretching them above his head. They strapped his wrists to the post, pulling the bindings taut until his body arched forward, his back bared to the punishment about to be inflicted.

A silence settled, heavy and expectant.

Then the first lash fell. The flagrum, a short whip braided with bits of metal, bone, and glass, bit into his flesh. Cinis did not flinch, but he wanted to look away.

The second lash came. And then a third, and then another, each strike digging deeper into skin and muscle. The jagged bits embedded in the leather tore the man's skin away in ribbons, leaving raw, open wounds.

Thirty-nine lashes; that was the Roman way. A man's body could not withstand forty.

Jesus bore them all, and in silence, he bore them.

Cinis had had enough.

His hopes of speaking to the man were all but gone, lost in the tide of blood and madness. This was not justice. This was not Rome. This was cruelty for cruelty's sake, and Cinis had no interest in bearing further witness to it.

He turned away, pushing through the edges of the crowd, trying to escape the sight of the butchered man who still had yet to cry out.

Then he heard the mocking laughter. A fresh wave of jeering rose from the soldiers, and Cinis turned one last time.

They had shoved a twisted ring of thorns onto Jesus' head, pressing it down until the spines pierced his skin, his blood mingling with the sweat of his agony.

A soldier draped a costly purple robe over his shoulders, the rich fabric soaking up the blood from his rent flesh. Another forced a reed into his hand, pressing it against his limp fingers like a scepter.

And then, with sickening amusement, they began to cheer him.

"Hail, King of the Jews!"

They knelt in mock reverence, smirking, laughing, spitting upon him.

And then, to Cinis' utter disgust, the chief priests and the elders themselves joined in.

Cinis turned away for good.

He could stomach battle. He could face death. He had seen men die horribly.

But this? This was not justice.

There was no honor in this.

❧ • ❧

CINIS STOOD AT the edge of the street, his arms crossed, his jaw tight. He had been finished watching. He had told himself he had seen enough.

Yet here he was.

The crowd had doubled in number since the sentencing at the Praetorium, the air thick with the stench of sweat and unwashed bodies, dust swirling beneath the tramping of countless feet. The jeers and shouts of the mob were louder now, a frenzied roar of contempt, as though each voice fed the others. The same priests who had demanded his death now walked among the people, stoking them to ensure the hatred did not wane.

Cinis stood at a sharp bend in the Via Dolorosa, where the road twisted suddenly southeast, forcing the condemned to adjust their footing. The sun was rising higher, the heat already pressing down, and he could see the blood-slicked stones where others had stumbled that very morning.

Then Jesus came.

Cinis' breath caught as he saw him again—not the man from the garden, calm and composed, nor the man in the Praetorium, silent before Pilate, but a man barely clinging to life.

A crossbeam was lashed across his shoulders, its weight forcing his upper body forward with every step. His back was torn and raw, his tunic long since clinging to his wounds. His face was almost unrecognizable, swollen from the beating, blood trickling from the jagged thorns pressed into his scalp.

The crowd mocked him as he passed. Cinis clenched his teeth.

Then it happened.

Just as Jesus reached the curve in the road, his steps faltered. His knees buckled, his body giving way beneath the weight of the wood, and he fell hard onto the stone. The cross tilted with the momentum, slamming into the ground beside him. A fresh cry rose from the crowd, half laughter, half frustration.

Jesus lay there, unmoving at first.

He wasn't going to make it.

Cinis felt something tighten in his chest.

"You!"

His voice rang out sharply, and for a moment, the voices around him quieted in confusion. The man beside him—very tall, broad-shouldered, a foreigner by his dress and bearing—flinched at the sound.

The man looked down at him, wide-eyed.

Cinis narrowed his eyes. "What is your name?"

The man swallowed hard. His hands, large and calloused, trembled slightly.

"Simon, master," he said quickly. "Simon of Cyrene."

Cinis scowled. "I don't care where you're from, dolt! Get to that man and carry the cross for him. He'll never make it on his own."

Simon hesitated, glancing toward Jesus.

Cinis shoved him forward.

Simon stumbled, barely catching himself, but he made no protest. He stepped toward Jesus, bending down, his large hands grasping the rough wood of the cross. Cinis watched as Simon of Cyrene lifted the burden that the condemned could no longer bear.

The soldiers, seeing the issue resolved, hurried them forward. The procession moved on. The shouting resumed. The dust rose again.

Cinis exhaled slowly, staring after them.

~ • ~

THE SUN HAD continued its slow ascent, casting long shadows over the barren hill. The third hour of the day had arrived.

Cinis stood on the edge of the execution site, his arms crossed tightly, his lips pressed into a firm line. He had seen men die in countless ways: on the battlefield, in riots, under the slow agony of starvation. But this...?

This was something else.

The nails had been driven through flesh and bone, pinning Jesus to the crossbeam with methodical precision. The Romans had perfected this means of death, ensuring it inflicted maximum suffering with minimal haste. This use of hammer and nail had nothing to do with efficiency, as one might expect from architectural discipline, but something cruder, baser.

This was a display, an example.

Cinis had noted every detail of the execution. The manner in which the soldiers lifted the cross upright, dropping it hard into the hole chiseled from stone, causing a fresh gasp of pain from the condemned. He had seen the man offered wine mixed with myrrh, the one minor mercy granted to those about to suffer.

And he had seen Jesus refuse it.

Cinis could not fathom why. Any man with sense would have taken whatever numbness could be found. But Jesus had turned his face from the cup as soon as he realized what it was. He had chosen to feel every moment.

Cinis watched. And with every passing second, his disgust grew.

Not for the crucifixion itself; he had seen them before. As a much younger man, he had even helped improve the design of the structures from which such torments were displayed. No, it was the masses, the insatiable hunger in their jeers, the laughter, the way even the so-called priests found themselves emboldened to mock him.

And the soldiers did nothing.

The four-man quaternion assigned to watch over the execution had not only failed to control the crowds, but they had also begun entertaining themselves. The tunic of Jesus had been stripped from him before his arms were affixed to the wood, and now the soldiers fought over it like beggars scrambling for scraps.

Cinis' stomach turned. Something inside him snapped.

He marched forward, his sandals grinding into the dry dirt as he ascended the hill. He passed through the throng without hesitation, weaving past those spitting, cursing, laughing.

His focus was fixed on the soldiers. They had been trying in vain to tear the garment apart, each man pulling at a corner, intent on claiming a piece.

"Enough!" Cinis barked.

The soldiers froze, looking at him.

The largest of them, a hulking brute with a thick gut, scarred knuckles, and arms like marble columns, turned slowly, his ice-blue eyes flicking over Cinis. Cinis recognized him immediately.

Cassius Brutus, a man he had dealt with before.

Like Cinis, Brutus was an evocatus, a veteran who had reenlisted after his original term of service. But while Cinis had pursued his skills as an engineer, overseeing fortifications and siege engines, Brutus had remained solely for blood.

He was a soldier for the sake of war itself.

The man straightened and stood at the foot of the cross, turning away from the cloak of Jesus and folding his thick arms across his chest. His scarred fingers, as thick around and stubby as links of blood sausage, tapped idly against the worn leather of his bracers, as if bored by the new arrival.

His huge gut cast a great shadow over the bloodstained rock beneath him in the morning sun. His gladius was absent—Cinis presumed it had been left in his tent as unnecessary for this light duty—but the wicked-looking pugio at his belt was worn in such a way to advertise that it was more than enough if needed. His broad shoulders strained against his armor, the segmented plates scuffed and dull, streaked with dust and sweat. His ice-blue eyes, cold, and predatory, swept over Cinis in recognition.

When Brutus spoke, his voice was thick with amusement.

"Ha! It's the little engineer!"

Cinis said nothing, his jaw tight.

"Hello, Appius Aurelius," Brutus went on, grinning. "Have you come to build a machine to help us tear this cloth? How can you serve me on such a fine and glorious morning?"

The stench of rotting teeth and stale wine wafted from his breath, and Cinis found himself half-wondering what killed the man's enemies first: his dagger, or his body odor.

Cinis exhaled sharply. "How can you serve Rome, is the question you should ask."

The grin vanished from Brutus' face.

The larger man straightened, his shadow darkening the dirt-stained rock beneath him. He inhaled deeply, the plates of his mail shifting and creaking as he squared his shoulders.

Then, after a pause, he laughed.

"I serve Rome as I always have! In glory and honor, and in mail with blade and blood!" Brutus spread his arms, as if mocking Cinis for even questioning him.

Cinis refused to back down. "You serve Rome like a pack of mange-ridden dogs, tearing at the scraps of the dead and dying."

Brutus' eyes narrowed.

Cinis turned his gaze on the others, sweeping over the three men standing beside Brutus, all of them still holding onto the bloodied garment as if it were a prize.

"Is this what Rome is?" he asked, his voice cutting through the morning air like a blade. "Is that all you are? Filthy curs pulling at the clothes of the Jews?"

Brutus' nostrils flared, but he did not speak.

Cinis took a step closer, his voice low and sharp. "Cast lots and be done with it. Show some honor in your actions."

A tense silence followed. Then, one of the men, a young munifex standing beside the two fledgling tirones, cleared his throat.

Cinis recognized the younger man. Titus Cornelius Scipio, the nephew of General Scipio himself.

The young soldier looked between Brutus and Cinis, and then, after a moment, nodded.

"He's right. We should cast lots."

Brutus exhaled through his nose, but he did not argue.

Titus Cornelius carried weight. Not because of his own reputation, but because of his name. A name that Brutus had no interest in coming against.

With reluctant grunts, the soldiers abandoned the pointless struggle, reaching instead for their dice.

Cinis did not wait to see who won; he had already turned away. His eyes lifted instinctively toward the cross.

And to his shock, Jesus was watching him.

The Nazarene's gaze met his, locking onto him with an intensity that sent a chill through Cinis' chest. There was no hatred in that expression. No blame. But neither was there sorrow.

Cinis could not place the emotion.

It was not fear, nor anger, nor resignation. It was something else entirely. It was as if the man knew him, knew everything about him. And for the first time in decades, Cinis felt vulnerable beneath the gaze of another man.

He tore his eyes away, forcing his feet to move.

Behind him, the mocking voices of the soldiers resumed.

And above them all, the dying man remained silent.

☙ • ❧

CINIS STOOD APART from the jeering crowd, his back against a low outcrop of rock, the weight of exhaustion heavy in his bones.

A wooden tub of sour wine had been placed near the base of the hill, intended to slake the thirst of the soldiers assigned to this miserable duty. The liquid was dark and acrid, a poor man's drink: little more than vinegar and fermented grape, thick and bitter.

He dipped a ladle into the cask and drank deeply, the sharp tang stinging his throat. As he lowered the cup, his eyes drifted back to the cross.

Jesus had been hanging there for nearly two hours now.

The mocking had not ceased. The crowd, emboldened by the presence of the priests and officials, had found new sport in tormenting him.

"You saved others!" they jeered, "Why do you not save yourself?"

Cinis wiped his mouth with the back of his hand and exhaled slowly.

He had seen men crucified.

Crucifixion was a punishment for slaves, rebels, and the lowest criminals—far too painful and humiliating for Roman citizens. It was meant to be a spectacle, a deterrent.

A slow death, drawn out by exposure and agony, designed to make an example of those who dared defy Rome.

But this was different.

Cinis was convinced that it was too painful for any man to endure. And yet, Jesus had not screamed, had not begged, had not cursed.

He endured.

Cinis wondered if it was too late to offer him another chance at the other wine: the one mixed with gall, meant to dull the mind, to make the pain somewhat less. But he knew he would be breaking protocol to offer the condemned any balm or comfort at this stage.

So Cinis drank his wine, and he watched.

Jesus endured the second hour of taunts, his body trembling from exhaustion, the thorns on his brow digging deeper into his flesh.

Brutus had been silent for some time now, standing near the base of the cross, arms folded across his massive chest. His pale blue eyes flicked toward Cinis, as if daring him to act.

Then, without breaking eye contact, Brutus turned deliberately toward the cask of sour wine placed there for him and his men.

Cinis narrowed his gaze, watching as the brute of a man scooped a flagon of the liquid into his cup.

I swear the man is incapable of independent thought, Cinis told himself, taking another slow sip from his cup.

Only when Brutus stepped back toward Jesus did Cinis understand what was happening. Brutus lifted his voice for all to hear, his booming tone thick with mockery.

"You! Up there!" he bellowed, his voice reaching the farthest onlookers.

Though Brutus stood at the base of the cross, his head was not far below that of Jesus—a testament to his sheer size. He grinned wickedly, lifting the cup toward the condemned man.

"Drink some wine!"

The crowd laughed, amused by the fresh spectacle.

Brutus turned to them, playing to their bloodlust.

"If you are the King of the Jews, as you have declared, then come down! Free yourself!"

And with that, Brutus flung the contents of his cup toward Jesus.

Cinis surged forward.

The crowd was still laughing, entertained by the cruelty, but Cinis' face was carved from stone, and those seeing it parted to make way.

Cinis reached Brutus, grabbed the larger man's arm, and spun him around.

Brutus' brow furrowed, surprised but unbothered. His expression became smug.

But before he could speak, Cinis cut him off.

"You're done here," Cinis said, his voice quiet but edged with undeniable authority. "I'm taking your place."

Cinis kept his grip firm on Brutus' thick wrist, his fingers digging into the leather of the larger man's bracer as he guided him away from the crowd, ensuring that their conflict would not become a spectacle.

"You're done here," Cinis repeated under his breath, his tone steely and final.

Brutus exhaled sharply through his nose, the sound more amused than irritated. His cold blue eyes flickered with something darker, something cruel and evil.

"You think you're in charge now, little engineer?" he sneered.

Cinis met his gaze without flinching. "If you want to dispute it, we can settle it here," he told the larger man, his voice low. "But if I were you, I'd choose a battle you can win."

Brutus' expression darkened.

The strike came fast.

Cinis barely had time to react before Brutus' fist smashed into his ribs, the impact reverberating through his chest. He staggered back slightly, but not before the second blow came: a brutal jab into his stomach. Cinis clenched his teeth, forcing himself to stay upright, to not give the brute the satisfaction of seeing him stumble.

Then, he felt it.

The hot, sharp sting of steel slipping between the plates of his armor—low, under the ribs.

Cinis grunted but did not cry out.

Brutus leaned in close, his breath rank, his lips curling into a wolfish grin.

“Still think you're in charge, little engineer?” he whispered.

The blade withdrew and struck again.

And again.

Cinis knew what was happening. Brutus wasn’t aiming to kill him outright.

He was going for quick, shallow jabs, slipping the short pugio between the gaps in Cinis’ breastplate, ensuring the wounds bled freely but did not cripple him immediately.

Coward.

A roaring heat flared through his side, and Cinis felt his own warm blood seeping into his tunic. But he would not fall.

He would not.

With a burst of strength, Cinis lashed out.

His elbow drove upward into Brutus' throat, causing the larger man to choke and recoil. Wasting no time, Cinis pivoted, bringing his knee up into Brutus' gut before slamming his fist across the man's jaw.

Brutus stumbled, shocked by the counterattack.

Cinis pressed forward, driving the larger man backward with each blow.

A punch to the gut.

A strike to the nose, sending blood spraying into the dust.

Cinis ignored the burning pain in his side, the wetness of blood dripping beneath his armor.

Brutus grunted in pain as Cinis delivered a final savage blow to his jaw, sending the big man crashing onto the rocky ground.

A breath. Two.

Then Brutus rolled onto his hands and knees, his bloody lips curling into a snarl. But he did not renew the attack.

Instead, he spat into the dirt, wiped his face, and pushed himself, wavering, to his feet. His cold blue gaze met Cinis' again, but this time, there was no amusement. Only hatred.

Brutus wiped his sleeve across his bloodied mouth, then, without a word, turned and stalked away.

Cinis watched him go, his breathing heavy, his hands trembling. He had won the fight, but the price was steep. His side burned. His vision swam slightly. But he had a duty to fulfill.

He turned back toward the cross.

Cinis walked with purpose, despite the pain, despite the sticky warmth of his blood seeping into his tunic.

He reached the foot of the cross, stepping into the place that Brutus had vacated.

The remaining three soldiers regarded their new watch commander, waiting. None of them spoke. They had seen what had just happened. They were wise enough not to question him.

Cinis stood tall, pressing his palm to his wound to slow the bleeding. If he could do nothing else, he could at least ensure that the man on the cross died with some dignity.

The jeering had lessened, the crowd uncertain now that a man of honor had taken command after dispatching a much larger adversary. The priests and mockers still whispered among themselves, but no one approached.

Cinis was an engineer by training, a soldier by necessity. But in the right moment, he could be something else entirely. He was very intimidating when it was required. The crowd shrank back.

And then, a movement from above.

Cinis turned his gaze upward.

Jesus was looking at him.

For a brief moment, despite the blood, despite the pain, despite the mockery surrounding them, their eyes met. Cinis swore that he saw something in the eyes of Jesus. Something that unsettled him more than the Roman soldiers, more than the Jews, more than the priests who had condemned him.

Something that made Cinis wonder... if this man knew him.

He looked away, feeling unworthy to hold this man's gaze for long.

A short span later, Cinis saw them coming up the hill before they arrived. A small group of weeping women approached, led by a man. A disciple, if Cinis had to guess.

He had seen them earlier. They had lingered on the outskirts of the crowd, just as he had. Watching. Waiting.

The Nazarene saw them too; his eyes softened. His gaze settled upon one woman in particular: small, frail, barely older than Cinis himself. She wept as if her soul was being torn from her body.

Jesus spoke.

His voice was weak, barely more than a whisper. But it carried.

"Woman, behold your son."

The women sobbed all the more, the one Cinis had noticed wailing openly as she fell against the man beside her. For his part, the man's face tightened, his sorrow barely contained as he wrapped an arm around the grieving woman.

Then, with great effort, Jesus turned his gaze to the man and spoke again.

"Behold your mother."

The man nodded.

Cinis swallowed hard.

He had seen men die before, but he had never seen a dying man give away his mother. Never seen a man in such suffering so unconcerned with his pain that he could expend his ebbing energy to ensure the welfare of someone else, family or not.

The small group withdrew, disappearing into the sea of bodies.

Cinis exhaled slowly.

He knew it could not be much longer now.

IT WAS THE sixth hour of the day.

The sun had reached its highest point in the sky, standing at its zenith, as it always did. And yet, a shadow fell upon the land.

At first, Cinis thought it was a cloud: a passing veil of shade before the sun would reassert itself. But then the darkness deepened. The air grew still, the cries of the crowd diminishing as people turned their eyes upward, murmuring among themselves.

The sun had hidden itself. Like a veiled witness to the travesty below, it had refused to watch. The light that had bathed the city only moments before was now gone, replaced by a thick, unnatural twilight that spread over the hills like ink spilled across a scroll.

Cinis felt a chill work its way down his spine.

The mocking voices died away, and in their absence came fear.

The weak-minded and the superstitious fled, their murmurs turning to whispers of bad omens. Some ran back toward the city, while others hurried down the hillside, their robes trailing behind them like spirits dissolving into the gloom.

Cinis was grateful for their absence.

The stillness was a relief, a moment of quiet in the wake of so much senseless cruelty.

For three hours, the darkness remained, as though the very heavens mourned.

Then, Jesus spoke. His voice rang out, strong despite the hours of suffering, cutting through the hush with a force that should not have been possible for a dying man.

"Eli, Eli, lama sabachthani?"

The words were foreign to Cinis, but their anguish needed no translation. He felt a tightness in his chest.

The brilliant, unshaken man he had encountered in the garden, the one who had stood calmly before Pilate, the one who had endured mockery, flogging, and crucifixion without a single cry of pain...

Now, at the end, he cried out.

Cinis did not understand the words, but he understood their weight: Jesus was alone. Forsaken. And it was not right.

Cinis tore his gaze from the cross and turned to Titus Cornelius, who stood nearby, his face pale in the eerie twilight.

"Wine," Cinis ordered.

Titus hesitated for only a second before nodding. Dropping his long spear, he moved quickly to the nearby cask. Pulling a hyssop sponge from a nearby vessel, he dipped it in the sour drinking wine. Then, he took a reed, thrust the soaked sponge onto its end, and raised it toward the dying man.

Cinis watched as Jesus' cracked lips parted just slightly, his swollen tongue barely moving to accept the dampness.

For the briefest moment, Cinis felt relief.

Then, Jesus exhaled a single, final breath.

And he died.

❧ • ❧

THE MOMENT JESUS breathed his last, the earth shuddered. A deep, thunderous groan rolled through the hills, rising from the depths of the land itself, as though the very foundations of the world had been shaken.

Cinis staggered, the force of the earthquake ripping the ground from beneath him. His knees buckled, and he crashed down onto the rocky earth, barely managing to throw his hands out in time to break his fall.

From all around him, the sound of breaking stone filled the air. Boulders tore loose from the ridges above, tumbling down the slopes like the fists of an angry god. The dry, cracked earth split apart in jagged seams, dust rising in sudden, choking clouds.

The three remaining soldiers—Titus Cornelius and the two young tirones—stood frozen, their faces pale, their eyes wide with terror as the world heaved and groaned around them.

And in that moment, he knew. In the darkness, in the shaking of the earth, in the shadow of the lifeless man upon the cross, Cinis knew.

He looked up at Jesus, at the man who had refused to save himself, at the man who had spoken of his father in heaven, at the man who had healed the sick, raised the dead, fed the multitudes, and forgiven even those who nailed him here.

Cinis knew. And he spoke.

His voice was hoarse, filled with something more than certainty: something deeper, something that burned through every doubt he had ever held.

"Do you have any doubt now," Cinis cried, his voice ringing out over the rumbling earth, "that this righteous man was the Son of God?"

None of them answered.

They only stared at the man on the cross, and the man on his knees before it.

❧ • ❧

CINIS MUST HAVE blacked out. One moment, he had been kneeling, his body weak from blood loss, his words still echoing over the shaking ground. The next, he was lying prone, his vision blurred, his breath ragged. The deep ache of his wounds pulsed with every beat of his heart, his tunic clinging wetly to his skin.

The screams brought him back.

Sharp, pained cries. Wet impacts. Bones cracking under the force of heavy blows.

Cinis' head snapped up, his vision sharpening at once.

Two new soldiers approached the base of the crosses on either side of Jesus, their armor clean: fresh reinforcements sent to finish the day's task. Their segmented plates gleamed, their helmets still polished, though dust from the road already clung to their greaves.

Their arms were bare beneath their armor, corded with muscle, and each man gripped a massive iron hammer, its two-cubit handle rough-forged in a single piece with the crossbar of its metal head. These were simple camp hammers, meant for driving stakes into solid rock, for splitting beams and stone. Now, they were instruments of death.

The legionnaire standing near the thief to Jesus' left raised his hammer high, his expression one of grim purpose. With a single, brutal swing, he brought the hammer head in an arc onto the man's left leg.

The crack of shattering bone rang out over the hilltop.

The thief screamed in agony, his body convulsing, his arms straining against the nails that bound him. Another sickening crunch followed soon after.

The second thief likewise howled as his legs too were snapped at the shin. The hammer-blows ensured he would die quickly now, unable to lift himself to breathe.

Cinis forced himself to his feet, his vision swimming. His limbs were unsteady, but his rage gave him strength.

The two soldiers turned toward Jesus, hammers resting on shoulders as they approached.

Cinis stepped forward.

"You will not desecrate this good man's body."

The two men paused, looking toward him, and to each other in bewilderment. The first legionnaire, a thick-set man with a scar running down his cheek, straightened. If he were confused about the blood drenching Cinis' armor and clothing, he gave no sign. "We were ordered by Pilate himself to do so. The Jews want this matter finished before their Sabbath."

Cinis' eyes burned. "It is already finished! The man said so himself, even as he died. Step away."

The second soldier, taller but leaner, shrugged. "We have orders."

Cinis felt his anger boil over. His head throbbed, his wounds ached, but he did not care. Knowing he was already a dead man gave him courage beyond recklessness.

“I care not for your orders! Nor do I care much for the coward who gave them.” His voice was sharp as a blade, cutting through the quiet that had settled over the hill since the last cries of the thieves had faded. “This man is dead, and you will not dishonor his body.”

The scarred soldier exhaled through his nose. "If he is dead, he cares not about honor. But what matter is it if he is dead or not when we break his legs? And what is it to you?"

The taller man shrugged again, gripping his hammer more tightly. “Besides, if he is dead, he won’t feel it. Let us do our job.”

“I will not,” growled Cinis, his fury surging to the surface. Before the two men could react, he grabbed the pilum that Titus Cornelius had set aside to give Jesus drink.

The two soldiers stepped back instinctively at sight of the spear; their hammers raised defensively. Their eyes flicked to the pilum's sharp iron tip, their stances shifting as they prepared to fight.

But Cinis did not attack them.

With the last of his strength, he spun toward the cross and thrust the spear upward, its iron tip sinking deep into the side of Jesus.

For a moment, stunned silence.

Then, a great gout of commingled blood and water poured forth, drenching Cinis from head to waist, the hot red mingling with the cool, clear flow. The gore mixed with Cinis' own blood, running down his arms, soaking into the fabric of his tunic.

The burning wounds Brutus had given him, torn open afresh by his effort, were strangely cooled by the flow. Cinis staggered back, breathing heavily.

The assembled legionnaires looked on in mute shock.

No one spoke as Cinis collapsed to the dampened earth.

Jesus was dead. There was no point in breaking his body.

And Cinis had given him what dignity he could.

❧ • ❧

PILATE SAT BEFORE him, perched on the edge of his stone bench, fingers pressed against his temples as he exhaled a long, irritated breath.

Cinis barely registered him. He barely registered his surroundings at all. The world had shrunk to a haze of pain and exhaustion, his body heavy and useless, his limbs numb except for the slow, constant throb of his wounds.

His head hung forward, chin nearly resting on his chest, his breath shallow. The tunic against his skin was stiff with dried blood: his own, and that of the man he had tried to protect.

Cinis could feel Pilate's eyes on him, cold and calculating, but he didn't have it in him to look back. He was bound at the wrists and ankles, though even he did not know why. He had no strength left to run. He had no fight left to give. And he had caused all the trouble he would this day.

Or, he feared, any other.

Brutus was there, bandaged and accusing, but smiling at Cinis' sorry state. The heavy bruising on the big man's face did little to lessen the self-satisfied gleam in his icy blue eyes. He stood with a relaxed posture, his arms crossed, his scarred fingers tapping idly against his bracer.

He had already won, and he knew it. He knew the wounds he had inflicted on Cinis were not long from taking their final toll.

Pilate watched them both in disdain, his mind turning over the problem like a gambler considering a poor roll of the dice. He had enough troubles to deal with, and yet his officers could not seem to refrain from creating more. He was in a quandary.

He hated being in quandaries.

Finally, with a growl of frustration, he made his decision.

"Imprison him."

Brutus smiled but said nothing.

Cinis did not react.

Pilate leaned forward slightly, his hard eyes locking onto the engineer's battered form.

"Twice, Appius Aurelius," he said, his voice a knife's edge of irritation. "Twice this day have I been faced with impossible decisions, caught between two choices, neither of them good. Neither of them good at all. You broke the rules, Appius Aurelius. Rules that I must enforce, whether I have patience for them or not."

He exhaled sharply, then waved a dismissive hand.

"But it is a temporary punishment. You won't be suffering it for long."

His gaze flicked to Brutus, then back to Cinis, and he shook his head.

"You will be dead by morning anyway."

Pilate stood, adjusting the folds of his toga. He was done with this.

"Get them both out of my sight."

The guards moved at once, yanking Cinis upright. His body protested, but he did not fight them. He had nothing left with which to fight.

And so, Appius Aurelius Cinis was taken off to prison to die.

❧ • ❧

THE CELL WAS dark and cool, the air thick with the damp stench of old stone and forgotten men. Cinis slumped against the wall, his body heavy, broken, spent.

He had seen so many men die in places like this. Now, his turn had come.

The ache in his side had become a dull, ever-present throb, pulsing in rhythm with his heartbeat. His vision swam, the pain dulling into something else: something distant and not quite real.

He could feel it beginning. The heat swept over him. It started in his chest, a slow, creeping warmth that spread outward, like embers catching on dry leaves.

The fever had come.

It would take him before the night was through, he knew. He let his head rest against the cold stone, his eyes slipping shut as the warmth consumed him.

And as darkness swallowed Appius Aurelius Cinis, the fever raged.

He knew not then that this would only be the first of so many such fevers.

Chapter 21 : THE END AND THE BEGINNING

ASHE STOPPED SPEAKING. His voice had burned out somewhere near the end, his throat raw, each word scraping its way past cracked lips. A fever sheen clung to his skin, sweat collecting in the hollows of his face, trickling down to mix with the blood and dust caking his body.

The fever was pulling him under, the long-familiar weight of it settling into his bones, his body beginning its slow, agonizing ritual of repair.

It was always like this, when he came too close to death. A descent into darkness and confusion, wet, suffocating: a drowning without water, a burial where the body would not be still.

His breath was uneven, ragged. He turned his head just enough to look at Standish. The jerk was already dead.

Or so Ashe thought.

Standish sat slumped against a rock outcropping, his body ragged and hollow, his face devoid of anything—no hate, no triumph, no final satisfaction. Just emptiness.

Then, the man blinked.

Standish's chest barely moved, the rise and fall so shallow it could have been mistaken for stillness.

His lips parted slightly, as if trying to speak. No words came.

He tried again, struggling against the weight of his own dying body. The tendons in his throat shifted, convulsed, but the words wouldn't come.

It didn't matter. Ashe could already see the end creeping up on him. His face was waxy, the skin around his mouth drained of color, his hands slack except for the one still clenched around the dead man's switch. He had held on for far too long. The weight of the fight, the wounds, the sheer force of his hatred had kept him tethered to this world, but there was nothing left. Except one final thought: one final reckoning.

Standish's lips moved one more time, his voice nothing but air at first, then—

"I... was..." His breath hitched, eyes fluttering. And then, clear as day, came the words of his judgment.

"I was wrong."

Ashe's chest tightened, though whether from the fever burning through him or the words themselves, he couldn't tell.

Standish's fingers twitched slightly, his grip loosening around the detonator.

"I was wrong to judge you," he whispered, barely audible.

Ashe could see it now: the weight pressing against the man. Not the weight of his wounds, but something far more painful.

Standish breathed his last, shuddering breath. His body sagged inward, curling slightly around his wounds. Then, his eyes closed and Lamentation Standish himself went off to be judged.

The silence that the man slipped off into was thick, absolute. There were no voices. No echoes. Only the slow drip, drip, drip of water from somewhere above, the cavernous ruin breathing in the absence of its final occupants.

Somewhere beyond the collapsed corridor, rats stirred. Waiting. Watching. Slinking through the cracks in the ancient stone, their whiskers twitching, their small, black eyes gleaming in the dark. They did not know that their feast, their moment of triumph over the fallen titans, would never come.

Because the moment Standish died, his hand began to loosen.

Ashe saw it happening, felt the last vestiges of life slip from Standish's fingers. His body relaxed in death, and with it?

His dead man's switch. The detonator.

Ashe's mind snapped into action, but his body would not respond.

His arms refused to move. His spine was still severed. He wasn't dead, but he might as well have been.

The only thing he had any control over was his leg.

His leg. His right leg had twitched.

He forced everything he had into that leg, every ounce of willpower, every fragment of control. Two thousand years of effort and strife culminated in that single moment as he tried to make his broken body respond.

With a clumsy, jerking movement, Ashe's leg flew upward, jerking his entire body after it. He flopped like a fish off of the bomb and onto the floor. The foot traveled in a mighty arc, and his boot came down. It landed directly on top of Standish's hand.

The switch didn't release.

The bomb didn't detonate.

For now.

Ashe let out a slow, shuddering breath. It had worked. He dripped sweat onto the dusty floor, mingling with the blood of his wounds he'd torn open in the effort to move.

He took another breath. He exhaled.

Then, softly, dryly—

"Great." His voice was hoarse, ragged. "Now all I have to do is lay here and hope my leg don't twitch."

A beat.

The distant dripping of water.

The quiet shuffle of rats in the darkness.

Ashe closed his eyes.

"Forever."

~ • ~

ASHE HATED HOSPITALS. He hated the sterile scent of antiseptic and despair, the muted voices of doctors speaking in hushed, tired tones, the mechanical beeping of monitors tracking the fragile line between life and death. He'd managed to avoid them for the most part, but on the rare occasions when he found himself trapped in one, he'd discovered that each one was different, each one had its own unique aspect that he hated more than anything else. This time, it was the looks. He hated the looks.

Knowing looks. The sidelong glances from doctors and nurses, their eyes flicking over him, over the scars, the wounds still fresh enough to tell a story. They didn't stare. No, they were professionals. But they looked. They looked and quickly looked away, some with curiosity, others with unease, and too many with something closer to understanding than Ashe was comfortable with.

The patients in the waiting area, of course, barely spared him a glance. They were absorbed in their suffering, too caught up in their pain, their bandages, their uncertain futures to care about a middle-aged man being wheeled toward the exit.

And that was just fine with Ashe.

Because he was finally getting out of here.

The wheels of the hospital-issued chair creaked faintly beneath him, the sturdy frame gliding over the cool tile floors as his escort maneuvered him through the last stretch of his medical imprisonment.

Somehow, his nurse had told him, Ashe ranked. His escort was no nameless orderly. She was Adina Ben-Tov, and she had made it very clear that he would not forget her name, as anonymous and mysterious as he himself tried to be.

"I know that look, Mr. Golding," she said, her accent crisp but lightly rolled, giving his wheelchair a firm push through the sliding doors. "You are sitting there, thinking about how much you hate hospitals. I see it all the time with men like you. I could set my watch by it."

Ashe ignored her, leaning forward to try and catch his first glimpse of freedom.

Adina was impossibly beautiful: a tall, strong Israeli woman with olive skin, sharp hazel eyes, and the kind of no-nonsense demeanor that came from years of military service. He had no doubt she could break a man's nose with a surgically-placed strike of her clipboard.

A glance upward revealed Adina to be smiling at him. She had enjoyed bossing him around these past few weeks.

"Men like me," Ashe muttered, shifting in the chair.

"Yes! You think you are invincible. You think that you do not need doctors, that you are just fine, with your battered stuntman thumb in the air. That you will live forever, and that lets you do stupid, stupid things. That, if you do ever land in a hospital like mine, you will walk out and be better than before. And yet—" She tapped a manicured fingernail against the handle of his wheelchair, "—look where you are."

Ashe rolled his eyes. "You're enjoying this, aren't you?"

"Immensely."

As they passed through the final set of glass doors, the bright, punishing heat of Tel Aviv slammed into Ashe like a wall. It was midday, and the sun hung high and merciless, reflecting off the hospital's white stone façade and casting a harsh, blinding glare across the pavement. The transition was jarring. Inside, the hospital had been dim and cool, a world of quiet hums and sterile peace. He'd hated every minute of the past weeks.

Outside? The world was loud, burning, alive. It smelled of citrus trees, exhaust fumes, and the distant briny bite of the Mediterranean.

Ashe almost smiled, but he fought back the urge.

Adina rolled him to a shaded patch of sidewalk near the drop-off area, setting the brakes on the wheelchair with two firm clicks.

"Mrs. Linder should be here shortly," she said, stepping in front of him, arms crossed. "I thought you might enjoy the sun while you wait."

Ashe grimaced. "That's debatable."

She ignored him.

"I don't know why you distrust hospitals so much, Mr. Golding." She leaned down slightly, eyes sharp and assessing. "You had one of the best surgeons in Israel, and Mrs. Linder made very sure your case was to be handled discreetly. We work with clandestine services often, you know. It is not so unusual. You are not as special as you think."

"Also debatable."

Something flickered in her eyes.

"In fact... I believe you may have met my fiancé. His name is Nehem."

Ashe blinked, frowning slightly against the glare. "Small world."

Adina grinned. "Very."

Before Ashe could respond, the low rumble of an engine and sound of tires hissing on hot pavement interrupted the conversation.

A black rented minivan pulled up to the curb, and before the vehicle had even fully stopped, the passenger-side door slid open along its rails with great force, slamming against the stop.

A blur of red hair and reckless energy burst out of the van like a torpedo launched from a submarine.

"ASHE!"

Any return greeting Ashe might have made was lost in a grunting exhale as Amber threw herself forward, colliding with him in a crushing embrace. Pain rocketed up his spine, and for a split second, Ashe was convinced she had just finished the job Standish started.

"Jiminy, kid—" He gritted his teeth, barely managing to keep from groaning out loud. As usual, Amber had zero situational awareness and no idea of how much force she was using.

"You're alive! You're in one piece! Well, mostly!" She pulled back slightly to regard his condition. "Holy cow, you look terrible!" She squeezed harder.

Ashe made a choked noise that might have been a laugh. Or a cry for help. He was unsure himself.

Dani stepped out from the driver's side, arms crossed, watching the scene with an amused smirk.

"Amber, you know he won't thank you if you put him back in the hospital."

Amber finally pulled back, eyes wide. "Oh! Right! Sorry, sorry!" She hovered in front of him, hands fluttering uselessly, unsure whether to help him stand or let him die on the spot.

Ashe, still trying to breathe, muttered, "This is why I hate hospitals. People get stupid ideas."

Still standing behind the wheelchair enjoying the scene, Adina rocked Ashe's head playfully to the side with a mock slap. "Yes, of course. It's the hospital that is the problem."

Ashe grunted, rubbing the side of his skull. "Ow. See, this is elder abuse."

Dani stepped around the van, hands in the pockets of her smart linen slacks as she exchanged a glance with Ashe's nurse. She smirked. "No, I think it's you being an idiot and getting what you deserve."

Dani turned to Ashe's nurse with a warm smile. "Good to see you again, Adina."

Adina nodded. "Mrs. Linder. I hope you have a solid exit plan. This one is trouble." She nudged Ashe's shoulder lightly.

"Oh, I know. He can be slippery," Dani grinned.

Adina smirked. "You could always steal his cane."

Amber gasped. "Yes! That's genius!"

"I hate all of you."

Dani chuckled, stepping forward. "Alright, let's get you in the car before Adina gives Amber any more ideas."

With great difficulty, Ashe moved to haul himself out of the wheelchair, gripping his cane with a firm but unsteady hand.

Dani stood back, watching him closely. A slow smirk graced her lips. "You know, Ashe? I really think you are getting better with age."

"Shut up."

Amber bumbled around him, trying to help but mostly getting in the way, while Dani just let him struggle. "Get in the car, grandpa," Dani told him, smiling, "before your legs give out, and I have to explain to Israeli security why we left such an ugly corpse outside their favorite hospital."

With far more effort than he wanted to admit, Ashe finally pulled himself upright.

Adina stepped back, watching with deep amusement. She reached down to disengage the locks on the chair's wheels. "Try to stay in one piece, Mr. Golding. I'd hate for my fiancé to have to carry you back into my hospital again."

Ashe grunted as he hobbled toward the van.

"You and me, both, kid."

Then, with gritted teeth, he climbed into the van, one slow, painful step at a time.

And for the first time in a long, long while...

Ashe felt almost human.

THE AIR INSIDE the Church of the Holy Sepulchre was thick with the weight of centuries. It clung to the stone walls, to the gold and silver lamps hanging low from the vaulted ceiling, to the very bones of the place. The smell of ancient incense and melted wax seeped into everything, curling around the pillars, drifting through the hushed murmurs of visiting pilgrims.

The flickering candlelight made the mosaics shimmer, halos of long-dead saints catching the glow, casting their solemn gazes over the faithful below. Priests in heavy robes moved like ghosts, their whispered prayers in Greek and Latin mingling with the sound of footsteps on marble, the occasional scrape of a cane against stone.

Ashe had been in holy places over the centuries, but none had carried the same gravity as this. Because here, he had once stood not as a pilgrim, not as a believer, but as a soldier, a watcher, a witness to something far greater than himself. A protector, if he had been able.

And now, nearly two thousand years later, he had returned.

Amber and Dani were probably furious by now.

By the time he returned to the hotel, Dani would have half of Israeli State Security searching for him. Amber would likely chew him out twice as long as Dani, because she had started to think she understood him, and he had gone and done something reckless anyway. The kid really should know better than that.

Anyway, they didn't belong here. Not this place. At least not right now, for this visit. This wasn't for them.

It was for him.

And after so many years, after carrying the weight of this place on his back, he wasn't about to pass up the chance to come back one last time.

He stood apart from the cluster of tourists, just close enough to see their hands reach through the hole in the silver disc beneath the altar. They were touching something sacred, or so they believed. He hoped so, anyway. But he knew that many of them just wanted to have an experience, to go home with a memory to make others jealous. Something to remember into their old age. Stone entombed in glass, the rock of Golgotha, the place where the cross had stood.

It had changed a lot, this place. He had not.

The limestone, rough and ancient, encased beneath layers of glass, looked more like a museum artifact than a relic of faith.

He remembered it differently. He remembered the heat of the sun that day, the dust dry and choking, the cries of the crowd rising and falling like the tide.

The cross had actually stood slightly to the right. He was pretty sure of that. A small detail, one that meant nothing to anyone but him.

He didn't reach out to touch the stone. He didn't need to.

He had already been there.

He had stood in the blood-soaked dirt, watching the sky darken, listening to the dying gasps of a man whose presence and passing had shaken the world.

Several men had died on that hill that day. Ashe had done so himself, in a way. But Ashe wasn't the one who mattered.

His grip on his cane tightened.

He stood there, his eyes tracing the flickering candlelight, the shadows shifting over the silver altar, the hushed voices of pilgrims kneeling before it.

So softly that no one else would hear it, and in a form of Latin so old they wouldn't understand it if they did, Ashe muttered a prayer.

Then, slowly, he turned away.

He walked down the path he had climbed so long ago.

He walked down, not with a spear, but with a cane.

* * *

About the Author

THE CREATIVE JOURNEY of pHil Rittenhouse has meandered from art to science to technology. Roughly in that order, and sometimes all at once. Once upon a time, pHil was a cartoonist. Of course, he also spent over a decade as a research chemist, so that probably cancels out any credibility he may have gained from cartooning.

As a chemist, he learned to approach the world through experiment and observation—habits that shaped his attention to detail as a storyteller. He also learned that explosions, while educational, are frowned upon in most laboratory settings.

These days, pHil (he insists on capitalizing his name that way for obscure reasons no one fully understands) works in software development at Microsoft, where logic and architecture meet imagination, and where he's spent nearly two decades wrangling SharePoint and Dynamics 365 into submission. The precision of coding and the chaos of creativity somehow coexist comfortably there, which might explain both his career longevity and his fiction.

A lifelong reader with a fondness for history, philosophy, and frequent esoteric rabbit holes, Rittenhouse draws from ancient texts, scientific theory, and forgotten myths to craft stories that blur the boundary between the known and the unknowable. His writing explores how obligation, guilt, and grace echo across time. Sometimes with explosions, but fewer than he'd probably like.

He lives in rural Illinois with his wife, four amazing kids, and a cast of household pets large enough to qualify as a small ecosystem. When not writing or debugging, he can often be found reading late into the night or volunteering at his church—still experimenting, still observing, and still sketching his next idea in the margins.

* * *

All statements of fact, opinion, or analysis expressed are those of the author and do not reflect the official positions or views of the US Government. Nothing in the contents should be construed as asserting or implying US Government authentication of information or endorsement of the author's views.

www.ingramcontent.com/pod-product-compliance
Lightning Source LLC
LaVergne TN
LVHW041057080826
845145LV00007B/1607

* 9 7 8 1 9 7 0 3 2 2 0 6 4 *